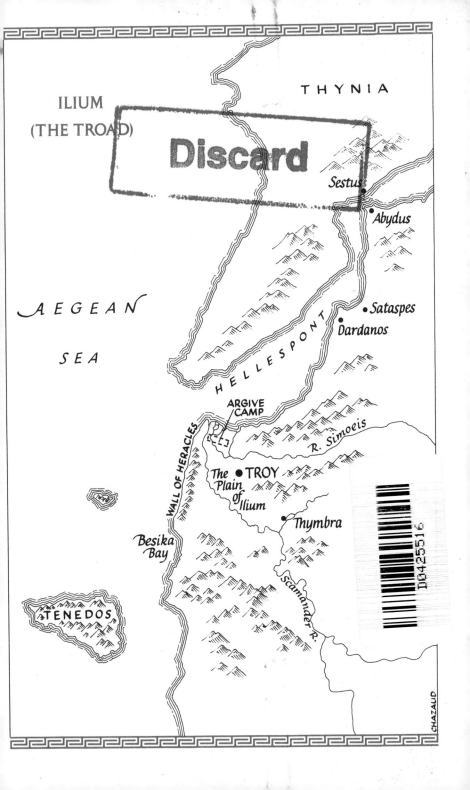

PAR   Parotti, Phillip
      Fires in the sky

$19.95

PAR   Parotti, Phillip
      Fires in the sky

BUFFALO SENIOR HIGH SCHOOL
023567
FIRES IN THE SKY

SENIOR HIGH LIBRARY
BUFFALO, MN

© THE BAKER & TAYLOR CO.

ASIA MINOR

FIRES
IN THE
SKY

PHILLIP
PAROTTI

23567

TICKNOR & FIELDS

NEW YORK

1990

For information about permission to reproduce selections
from this book, write to Permissions, Ticknor & Fields,
215 Park Avenue South, New York, New York 10003.

Library of Congress Cataloging-in-Publication Data

Parotti, Phillip.
Fires in the sky / Phillip Parotti.
p.   cm.
ISBN 0-89919-930-5
1. Troy (Ancient city) — Fiction.   2. Mysia (Turkey) —
History — Fiction. I. Title.
PS3566.A7525F57   1990   90-34323
813'.54 — dc20   CIP

Printed in the United States of America

BVG 10 9 8 7 6 5 4 3 2 1

Maps by Jacques Chazaud

Book design by Ann Stewart

for my wife

Man, supposing you and I, escaping this battle,
would be able to live on forever, ageless, immortal,
so neither would I myself go on fighting in the foremost
nor would I urge you into the fighting where men win
   glory.
But now, seeing that the spirits of death stand close
   about us
in their thousands, no man can turn aside nor escape
   them,
let us go on and win glory for ourselves, or yield it to
   others.

SARPEDON TO GLAUCOS
The Iliad 12.322–328
Richmond Lattimore translation

Of all creatures that breathe and creep about on Mother
Earth, there is none so helpless as a man. As long as heaven
leaves him in prosperity and health, he never thinks hard
times are on their way. Yet when the blessed gods have
brought misfortune on his head, he simply has to steel
himself and bear it.

ODYSSEUS TO AMPHINOMUS
The Odyssey 18.131ff
E. V. Rieu translation

CONTENTS

MAPS

PREFACE

In the beginning, long before the sacred walls of Ilium rose high above the Plain, Dardanos came into the land, gathered his clans, and shaped them into a people. Peerless Erichthonius became their king, and his son, Tros, became Lord of the Trojans. Tros sired three noble sons, Ilus, dark-eyed Assaracus, and handsome Ganymede, who was made cupbearer to the gods. Ilus became father of bronze-armed Laomedon, and in time Laomedon prospered, erecting the high white towers of Troy to overlook the Plain. To Laomedon in the grace of age were born five noble sons, of whom Priam was ascendant, becoming King of Troy and Lord of holy Ilium.

According to the Muse, Priam became a lordly leader to his people; he seized control of the Hellespont by striking north into Thynia while consolidating his power in the Troad. In his youth, hard by the waters of Scamander, Priam had ranged the Plain in company with noble Antenor and a third companion, a commoner known to myth only as the Gray, and when he finally rose to the throne, Priam embraced these friends, making them leaders of his Grand Council and generals in command. During the northern wars, by means of their sharp intelligence and astute choice of subordinates, they served him well, first invading Thynia and then, after defeating a desperate enemy, moving hard into Thrace, civilizing the people and spreading broad Trojan power, even to the limits of the dark, black sea. In time, Priam prospered; in time, the vast treasure rooms of Ilium rivaled even those of the gods, and in the end, the envious gods struck Troy down.

The first blow fell from the south, from beyond Mount Ida, where Ares, Butcher of Men, incited the dark-hearted Mysian nation to covet Priam's Plain. Crude, harsh, and primitive, the Mysian warlords, led by a sly and greedy king, looked north from their stone keeps and squalid, mud-brick warrens, watched as Priam's power increased, and viewed with insatiable envy the wealth and cultivation of the Troad. At last, mad for plunder, the Mysians marshaled their strength, struck north, and drove straight for the Trojan stronghold at Thymbra, their fierce, bare-footed regiments pouring from the heights of Ida into the fertile valleys below. Clad only in skins and coarse brown cloth but armed with bows, bronze axes, and spears, the black-haired Mysians drove down hard on the Troad, launching the first in a series of four wars that, by the measure of man, ranged blood red across a span of more than a score of bitter years. Each time they made war on Troy, the Mysians were narrowly defeated, but owing to a variety of palace intrigues — all of them initiated secretly by Hecuba, the ambitious queen, who sought only the promotion of her own line — capable Antenor had been pushed from command of the Grand Council, and with him fell the Gray. As a result, new forms of strategic thought, all of them defensive by nature, prevailed with the Trojan elders, and Mysia, having once seized the initiative, was able to go on exploiting it. The effect was grim. As a result of Troy's failure to take the war into the enemy's heartland, the Mysian Wars dragged on and on, sapping Troy's wealth and strength and will, bleeding the Troad white, and when at last the Fourth War was won, tired but victorious Ilium awoke to the fierce threat on her flank, the Achaian Greeks, who, through the long duration of the Mysian Wars, perched along the western edge of the Aegean, waiting like hungry wolves to devour a weakened prey. With Troy's triumph, with Mysia now subdued, subjected, and brought fully into the Trojan camp as a client state, Priam, awake at last to the threat from the west, made a sharply threatening gesture against the Greeks, striking from the sea, raiding the Greek stronghold at Scyros. Then, hard on the raid's heels, he sent the Greeks an ambassador to cry a warning before offering them the olive branch of peace. But the man Priam sent to reason his case became the instrument of Troy's undoing.

To the sons of Atreus, leaders of the Greek alliance, to Agamemnon of Mycenae and Menelaus of Sparta, Priam sent as envoy his beloved youngest son, Paris, the newly recovered prince of Ilium. At birth, in response to prophecies portending Troy's destruction, Paris had been snatched from his mother, taken from Troy, and exposed on Ida's slopes. But found there by a goatherd, who raised the boy as his own, he survived, and grew to handsome manhood in the shelter of the pines. There, near Ida's peaks, golden Aphrodite sought and found him during the springtime of his youth, and implored his help in winning a trial of beauty among three contesting goddesses. She bribed his favor, promising to quench his desire with the most beautiful woman in the world. Eventually, Paris returned to Troy, where his loving parents rejoiced in the hour of his recovery. To make manifest his joy, Priam appointed this son his ambassador to the House of Atreus. Not long after, catching a fast tide, Paris sailed to Greece, and there, in the Spartan palace, he first laid eyes on Helen, wife of Menelaus, and knew her to be the woman of his dreams. With Aphrodite's help — indeed, at her urging — Paris seized the beautiful Helen, kidnapped her, seduced her, and sailed away with her, returning to Troy, where he made her his wife, and where, obsessed by parental love, both Priam and Hecuba turned a blind eye to the nature of his crime.

Enraged by what Paris had done, incredulous over Priam's response, lordly Agamemnon, acting on his brother's behalf,

gathered a thousand high-beaked ships in the bay at Aulis, sacri-
ficed his own blushing daughter in order to obtain favorable
winds, and sailed for Ilium, hot in wrathful pursuit. There, the
sons of Atreus made long, hard, and bitterly sharp war on Priam,
striking all the fine brave Trojans to their knees. And when ten
endless years had passed, owing to the depth of Trojan exhaustion and to the cunning Greek ruse of a hollow wooden horse
filled with Argive warriors, merciless Agamemnon avenged the
insult to his family by putting the whole Troad to the torch and
almost all of the remaining Trojans to the sword. Some few,
isolated Trojans survived. Prince Helenus, leading a small band,
made his way into Thrace; lordly Aeneas, with his father, son, and
a few companions, sailed to the west; and the frail daughter of
Antenor found refuge with the Cicones. And on the field, cornered, surrounded, fighting bitterly in the shadow of the Abydian
hills, the last Trojan warriors went down hard to bright Greek
bronze, and in the battle's wake, the Argive Greeks came away
with a single, wounded captive, a young Trojan general, who
identified himself only as Dymas, son of Kalitor, a defeated commander from blue Abydus-by-the-sea.

FIRES
IN THE
SKY

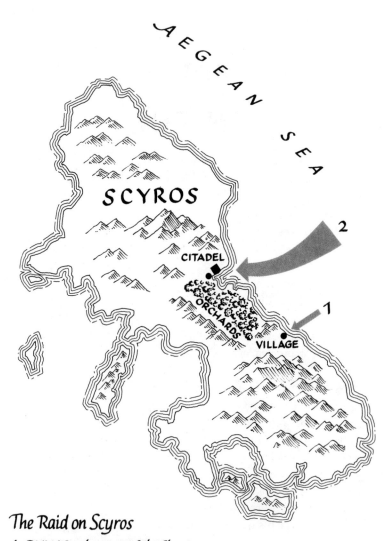

The Raid on Scyros
1. DYMAS - elements of the Shark
2. POLYDAMAS - main force

CHAZAUD

PROLOGUE

Stretching before us like a black serpent, the isle of Scyros emerged from the sea. Over the high beak of our bow, far in the distance above the island's northern coast, watch fires twinkled like fading fireflies, and in the direction of Ilium, Aurora's first blush became broadly visible. Before me, their bearded faces stinging beneath a sharp salt spray, my bronzed men wrapped their shoulders in their cloaks, shielding themselves behind the shipped pine shafts of their oars. One, a boy from Percote whose beard had not yet ripened into growth, became ill, vomiting over the side, but the rest, older men and more seasoned, although buffeted by a rising sea, absorbed its motion and held on, waiting silently for the dawn.

Whitecaps appeared, and foam, whipping from the crests with Borean force. Somewhere to starboard, riding the hard currents of the wind, an eagle screamed, and in that instant Tropos came from the sail well to join me before the helm.

"Now, my Lord Dymas?" Thick, swart, his short black beard streaming with spray, Tropos reminded me of a crag: pounded for years by Poseidon's trident, he still stood — hard, dark, and firm, unyielding before the blows of the sea.

I did not answer his question. Instead, compensating for a roll that caught us in the trough, I snapped like a whip to scan the horizon in the direction of Troy. My orders had been clear; my Lord Polydamas had issued them himself.

"Dymas," he had said, "remain well to sea until dawn. Then, when Aurora unveils her last faint blush, *move.* Too soon, and the feint is wasted. Too late, and before noon, Greek kites will feast on your bones."

I understood exactly what Polydamas wanted. I waited; then, concentrating my senses, saying nothing, I stood, watching the dim sky brighten above the sea path. When the last traces of Aurorean pink had changed to burning gold, I lifted the wineskin and poured three generous libations, one for the son of Cronos, one for the Earthshaker, and one for Ares, Butcher of Men.

"Now?" Tropos asked.

"Now," I said.

Tropos whirled, faced forward into a rising sea, and roared, *"Oars!"*

Like thunder, his order rolled over the heads of our men, and the reverberating echo came back to us in the sound of all oars going out, their flat pine blades flashing bright beneath the first rays of the sun.

"Steady!" Tropos roared again. "Steady — STROKE!"

Like tongues of flame, all oars struck the foam, and all our fine bronzed men pulled away together, straining like bulls. Beneath us, the hull shuddered, poised on the crest of a swell, and then it lunged violently forward.

"STRO-O-OKE!"

Again, the shudder. Again, the thrusting lunge. And again, the wind, whipping tart spray against our faces as we surged over the wine-dark sea. Up forward, the mallet swinger took up the rhythm, striking hard on a thwart for each long stroke of the oars; then, as our high-beaked hull gathered speed, driving hard across each mountainous swell and down through each successive trough, the men caught the beat, locking their strokes to the deep, pounding tones of their sea chant.

Off the port quarter, Agelaos' keel broke furiously across the crest of a swell and plunged again into the trough, all oars flashing like fire. Farther south, skimming the swells like a kite, Orthaios' red-beaked prow gleamed in the morning sun, its dark green eyes looking lean and sharp. Only Tarsos lagged, his flatter, wider hull gathering momentum, humping the waves like an angry grayback whale.

Ahead, the serpentine hills of Scyros loomed larger, blacker, closing in fast to fill the horizon. Suddenly, to the north, the citadel came into view, first as a speck, then as a series of dark low walls and slate-gray keeps. Compared with Troy, it seemed dull, hardly a city, nothing more than a stone redoubt fit to shelter the squat, ugly villages below. It was that, certainly, but the facts suggested a greater importance, an importance that our agents had established beyond doubt: the citadel at Scyros was the administrative and logistic center for the Argives' eastern sea frontier. Argive Greeks, sailing from anywhere in the alliance, going anywhere east, put in at Scyros to water, replenish, or combine in convoy before crossing the wide Aegean. That citadel, which looked so flat, so dull, so utterly undistinguished, was really a hive. Every corridor swarmed with activity; every room functioned as an office, storehouse, or barracks; every wall sheltered ships' crews or passengers or hard military companies in transit and — in times of trouble — farmers and villagers from the countryside. But our agents had penetrated even farther, even into the depths of the keep, and there they had seen prodigious weights of salt, grain, and oil; dried meat and fruit enough to feed an army and water enough to replenish a fleet; bales of sailcloth, scores of spare pine oars, and an immense armory filled with long ash spears. The citadel on Scyros was more than it seemed: it was at once a rock capable of holding fourteen or fifteen hundred defenders and a strategic key for controlling all traffic through the central Aegean. As such, Scyros had become a serpent's tooth, a fang capable of stinging Troy to death by shooting sharp Argive poison into all our veins of trade.

"The citadel, my Lord Dymas!" Shouting above the wind,

Tropos pointed a blunt finger toward the rising northern heights.

I nodded, turned, and squinted over the bow. We were less than a league from the beach, running hard, skimming the waves like hawks, the feathers of our oars barely touching the surface. Suddenly, the wind turned, and we found ourselves racing in on a flooding tide.

Squinting into the spray, I focused my eyes on the shore. Ahead, a white beach rapidly revealed itself like the glittering belly of a snake. Up from the beach, I saw a village, and beyond, rising high into the hills, barley fields in tiers and clumps of woods. Here and there, I made out olive groves and, I thought, orchards, but before I was sure, something at the edge of the village caught my eye. In the instant, a beacon fire flared and then, on the heights behind the village, another. We were discovered — in good time, I thought — but discovery was only the first step toward success. Would the Greeks allow themselves to be drawn? I did not know. Darting a glance north, I scanned the citadel and found no response. Some two leagues away, that massive fortress sprawled silently on its mound, slumbering above the island's harbor like a satiated beast. Half a league to starboard, between the beach we were preparing to assault and the Argive keep, a rib of land was fast rising up, jutting into the sea before dying on the lip of a crag. Once we passed beneath it, all sight of the citadel would be lost; from that moment on, we would move as if blind, racing against time, never knowing until the last instant what danger threatened, never knowing until the last moment whether the draw had succeeded. I looked once more toward the citadel and, in the fleeting second before it disappeared from view, saw an answering beacon burst into flame atop the keep. We had been discovered. Sweeping away all doubts, I took up my shield and my long ash spear and made ready to beach.

The Greek village resembled a suddenly scattered anthill. As the low, whitewashed walls hurtled toward us, men, women, and children, some with bundles, some without, leapt from their doors, stopped briefly to assay the danger, and then bolted, fleeing desperately up narrow streets toward the protecting hills. We were not yet close enough to distinguish their faces, but clearly, panic prevailed. People collided furiously, fell to the ground, rose, and ran on, seized by terror, intent only on putting as much distance as possible between themselves and the points of our spears. At the village's eastern edge, a house suddenly caught fire, and farther back near the base of a field, black smoke began to pour from yet another hovel; within seconds, it, too, burst into flame.

"There!" I shouted to Tropos. "As soon as we beach, lead the men forward to *that* house and set fire to the fields. I want fire, as much as possible, as soon as you can make it. Burn everything in sight!"

We were close when I finally gave the order to ship oars, and we beached hard, riding up onto the wet sand with such grinding force that men were thrown from their rowing benches. It did not matter; we landed unopposed, and as I ran forward, leaping to earth across the bow, shouting my war cry and holding my long ash spear at the ready, all my fine bronzed men poured over the sides behind me and lunged forward in a bristle of spears. Within seconds, they were hurtling through the village, Tropos at their head, moving toward the burning house and the exposed fields beyond.

Agelaos scudded ashore, and Orthaios, their salt-rimed men leaping onto the beach amidst a hail of war shouts and the brazen clatter of arms. I raised my spear once, and Orthaios deployed south, scattering his warriors like angry hornets so as to cover our flank. To Agelaos, I gave one command: "Burn the village!" On the instant, he was away, his men — tall, dark men from Sestus and the Thynian coast — racing behind him, their black Thracian topknots shining in the sun.

Finally, Tarsos landed. He brought in his own wide hull on the northern flank, anchoring with at least a sword's length of water beneath his keel. He was an old soldier, Tarsos; he knew what to do. He'd been with me in the Mysian Wars, and as rapidly as his anchors hit the surf, so did his men, wearing full bronze armor. As they stormed ashore, streaming salt and foam, they looked, I remember, like bronze gods rising from the depths of the sea.

By that time, my staff had assembled: four runners, two spearmen, and a dark Mysian archer from Thymbra. Turning to one of the runners, I recognized him instantly as the boy from Percote. "To Lord Tarsos," I barked. "Lord Dymas sends respects and orders him into position along the top of the land rib. He is to block the road from the citadel until I move to support him." Sprinting hard along the tide's edge, the boy was away, but Tarsos moved even before the boy reached him. As I said, Tarsos was an old soldier, a good one, and during our war council, I had made my intentions clear. Without waiting, he moved swiftly off the beach, skirting the village, and ran his company toward the sloping heights of the rib. Somewhere up there he would find the road and block it at the crest.

My command was ashore, then, nearly three hundred Trojans — men from Percote, Sestus, Abydus, Arisbe, and holy Ilium — all hard, all well trained, all proven warriors. And one party of swart Mysian archers, in whom I placed little trust. We had achieved surprise, effecting our assault without casualties, and made rapid progress toward the objective, but still, the matter was beyond my control — feints depending entirely on the response of the enemy. We would do what we came to do, I remember thinking, do it well, do it for as long as we could hold, and trust in the gods. That would have to be enough.

Beyond the village, barley fields blossomed into flame. Streaming up the slopes, their bronze arms barely visible in the distance, Tropos' men hurled burning brands into the thickly ripening grain while breezes, strong from the sea, fanned the flames, turning one field after another into a red-hot pyre.

Close in, my topknotted Thynians fired the village. Running from street to street, issuing sharp commands, Agelaos set his war parties in motion; as I watched, three or four of his warriors would enter a dwelling, overturn the cooking fires, and rush out to hurl firebrands onto the roof. Already, the southern quarter was on fire, and within a short time, the wind-whipped flames leapt from house to house. Animals ran everywhere in terror, and soon a few captives were being herded down to the beach. Two old women stumbled in the van, followed by a small female child and finally a crippled graybeard, who tried to strike his captor and was pinked in response by the tip of Thynian bronze. "Carrion!" the old man screamed at me. "Fly dung! Anus of Ares! You will pay for this, by the law! The doer must suffer! That is the law! The law — " He was cut off from further recrimination by the Thynian, who, before I could prevent him, flattened the old man with the butt of his spear.

"Report to your commander," I ordered. "Strike no old men unless they threaten you with arms!"

Abashed, the Thynian withdrew, disappearing swiftly into the smoke of the village.

Over my shoulder, Helios climbed a degree or two higher. I knew that it was time to move, time to press the feint, and I sent runners to Tropos and Agelaos, ordering each to move his company to the top of the land rib so as to reinforce Tarsos. Moments later, I myself started for the rim, skirting the village to the northeast before turning inland, my remaining spearman and the Mysian archer running behind me, breathing hard but holding the pace.

As I started upcountry, topknotted Thynians poured from the village, their arms and faces blackened with smoke. Farther back, I could see Tropos' company running north, hurtling across the charred stubble of the fields, not sounding their war cries now, merely running hard, concentrating on the task ahead, holding their spears and their shields and their eyes at the ready, sucking air like the strong white horses of Troy when, after a morning's swim in the sea, they are loosed by their keepers across the breadth of the Plain.

We came together halfway up the slope of the rib, Tropos' bronzed but blackened warriors hurtling over a low stone wall and onto the road from an olive grove, Agelaos' moving up quickly through neat terraced rows of grapes. Streams of sweat trickled down their arms and faces, but once on the road, the pace quickened as Thynians competed with their Dardanian peers for the summit of the rib. I put on speed there, bolting forward, racing for the forefront, overtaking man after man, and all my fine bronzed men cheered me as I ran. Ahead, Tropos came into view and then Agelaos, and then we were all running together, strong in the depth of our wind.

As we approached the summit, Tarsos' men rose to greet us and to cheer our coming. Things had been quiet on the rib, but they might not remain so for long, and we were welcomed openly, even by those hardened warriors. Without hesitation, Agelaos reinforced our position on the inland side of the saddle-shaped pass while Tropos' command moved seaward along the rib's rim. Meanwhile, I moved on over the saddle. Not twenty paces beyond, wearing nothing more than light leather armor, lay a party of dead Greeks, some ten or twelve in number, their twisted bodies lined up beside the road, black flies already swarming over their wounds. Tarsos came up to me from farther down the reverse slope, where his advance guard watched the road as it disappeared across a smoking wheat field into an orchard.

"From the village," he said, pointing to the bodies with the bloodied tip of his spear, "a rear guard, to cover the flight of their people." When he spoke, Tarsos' jaw barely moved, his thick black beard extending from his chin like a fan of pine needles. "We caught them on the summit; they made a sharp fight but a short one, and we dropped them where they stood. Their people had plenty of time to get away."

"And up ahead?"

"I sent one party down," he said, "to fire the fields. They're scouting the orchard now." Then he told me what I'd been waiting to hear. "The Greeks have taken the bait."

"How do you know?" I charged. I had examined the citadel myself, carefully, as soon as I crossed the saddle, as soon as the distant mass had come back into view, and I had looked in vain for signs of activity. Only the beacon fires, smoldering from the top of the easternmost keep, suggested that the walls were manned, that human life persisted on the far northern shore.

"There," Tarsos said, raising his spear.

And then I saw them, dust clouds rising above the lime trees no more than a league distant. They had left the road, masking their numbers beneath the green foliage of the trees. Judging from the dust, I knew that a large force was marching against us.

"Estimate?"

"Six, maybe seven hundred," said Tarsos, leaning on his spear. "We saw them leave the citadel as we came onto the ridge, about the same time that the last villagers disappeared into the orchards, running from our spears. They moved rapidly out of the keeps, fully armed: we could see the sun glittering from their bronze. At the pace they have set, it won't take them long to reach us, and . . . *there,*" he said suddenly, his dark eyes narrowing as he shifted his gaze toward the sea and lifted the point of his spear. "Those could be trouble."

He had not seen them before because their sails had been down, and their light gray hulls had blended with the rocky background of the harbor. But now, to catch a land breeze, their sails were going up, making each Greek hull, at the distance, darkly visible.

"My lord," he said quickly, "they intend to cut off our withdrawal!"

"There's a risk," I said flatly, "but we are committed. We will have to go the course. Has the beacon fire been laid?"

"Aye, my lord."

"We must trust in the gods," I said, giving him a quick grin, "and in the hard strength of our Lord Polydamas' right arm."

"And cunning," Tarsos said, grunting.

"And that, too." I laughed, bringing up the point of my spear. "Call in your scouts, and keep me informed. Follow the Greeks' progress by their dust. And keep an eye to the flank; there is no way of knowing what they may have tucked away in these hills."

I regained the saddle and turned once more to study our position. To my right, beyond the point, the sea shone gold beneath the sun. Ahead, beyond the wheat fields, beyond the orchard, other fields and orchards stretched north toward Scyros, and in the midst of those groves, running feet stirred clouds of dust, warning us that Greeks were on the march, warning us that they were coming in large numbers bent upon our destruction. On our left, the rib ascended gradually, shaded by boulders and squat trees, until it became one with the island's spine. Here and there, late summer wildflowers remained in bloom, their pale pinks and reds standing out sharply against the browns and grays of the hillside. Finally, I looked back over my shoulder toward the village. Huge plumes of smoke billowed above it, but in the center, still, orange flames swirled furiously from the rooftops. And in that instant, from the hills, we came under attack.

Pouring from the heights, the Greeks hit us hard on the flank but with a small force. Who they were or where they had massed, I do not know; regardless, they achieved surprise, and within seconds, seven of Agelaos' Thynians had fallen to their spear casts. There couldn't have been many of them — no more than forty at the most, but they were fearless and drove their assault hard. That they were not a part of the main body, I am certain; rather, I think they were a scratch force made from watch parties that manned the warning beacons atop the island's spine.

At this distance, it no longer seems to matter, for all but one have moved deep into the chambers of decay.

They hit us very hard, very quickly, and started to roll up our line. Reacting swiftly, Agelaos shouted a single shrill command, and his topknotted Thynians recoiled into a new line, but the Greeks hurtled down on his center in too powerful a bolt for this tactic to have been effective, and had I not moved forward with some of Tarsos' warriors, the Argives might have broken through, shattering our command into disordered fragments. Then we would have had to withdraw, leaving a mere handful of Greeks in control of the heights.

I lunged forward, roaring my war cry, urging Tarsos' men to follow me, and like a wolf pack hot on the trail of a deer, they snarled up the hill behind me, their long ash spears gleaming like teeth. Agelaos' line fell back, but in the moment I hurled my spear, struck the leading Greek on the ridge of his helmet, and brought him crashing to earth like a felled tree. He had scarcely uttered his death rattle before Tarsos' strong warriors rushed into the melee, driving the points of their spears against the massed Greek shields. Oiax of Percote was the first to kill his man; a black-eyed rider of the sea, he drove sharp bronze through the throat of an onrushing Greek, spitting him like a piece of dead meat. Aphlaston was next into battle, and then Chaledon, and like angry wasps when a small animal disturbs their nest, my bronzed warriors began stinging the enemy to death.

Faced with this response, the Greeks hesitated, stumbled, and came to a halt. Our sudden thrust had blunted their resolve, throwing them instantly onto the defensive, and in the same moment, our Thynians recovered, sprinting in from the extremities of their line to fall on the Greek flanks. In short order, we had them surrounded, their means of escape cut off. Then, there was much fighting and much hard killing, and the ground ran red with Greek blood. Terrified, the Greeks fought like cornered beasts, but the battle, once begun, ended swiftly, leaving the hillside littered with Greek dead and not a few of my Thynians. Iastros of Sestus went down there, and the swift-footed Kamax, who hailed from Arisbe, and many were our wounded, but we came away with victory and fourteen captives, whom we later bound in the holds of our ships.

I had been pinked on the forearm by an Argive spear, and as I bound my wound with linen, Tarsos sprinted up to me, his thick body streaming with sweat, his hard black eyes blazing like coals.

"You have been long about it, my lord. The main body of Greeks is no more than a quarter league distant. It is time to move."

"Fire the beacon," I commanded, turning swiftly, beckoning Agelaos and his company to follow as I raced downhill with Tarsos in my wake. "Put out the Mysian archers, just behind the lip of the pass's saddle. As soon as the Greeks close to within two hundred paces, release their volleys."

"It is done, that of the archers, my lord. I came only about the beacon." Tarsos puffed hard as he spoke, and spoke as he ran, plunging down the slope behind me.

It would be as he said: the Mysians would be arrayed beneath the lip of the saddle, their quivers by their knees, their bowstrings taut, ready, waiting to blunt the first line of the Greek attack that would pour from the orchards and up across the fields toward our positions on the rib.

Passing through scrub, I came out on the saddle and stopped, collecting myself while I studied the ground. The Greeks were there, already massing beneath the nearest orchard. I could see their front ranks clearly, standing in thick bronzed rows like stands of summer wheat. There wasn't much movement; they were preparing to attack; but the air above the orchards held still the clouds of dust, their fine particles glistening in the sunlight.

My staff collected, my runners, my spearmen, and the lone Mysian archer who went to his knees over a pile of dry twigs, blowing a flame into them from a tinder. I snapped my fingers once in the Mysian's direction, and he immediately loosed an arrow in the enemy's direction. On that signal, my warriors leapt to their feet, beating the ash shafts of their spears against the dark, hardened rims of their shields, and within seconds, each man caught the rhythm, and the din became deafening, the fury of our intent pouring across those blackened fields like slow-rolling thunder.

Glorying in the courage of my warriors, I waited. We had masked our numbers, but the noise we made was enough to strike terror into a thousand men. Below, near the edge of the orchard, the Greeks began to move, their close ranks stepping forward with slow, determined restraint, advancing at the walk, in silence, hoping by means of their unblunted resolve to frighten us off the rib. They were disciplined men, those Greeks, no mere collection of random villagers, and as rank after rank emerged from the trees and started up, across the smoking stubble of the fields, I had to admire the skill with which they maintained order in the face of the unknown. They were pitting themselves against us, sight unseen, and they had no fear. There were, I thought, more than eight hundred of them, and all were well armed.

On the rib's point, our beacon burst suddenly into flame, shooting sparks and smoke high into the air, filling the morning sky with brilliant beams of light.

They should have known, then, known that they had been drawn, but they could not be sure, and in their uncertainty lay the success of our plan. Having dispatched eight hulls — hulls that were plainly visible — to secure their seaward flank, the Greeks might reasonably have believed anything: that our beacon fire was a warning to our ships, or that it called for reinforcements, or . . . at this distance, speculation is pointless. Swiftly, I acted to increase their confusion and draw them on, running Tropos' command down onto the field in a seventy-man front. We moved forward no more than the flight of an arrow, the Mysian archers coming up behind us while Tarsos and Agelaos formed in line of battle across the saddle, but all the while, I kept a steady eye on the sea.

We had given the Greeks no choice. They saw us as a force to be reckoned with, apparently small, much smaller than their own, but possibly the advance guard of a larger army massed behind the rib. We were committed. They knew it, and they had to commit themselves or risk our doing the unexpected. It was clear by that time that we had come with larger intent than a mere raid. They could not ignore that we had struck hard and elected to hold our ground, threatening them face to face across their own fields. As I said, they should have known, but they did not and continued to move forward, their horse-hair plumes glistening and swaying beneath a warm morning sun.

When I could make out the designs on the Greeks' shields, I sent the Mysians forward and loosed a volley. Some of our bronze-tipped arrows fell short, but some found their mark, and along the Argive front a number of men went down with sharp barbed arrows through their necks. In the same moment, I turned, signaling toward the saddle with my shield, and there, my own Mysian shot a flaming arrow high into the air, out beyond our lines. The moment the arrow fell, Agelaos and Tarsos melted away from their positions, running hard for our ships. Tropos' warriors were the next to go, moving swiftly to his command while the Mysians loosed volley after volley in the direction of the Greeks. I did not have enough archers to be very effective, but as the enraged Greeks charged forward, furious to see us slipping away, Mysian arrows dropped like bolts from the sky, killing some, wounding many more, doing serious damage to the Greek front until we had cut its number by as much as a third. And then I had those thirty archers up and running. They were Mysians, of course, as fleet of foot as they were wary of battle. I never trusted them, but on that day they did me good service, earning the right to be called Trojans.

Tropos' infantry had turned as soon as they had reached the rib, planting their spears across the saddle's seat so as to cover our withdrawal. As the Mysians rushed up, just below Tropos' spear points, I shouted sharp commands, and all archers loosed three more volleys into the onrushing Greeks. I barked again, and the Mysians were up, sprinting between the files of infantry, racing over the rise and down into the valley beyond; two hundred yards below, they would turn and cover Tropos' withdrawal.

The Greeks — winded, outpaced by our fresher, more lightly armed men, hurt, bleeding, howling with rage — continued to run forward like swarms of angry ants when man or beast has purposely trampled their mound. Their fallen comrades they left behind them, writhing on the dark ash of the fields, their fast-flowing blood mingling with the earth and the sooty dust thrown skyward by pounding feet. In that moment, it was a grim scene that presented itself, but a grimmer event was in the making, for at last, far out to sea, riding forward on the wings of eagles, came the fleet, my Lord Polydamas' high-beaked ship skimming the wave path in its van. Our high-prowed hulls looked like fifty feathered darts whipping across the whitecaps and onward, into the main harbor of Scyros, bent upon fearsome destruction. I waited no longer, but shouted orders for withdrawal, sending Tropos and the infantry hurtling over the saddle and down the reverse slope toward the beach. And when I finally saw the eight Greek hulls turn back toward their harbor, too late to blunt the main Trojan assault, I knew my feint had succeeded. I turned, found my legs, and ran like the wind toward the sea.

By the time I reached the beach, my fine bronzed captains were already launching their ships. Orthaios was first away and then Agelaos, and as I sprinted through the still smoldering remains of the village, Tropos' infantry and the Mysian archers passed quickly through the rear guard, launched their own high-beaked hulls, and clambered aboard. Shouting my war cry, I flung myself toward the sea, and in response, Tarsos' rear guard faded back swiftly, wading out through the surf to scramble aboard their well-anchored hull. And then I too struck the beach and felt the warm sand beneath my feet as I plunged into the rush of the tide.

The anchor stones were already coming up when Tarsos and

three of his henchmen leaned far over the side to hoist me from the sea. I was the last man to board, the last man away, the last man to face the enemy and shout my war cry, and with warm thanks to Tarsos for his gesture, I ordered my hulls away. Like greased poles, the long oars shot out, their flat blades flashing, and then all hands pulled away together, and all four hulls lunged toward the open sea.

On the beach, armed Greeks straggled into the surf, cursing us, shaking their spears in signs of defiance, but they were spent, and we were well beyond their range; not very many of them, I think, had followed us down from the saddle. By that time, they must have seen in full the disaster that was befalling their citadel, where flint-eyed Polydamas had put ashore five thousand war-hungry Trojans in a matter of seconds. I did not witness the main assault, but I know from my lord that it developed swiftly, realizing complete success when Trojans — disguised as Rhodian merchants and sent into Scyros on the day before — overpowered the gate guards from within. There was fearsome fighting and much killing as our Trojans drove the Greeks back into the keeps, slaughtering them as they went. Had it not been for my feint, our main assault would have had to contend with four times the defenders they actually met, and Polydamas himself told me that against such a citadel he could not have prevailed without a siege lasting many months. We won on cunning and on the strength of our strong right arms, and the Greeks who attacked us must have known what was coming as soon as they saw our battle fleet speeding in from the east.

I took my ships to sea, coming away with my command intact. In the distance, the citadel was already on fire, huge clouds of smoke leaping from its keeps. As we moved closer, the flames became visible, raging above the walls; but only gradually, as we neared the mouth of the harbor, did the immensity of the Argive disaster become fully apparent. Close in, we could see that the whole citadel roared, the enraged flames leaping high into the air. Below the smoke-belching walls of the keeps, stretching all the way down to the harbor, Scyros itself was in flames, its narrow streets thick with smoke, its rooftops crawling with fire. Out beyond the edge of the town, isolated fields were burning and individual country homes; and farther back against the sides of the high hills that formed the island's spine, we could make out the tiny streams of people, running away from disaster.

Inside the bay, along uninhabited stretches of beach, our sleek ships were drawn up on the shore, their command pennants still fluttering from their masts, indicating what units were ashore and where, showing me at a glance that the assault had gone according to plan. My Lord Polydamas and the Shark had, indeed, struck the citadel. Lordly Asius had led the combined might of Percote and holy Arisbe against the town, and Acamas, warrior of the bright eye, had put his men forward to ravage the fields and the country hamlets.

Three of our hulls had been on patrol, but as soon as my own crews scudded into view, they turned and drove hard for shore, beaching just north of the citadel, where their companies, looking like mites at the distance, swarmed up the hillside to attack some small outlying structures that were soon consumed by flame.

We patrolled the harbor entrance throughout the morning, but when Helios reached his zenith, I hoisted my signal pennant, and all four of my hulls, like gliding swans, turned broadly east. We put out full canvas then and pointed our prows toward Ilium.

Behind us, Scyros was a pillar of fire and the citadel absolutely lost in blackness. Upcountry, wheat and barley fields had long since burned, but now, beneath towering flames, whole orchards and olive groves went up and, farther back still, thick clumps of mast-high pines. And along the shore, our ships were coming away, launching themselves in groups onto the outgoing tide.

Long after the island disappeared behind us, mere moments

before Night descended, the entire fleet came together, put itself in order, and set a sharp course for the slave markets of Antissa, my own dark command screening the van. We had come away with much plunder, and as the lanterns went up that night, marking the high masts of our ships, we thought that the Greek threat had been blunted, that the coiled serpent of Scyros had been crushed in its den.

Three days later we returned to Troy.

1

My HISTORY? You want to hear *my* chronicle? What does it matter, since I am already hard by the chambers of decay? Are Greek bards to sing of *my* achievements? I think not: Troy dies with me, and there's an end.

You say that it is the foundation of generalship to study your enemy, to analyze his victories and defeats, to know him inside out? Look about you, lords. What enemy remains? Troy's raid on Scyros is ten years past, a mere prelude to your ten years' war on the Troad. Have I not already laid bare the details? For your purposes, it is a pity that you did not capture Polydamas himself, for he was the chief planner.

Know your enemy, you say? Frankly, I suspect your motives. You have annihilated Troy. On the dusty Plain, Trojan bones will soon bleach white, so what does it matter, unless you have doubts — unless you wish to know not your victims but yourselves, now ... here ... at the bitter end, searching your own fate by weighing ours.

Ah, I light upon the truth. Do not bother to answer; I see it in Agamemnon's kingly eyes and there, on the faces of Ithacan Odysseus, hawk-eyed Idomeneus, and lordly Nestor. You doubt yourselves, the righteousness of your cause, the finality of your victory. Small wonder — victories are never complete; invariably, they carry the seeds of the victor's own destruction. Know you not that Troy too was once victorious, first over Thynia and Thrace, and then, across more than a score of years and four successive wars, over the hardhearted Mysians to the south? Troy won a stunning victory over Mysia, a victory that completely shattered the Mysian nation, and in the process, we bled so white that you, my lords of Greece, found us easy prey. So why the question? Such is the way of the warrior. As for the righteousness of your cause, leave that to Zeus. How the dread son of Cronos may weigh your portion, I have no way of knowing. You must make your peace with the gods as best you can, with no help from me, for I am a mere mortal. Let *be* what *is*. The glory that was Troy's has now gone up in flames, and the wide, dusty Plain blows gray with Trojan ash. You, my lords, have cast the die; in the scheme of things, you must play on. But I am no longer part of the game.

As you wish, but do not expect to learn much from me, for I will not speak for the gods, whose mysteries are beyond my sight.

You ask me to begin with the beginning, and I will, although why you should want to know the facts of my life, I am at a loss to understand. As I said, I am mortal, no more, and lowborn. And in the hour of my birth, I killed my mother, whose womb had to be ripped open in order to make me free. I came into the world violently, kicking — so I am told — screaming, covered with blood, much the way I may leave it.

My mother was a concubine, an attendant in Aphrodite's shrine. My father captured her in one of his Thracian campaigns, brought her back to Troy, and installed her in the temple, but later, she was awarded to my father as a war prize. When he was ordered to command at Dardanos, he took her with him, and I was born there in a high chamber overlooking the harbor.

I never knew my father; he was killed in the First Mysian War, less than a month before my birth. I am told that he was a hard man and a great warrior; apparently he was, because during the northern wars, under his generalship, Sestus, greater Thynia, and all of southern Thrace were first brought under Trojan control. I have heard descriptions of him; they suggest that he was broad-shouldered and tall, with a dark beard, a thick hooknose, and beetle brows. Those characteristics, I have from him, but the blue eyes come from my mother, for I have heard that she was fair. That my father rose from the ranks, there can be no doubt; the records are clear. About his birth, facts remain obscure. I have assumed always that he was lowborn, and that is the claim that I make for myself, but it may not be so. Laomedon, as is well known, had five sons: Tithonus, Priam, Lampus, Clytius, and Hicetaon; according to my uncle, he and my father were the twin offspring of an illegitimate liaison between Lampus and a priestess of Artemis. Their mother, he said, had slipped from virtue during the summer of her youth, survived long enough to give birth to her sons, and then been struck dead by the angry goddess. My uncle was in his cups when he recited that story, so I have discounted it as the delusion of an intoxicated mind, but if what he said was true, such bitter truth would make my father and my uncle bastard cousins to Priam's wretched brood, dragging me along in their wake. If we were allied to the House of Dardanos through any blood tie whatsoever, that tie was never acknowledged, so my father attained his rank on merit alone and on the strength of his own right arm, and when he died, fighting against hard odds in the mountain fastness of Mysia, his body came home on his shield and was buried with honors beneath the walls of Troy.

Orphaned by my mother's death, wearing naught but swaddling clothes, I was carried north to Abydus, blue city by the water's edge, to the house of my uncle, and delivered into the arms of my aunt, a pretty woman from Percote who bathed me, changed me, and suckled me until such time as I was able to hold a cup. When that day came, without heat or ceremony, I was pushed from my aunt's bed by my uncle's heel and taught to take my sleep on a pallet. My aunt still fed me, with a spoon from a wooden bowl, and without suck, I began to grow. A year later, struck hard by the shafts of disease, my aunt went down to meet Charon with a coin in her mouth, and my uncle and I were left alone and stunned in that low blue house in Abydus-by-the-sea. In that hour, my uncle first turned for solace to the juice of the grape.

I may seem hard on my uncle. If so, I do him an injustice. He was not a bad man by any measure of his character. He drank, but only after my aunt died and only at night when he was home and alone. He never drank during the day. He held an important post, as Harbor Master in Abydus, and he needed to be alert during the day, and he was. He had been a soldier before and, according to his friends, a good one, having campaigned at Sestus, in Thynia, and in Thrace alongside my father. Apparently my father relied heavily on my uncle for a particular skill: the ability to organize logistical support for a campaigning army in the field. My father's talents seem to have shown best when fighting at the forefront; I have heard it said that he was a master tactician — my uncle declared that in their day there was none better. If so, my uncle was my father's mainstay, and the many victories they won in Thrace still bear the mark of their combined effort.

My father's partnership with my uncle, so successful that no opponent had ever defeated them, ended suddenly on a grim day during the last Thracian War. In that hour, a topknotted party of horse archers appeared behind my father's line, attacking his supply depots on the beach. Responding to the threat, my uncle gave battle and, without taking time to don armor, led the fighting strength of his supply companies immediately forward, their sea darts and bucklers at the ready. Somehow, this scratch force defeated the Thracians: my uncle said that he merely frightened their horses, throwing the entire Thracian attack into confusion. Whatever the case, my uncle annihilated the enemy to the last man, but not before topknotted archers put three of their stone-

tipped arrows into various parts of his body. He was still standing, still facing the field, when the battle ended, but he had
wedged himself into the fork of an oak in order to hold his body
in place, and after his men took him down, twelve moons elapsed
before he could stand again without pain. My uncle's campaigns
ended in Thrace; by royal decree, he was discharged from the
army and callously forgotten by the House of Dardanos. Later,
at the urging of some sound military minds, my father's among
them, my uncle was placed on pension, recalled, and sent north
to Abydus to fill the new post of Harbor Master.

At the time, blue Abydus-by-the-sea was only beginning to
become important in the grand Trojan design, and from all appearances, my uncle achieved marked success as an administrator. "When I first came up here," he used to rumble from his
cups, "Abydus was nothing but a village, a swine yard, a manure
pile — not a very big village but a very, very big dung heap!" He
never went on to say what his friends said, that he had made
Abydus into what it was, a fortified trade center, the hub of the
Trojan merchant fleet. In place of the village, my uncle had raised
a town of some ten thousand; in place of the swine yard, he had
erected a barracks block, an armory, and a stone stronghold in
keeping with the defensive needs of the frontier environment,
and in place of the numerous dung heaps, he had built the largest
shipyards anywhere in Dardania and a series of long, low warehouses in which to collect and store cargo against the vagaries of
the weather and the unpredictable movements of our ships. And
he had done all of this before I was born, even before my father
had been appointed to command at Dardanos. And he did more
as Trojan trade expanded, shifting the overflow gradually north
until holy Arisbe enjoyed its benefits, and even Percote. It was on
a visit to Percote that he met my aunt, married her, and, after an
interval, brought her back to Abydus to their blue house by the
water's edge. That theirs was a love match, I am certain, although
later, that surprised me, for my uncle remained much the general

in manner, continuing hard, bluff, and irascible even through our last meeting. Perhaps he was gentle with my aunt; perhaps she called forth a side of him that I never saw. I do not say, understand, that he failed to show concern for me; he did, although by and large, it was the concern of duty, a duty unlooked for but, once accepted, properly performed: I had a roof over my head, I was fed and clothed, I was given plenty of fresh air, and I was kept from harm by an old slave, a deaf mute who came to us to cook our meals and see to our general upkeep. This she did competently enough, without a trace of warmth, in exchange for food and a dry place to sleep. And at the beginning of my ninth year, my uncle went down to Troy and brought back Pharos to be my tutor.

2

I SAW PHAROS first in my uncle's wake, on the night they returned from Troy. Beyond our walls, white-winged Boreas blew down fiercely from the mountain fastness of Thrace, whipping sharp autumn sleet across the Hellespont and up our windy streets, but inside, wrapped in a goatskin beside the hearth, I was warm enough as I bent over a bowl, eating whatever meats the deaf mute had boiled for me. Suddenly the door flew open and Boreas leapt through, flickering the lamps, to be quickly followed by my uncle, clouds of steam blowing from his nostrils, the hard November chill dripping from his hair onto the fleece that wrapped his shoulders. Without so much as a word, he cast his fleece into a corner and strode forward, shaking two blunt fingers, indicating to the deaf mute that he wanted her to draw two bowls of stew and set them on the table. According to custom, I stood, making him my mark of respect, and as he moved forward, unmasking the door, I saw Pharos for the first time.

I gawked, I'm afraid, for I had never seen so strange a sight, and while I remember being apprehensive — perhaps even afraid — I nevertheless thrust myself forward to satisfy my curiosity. What I saw seemed almost mystical, an immensely tall, bald-headed, bearded apparition in soaking white with the deepest, darkest, most penetrating gray eyes that I had ever seen. The apparition had stooped, coming through the door; it had been forced to stoop because, when it finally straightened up immediately inside the jamb, its hairless head rose almost to the roof beams. Below this specter's right eye, purple scar tissue ran in ridges across the sunken bridge of the nose, coming to a blunt point near the leading edge of the earlap. Beneath, the apparition appeared both lean and hard, its thick gray beard contrasting sharply with the drenched folds of its sailcloth cloak.

The moment I stepped forward, those sea-deep eyes caught me, held me, and almost, I think, twinkled. Then the beard parted, and a voice rumbled in tones so low that my hair straightened along the back of my neck.

"This is the boy?"

My uncle nodded.

"The son of Kalitor?"

My uncle turned and looked at me from across the table while I still gawked at the sight before me. "So it would seem," he said thickly, "from the shape of the nose and the brow, but the eyes he must have from his mother." He looked at me for one or two more seconds before leaning forward, intent on his bowl; but just as he was about to sit down, he looked up and made a sharp, parting comment — without heat — in a matter-of-fact voice. "He's small for his age. And he lacks luster. You don't have much to work with."

"Oh?" said the other, throwing my uncle a hard glance. "We shall see.

"Boy," he shouted suddenly, "remove that goatskin; show me your limbs!"

Instinctively, I shouted back. "My name is Dymas! And *I* will remove *my* skin when *you* remove *yours!*"

That the man's eyes twinkled, I am sure, and in the last second before my uncle's flat, hard hand knocked me reeling to the wall, I can still remember that bald head nodding in affirmation. Regardless, I came up bleeding, my ears ringing.

". . . pointless!" the apparition was saying to my uncle. "And insofar as raw material, there seems to be more of it than you realized."

"That may be so," growled my uncle, who glared angrily in my direction, "but I brook no disrespect toward anyone who enters my door.

"Do you hear that, Dymas? Hospitality is protected by Zeus!"

As the apparition fumed, I acknowledged my uncle's words.

"Good," my uncle said roughly; "the matter is ended. Don't ever make that mistake again." And so saying, he settled himself on a stool. "Sit," he said to the apparition, "and eat. The food grows cold."

"No," said the stranger, "not yet. Not before you and I reach agreement about this boy. Either he is to be my responsibility and I am to have a free hand, or he is not, in which case, I return to Troy, tonight. Make your choice."

That was the only time in my life that I ever saw anyone give my uncle an ultimatum.

"In matters of discipline," my uncle barked angrily, "I — "

"In matters of discipline," the stranger rasped back, "*I* am to have total control, and I will exercise it by being responsible for the boy's conduct, but I will tolerate no interference — not now, not ever. Agreed? If not, I will go my way, and you may do the job yourself."

The moment froze, and like the Borean wind sweeping down from Thrace, the silence carried the breath of sleet. I did not know that my fate was being decided — there, in that ill-lighted room, in a test of wills between my last surviving relative and a stranger, but it was, and the tension became overpowering.

Here, tonight, beside the cold ash of Troy, I cannot say that Pharos or my uncle knew fully what was at stake; in fact, I am certain that neither had so much as an inkling of the truth, for who but an augur can read the thoughts of Zeus? Not my uncle, certainly, and not Pharos, for both were mortal men.

The veins on my uncle's forehead flushed thick to the point of bursting, and his jaw muscles set so tight across his face that they seemed ready to snap. Then he took one look at me and gave in.

"Done!" he thundered, and the tension went suddenly from his face.

The disagreement ended almost before it began. Not only had my uncle stood still for the stranger's ultimatum, he had given in, accepting all terms. I was thunderstruck, for I had never seen him do the like before, and in the years that followed, I was never to see him do so again. But on that November night, I watched him take a stand and back away from it, without an ounce of shame or regret, in the face of a stranger.

"Let that be a lesson to you," my uncle said to me in his most gravelly voice; "never try to hold an untenable position."

At the time, I didn't know what he was talking about. Now, I think he was making me an apology, but if I waited for something explicit, it never came, and besides, he'd already made his point. I had no illusions about why he'd struck me; even if the blow had been unjust, the lesson it delivered was well learned.

The stranger walked to my side of the table, stopped just short of me, looked quickly down, and gave me a broad smile. I could not see his teeth for the thickness of his beard, but his eyes brightened, conveying an unmistakable message.

"I am Pharos," he said, removing his dripping cape and hanging it from a roof beam. "I am to be your tutor."

With a short bow from the hips, I made him my mark of respect, cementing our relationship, and he immediately pulled up a stool and sat down before a cold bowl of stew. "Now, young Dymas," he said, "take your place at your uncle's right hand as a sign of your obedience. For the remainder of the meal, act as his cupbearer."

I did as I was told, and as though nothing had happened, Pharos and my uncle poured their libations and fell to the main course amidst an earnest discussion of the Mysian threat to the south.

*

From that moment, Pharos became my constant companion, and through the years that followed, I seldom found myself separated from his person. As good as his word, he made himself responsible for my conduct, and in fulfilling his charge, he saw that I remained ever under alert supervision. Not a moment went to waste. Daily, even before Aurora's first blush, we rose and left the house without waking my uncle. Once beyond the door, Pharos started me running, slowly at first, but always in the direction of the beach. On that first morning, the air was bitter cold, and ice had formed in the street, leaving the earth's surface hard and slick. Ignoring everything, Pharos pointed toward the beach and said, "Run, boy. Show me your speed." And I ran, slipping, sliding, breaking through ice into puddles, going up to my ankles in cold mud beneath. I shivered as I ran, Boreas biting at my bones, but as I plunged through the streets, racing down toward the sea, the chill left me, my pace quickened, and, as I passed a harbor man stepping from his door, my pride took command and I ran like the wind, breaking from the town's edge in a final burst of speed that sent me scudding across the beach with the strength of an outgoing tide. Once, I looked back over my shoulder, and behind me, his sea cape billowing in the wind, Pharos followed, running smoothly with long, easy strides. I drew up, finally, at the water's edge, breathing hard, as Pharos eased to a halt beside me.

"Good enough," he said to me, "but we must work on your form. Now, off with your tunic and into the sea." I couldn't believe my ears. As I'd made my way to the beach, Aurora had at last shown her face, but if anything, Boreas had only blown harder, and there, on the edge of the Hellespont, sleet blew down from Thrace with gale force. No matter; Pharos made himself naked and plunged instantly into the surf, and, eager to please, I plunged after him, though I knew not how to swim. I was knocked immediately from my feet by the surf's blows, and after going down hard beneath two successive waves, I came up spluttering, screaming, stung by jellyfish, which had wrapped their tentacles about my thigh. Pharos came back to me, then, where

I leapt frantically in the waist-high surf, and showed me the forceful wrinkles of his brow.

"You should have told me that you did not know how to swim," he said flatly. "When a thing is beyond your capabilities, make it known to me, and we will find a remedy. Now, wade forward, and I will teach you to swim."

And there in those icy waters, on that first morning, he did, and I was quick to learn. And when I had learned, we stepped again from the waves, pulled our tunics over our heads, and ran back to my uncle's house, where we applied coatings of oil and breakfasted with my uncle on fried fillets of fish.

The moment my uncle departed for his headquarters, Pharos drew a brand from the fire and made a series of marks across the hearthstones. "These are numbers, Dymas; you must learn their shapes and commit them to memory. As soon as you do, I am going to start showing you some amazing things about their manipulation." We spent the remainder of the morning at what Pharos called "my numbers," and by the time my uncle returned for his midday meal, I knew their shapes and, at Pharos' prompting, could draw most of them on the hearthstones. Following the meal, I was eager to continue, but Pharos said no. "This afternoon, we have other work," he said quickly. "Hoist your sail."

In the street, beneath Borean buffeting, we made our way past the barracks block where the Mustang trained for war and on into Armorer's Lane, and there, as I watched with delight, a one-eyed smith made Pharos his mark of respect, handing him a long ash spear. Then the sooty smith turned to me, casting his eye from my head to my toe. "A sea dart?" he said.

"A sea dart," Pharos confirmed.

From a stand of shafts, the grimy smith retrieved a bronze-headed javelin, the shortened version that we use at sea, and placed it in my hands. I had never held a weapon before, and as the polished olive shaft rested lightly in my hands, I hefted it, thrilling to its touch. Turning swiftly, I took up the same stance

I had seen our warriors take when they practiced on the Field of Ares.

"Ho!" The smith chortled. "The mighty Hercules."

"More like the mighty Ares!" I shouted in a burst of enthusiasm.

"Blasphemy," Pharos snapped, rapping me hard above the right ear with the butt of his spear. "Show a proper respect for the gods, Dymas; you are no more than a man."

Abashed for having prompted me, the smith became serious, beckoned me forward, and smudged my forehead with a sooty line. "May your spear cast always fly true," he said to me, "and may you heave your weapon with a recognition of your own mortality."

Pharos paid down a coin, and, bearing both my shame and my dart, I followed him outside.

Once in the open air, with the armory behind us, I received the first of many stern lectures that were to come to me through the years.

"You will purify yourself before supper," he said hotly while I ran stumbling beside him. "And you will pour three libations from your cup for each word of your blasphemy. You are not the mighty war god, and you are never going to be. Never speak the like again! You are a man, Dymas, or you will be one day, and men die, but the gods live forever. A proper recollection of that will keep you mindful of the scheme of things. The world is filled with evils, boy, but there is none so great as pride: pride is an insult to the gods — it is a denial of your own birthright as a human being and an attempt to make yourself into the gods' equal. It is always punished and punished hard. Do you not know the history of Tithonus? Well?"

I replied that I did not.

"Long ago," he said, heading toward the hills, "Lord Tithonus ran swiftly beside the sea. At that moment, blushing Aurora saw and fell instantly in love with him. She came to earth, declaring her passion, and so overpowered did both of them become that they fell instantly to lovemaking, goddess and man, their youthful bodies joined together. In time, Aurora brought her paramour before Zeus, begging him to make Tithonus immortal. 'And this is *your* wish?' the Master of Thunder asked. 'Yes,' Tithonus said. Zeus granted his wish, and the lovers went away, and years later Tithonus struggled awake one morning to find that vulture's feet had made their marks at the corners of his eyes. Suddenly, he realized that he was growing old.

"Time passed, and finally Tithonus knew that he could no longer satisfy Aurora's desires. He went back, then, to Ida and begged Zeus to let him die. At first, Zeus refused to relent, saying only that Tithonus should also have asked for immortal youth, but much later, when Tithonus had shrunk to the size of a hazel-nut, Zeus agreed to hear him once more. 'I thought,' Zeus thundered, 'that you wanted to be immortal like the gods.' 'I was wrong,' Tithonus replied; 'I should have remained a man. Now, I beg you to let me die like one.' 'Wisdom,' said Zeus, 'is often difficult to acquire,' and so saying, he changed Tithonus into a cicada so that he would expire on the night wind."

Pharos stopped, leaning on his spear. "Now tell me," he said, "do you understand the story?"

"Not the part about satisfying Aurora's desires. What does that — "

"Never mind that," Pharos snapped, showing me a pair of narrow eyes. "What about the rest of it?"

"Lord Tithonus wanted something that wasn't good for him?" I said.

"Exactly," said Pharos. "What?"

"To be like the gods?"

"That's right," Pharos said, "and be sure you don't forget it. A man is a man, Dymas, nothing more . . . but nothing less. To want to be other than a man is *hubris;* avoid *hubris,* for it rots the soul. Practice *aidos,* a proper respect for all things in their place.

Do it and be mindful of your mortality. We call that *sophrosyne,* Dymas . . . a virtue . . . that shamefastness in all men which reminds us that we must die."

And without another word, Pharos spun on his heel and started up the path while I leapt forward behind him, trying to keep up the pace.

We entered the hills, and for the remainder of the afternoon I practiced throwing my dart. Slowly, I learned to stand fast, whirl where I stood, and cast my shaft as I might a stone, and gradually I learned what Pharos meant by the suppleness of the wrist and how to point my head in the direction of my aim.

"Never mind the distance," Pharos chided; "control is the most important skill, and you have done far better than I expected. Now, Dymas, on with your cloak. Apollo descends, and we have a long run if we are to reach your uncle's door before nightfall."

We were away, then, beneath long evening shadows, moving swiftly over stones and across shallow watercourses still wet from the previous night's runoff. When we finally topped the last rise and started down into silent Abydus, Apollo's chariot was long gone, the only remaining light coming from windows where oil lamps filtered tiny beams through shutters that had been closed tightly against the chill.

3

FROM THE FIRST DAY, my training went forward at a steady pace, never much altered from the pattern I have described to you. Winter, summer, spring, or fall, we rose daily and ran to the sea for an hour's swim, and then we jogged home again for breakfast and the morning's lessons. Pharos permitted no skylarking, and if he caught my concentration drifting, he was quick to bring me up, shouting, "The enemy!" in my ear — Pharos always called a failure in concentration *the enemy* — before prodding me with the hard butt of his spear. More than once, I let out a yelp, responding to the cold bronze of his spear point, which always found me when I least expected it; in every instance, my surprise brought a second jab, for it was Pharos' rule that one must never let on that one had been caught off guard. "Far better," he would tell me, "not to have been caught off guard in the first place. Be alert, Dymas; it may save your life!"

During the afternoons, invariably, we practiced at arms or hunted in the hills, and throughout that first year, I worked daily with my dart, learning to command my cast. My strength improved as I grew, but Pharos also insisted that I eat meat with every meal, saying that the animal strength would add to my own, and on the whole, I am certain that he was right.

We hunted much, of course, supplying meat for my uncle's table, and Pharos taught me everything he knew about the art. My uncle, as I remember, became tired of eating so much wild hare during that first winter, so as a result, even before spring, Pharos found it necessary to take me higher into the hills, and there, hunting like a wolf in snow, I could sometimes take a wild goat or a small boar. Once, from the fork of a tree, downwind from a small drinking pool, I brought down a buck, and when we finally came down from the hills, long after dark, Pharos carrying the carcass over his shoulders while I carried our spears, my uncle seemed truly impressed.

We hunted in the afternoons in the hills behind Abydus, and then, during my tenth winter, Pharos began teaching me to use a sling.

"It is hardly a heroic weapon," he said to me, "but it is accurate at long distance, and it kills well."

Within a space of six months, I had learned the sling well enough to bring down a hare or goat on the run, and once, between Abydus and holy Arisbe, I stunned a gazelle and brought it home for the week's meals. Afterward, Pharos made me alternate weapons, hunting one day with the dart but on the next with my sling, and I grew gradually more proficient with both. And at the beginning of my eleventh summer, I was issued my first bow and two bronze-tipped arrows, to be used in practice against the straw targets on Ares' Field.

With the bow, and under Pharos' watchful instruction, I competed for the first time with boys my own age, and older, who practiced daily, learning the way of the warrior. In the beginning, I shot poorly; the horn bow was stiff, and I required some time before I could string it properly; but as I looked about and saw the other boys having difficulty, I willed myself to master it.

"Like the sling," Pharos told me once as I notched an arrow, "the bow is not a heroic weapon, but it is a superior hunting instrument, and its use in warfare is becoming more common. Your uncle's wounds in Thrace brought home the living proof.

Since, Lord Priam has ordered all Trojans to be well trained with the bow.''

"Am I to become a bowman?" I asked, releasing the tension on my bowstring.

"None of that," Pharos said sharply, thumping me with the butt of his spear. "Today, you shoot; for the moment, be an archer. What the Fates may have in store for you only Zeus knows, and idle speculation is foolish. Now, concentrate; let me see you hit the mark."

About the same time, I learned to box and wrestle. One hundred targets flanked Ares' Field, but Abydian youth were numerous, and each had to wait his turn. During the intervals, wrestling masters from the barracks block put us through our paces. Biting and eye gouging were not allowed, but otherwise we were encouraged to show no mercy toward our opponents. If a boy looked slack, the wrestling masters applied hard falls of their own, but if an officer from the Mustang or someone like my uncle found anyone holding back, the cat was applied with a strong stroke that left the offender bleeding.

Later in that same year, Pharos altered my training schedule again, taking me down to the harbor to begin learning about the sea and our high-beaked ships. Pharos was a good teacher, astute in his knowledge of winds and tides, and when he thought I was ready, he entered me at the barracks as a cadet, joining me with a crew of seven other boys, and took me to sea for the first time in a training hull commanding six pine oars.

In the beginning, we were clumsy, and we hadn't the slightest idea what to do. First, we learned to row, but it seemed that we could never find the rhythm, so after two or three successful strokes, one of us would invariably catch a crab and be swept painfully from the rowing bench by the butt of an oar. But with Pharos at the helm, with his firm but patient instruction, we learned gradually to control the stroke, and within a week or two, we found that we could launch our hull and beat up the edge of the channel until we were within sight of holy Arisbe. From there, we would turn seaward toward Thynia, catch the race, and ride swiftly back down the Hellespont to our starting point before Abydus-by-the-sea. When we had mastered this exercise, Pharos next taught us to make the circuit under sail.

Under Pharos' direction and within a space of two spring months, all eight of us were well on our way toward becoming competent sailors. Then, truly, each of us learned to rely on his fellow and on himself. For courtesy, I remember, because my tutor was in charge, I was the last among us to take my turn at command. I still recall the muscles in my jaw tightening as I set my mind to the task, and on that day, luck was with me, so I made no mistakes. By the time we reached our usual turning point, Apollo's chariot had already climbed to midmorning height. As I was about to turn, Pharos called to me from the bow, "Make Percote, Dymas, and beach your ship on the white shore!" My crew, as excited as I was, held to their oars and pulled away together, throwing up a new spray over our high-peaked prow, and with speed we scudded north in the lee of the shore, bent on seeing the unknown.

We beat up into Percote in late afternoon, tired, hungry, and sore from straining behind our oars. As soon as the matter of our landing had been settled, we moved forward up the beach toward the town gates, and very quickly I experienced a revelation.

On that day, I think for the first time, I became aware of Troy's precarious existence, and while we toured both the walled town and the citadel, guided by Pharos, who seemed to have intimate knowledge of the site, the lesson became ever more forceful. Everywhere I looked, I saw quantities of arms and supplies stacked as though the garrison commander expected an attack, and in the granaries and cisterns beneath the keep, Pharos showed us enough reserves to last Percote for two full years. Soldiers moved everywhere under arms, and on Ares' Field in particular, the training went forward with a sense of purpose and intensity that I had never seen in Abydus. Percote's warriors, I remember, looked lean to me and immeasurably hard. Even with the Thracian Wars ended, Percote's citizens occupied an exposed position on the Trojan flank and adjusted their lives accordingly, bearing arms wherever they went and fortifying their houses with an intensity elsewhere unknown in Dardania. This much, at least, Pharos explained to us as he guided us through the narrow streets toward the food vendors, whose stalls rose like mushrooms around the base of the citadel.

We camped that night at the foot of the keep, just outside a grove made sacred to Aphrodite. The night was warm, and the stars shone brightly, and on the walls, watch fires cast a flickering light over the streets below. Because Percote was a garrison town, large numbers of off-duty warriors — most of them wearing the Lion's crest — haunted the wine shops and the food stalls and what Pharos euphemistically referred to as "the Quarter of the Maidens," and then, too, large contingents of the armed watch moved back and forth throughout the night between the citadel and the beach, where sharp-eyed guards tended a long chain of watch fires that burned beneath the beaks of our ships.

In the meantime, from the surrounding farms and hamlets, the next day's food supply began to enter the town through the inland gate. Melon farmers, drovers, grain merchants, and even nut gatherers, all alike, came forward one by one, with their wagons or herds or pack animals or merely the loads on their backs, ascended the long, sloping ramp, stood fast at the gate for inspection, and then entered the town, making steady progress toward the heart of the market square. Exhausted, my companions had wrapped themselves in their cloaks and given themselves over to the night, but fixed by the wonder, I took in all that I could see.

"You seem vigilant," Pharos said, sitting down beside me, "but we've a long journey home. You ought to be asleep. A commander, especially at sea, needs to be alert. If you remain awake, you will be numb in the morning, and I may have to appoint Agelaos to command the return voyage."

Against the watch fires, I could just make out his beard and the gray sunken profile of his nose.

"Is that not why you brought us here?" I wanted to know.

"Speak plainly."

"To teach us vigilance?" I asked.

For a moment, Pharos remained silent. Then, propping his spear against the fork of a tree, he leaned against the trunk. "That, too," he said finally.

"There was another reason?" I said.

"To teach you to rely on yourselves."

"Vigilance was secondary?"

"Equal."

I hesitated, not knowing which question to ask him next. Finally, I couldn't hold myself back. "How much have we to fear?"

Immediately, Pharos chuckled, but then he sharpened his tone. "As I have told you, boy, we have much to fear, always; the trick is to know and ignore it."

"That's not what I mean," I protested. "What I mean is, how great is the threat against Troy?"

"Great," said Pharos.

"And from what quarter are we expecting it?"

Then Pharos fell silent, and his silence lasted for several seconds. "Consider," he finally said, "in the garden of Dardania, there are many adders. You know about them; you have seen them sunning themselves on the tops of rocks or lurking beneath shrubs or coiling in the shadows of their dens, and I have always taught you that their bite is fatal. We live in a world of lurking adders, Dymas, and the bite of each remains fatal until the serpent's fang has been removed or its head has been cut off. But from which corner the serpent may strike — whether from the warm rock or from the shadow of its den or from the hollow beneath the bush — it is not given us to know, so we must be wary of all and walk with a watchful eye."

He was speaking in metaphors again, a practice that to my

mind was becoming unreasonably frequent in his speech, and I told him so, only to be cracked on the head with the flat of his flint knife.

"Forbearance is a virtue," Pharos snapped, "and it is a virtue you should cultivate. I will be sure to devise you exercises for its practice."

And that he would, I knew, and I felt like kicking myself for having nettled him.

"Now," he went on, "if you think that you can hold your tongue long enough for me to finish . . . ?"

I remained silent.

". . . and if the principle is clear to you, the political specifics should not be hard to follow. The Argive serpent lazes presently along the shores of the western Aegean, its fat coils glistening beneath a warm Greek sun. To the north, the Thracian snake has retired to its den, but to the south, down the reverse slope of Ida and beyond, the Mysian adder lurks even more aggressively beneath each bush and root. Such is the threat of the hour, but remember, Dymas, that at any moment the threat may change, because the innate quality of the serpent is its mobility; it becomes sluggish only when the dread fist of winter slams down hard onto the face of the land."

"Then, what if — " I started to ask.

"No more," Pharos commanded, cutting me off in midsentence. "You are young, and you need sleep. And if we talk too long about serpents and threats near this, her sacred grove, the Lady Aphrodite may take umbrage and punish us."

"Perhaps," I ventured, "she would be less offended if you explained to me about that Quarter of the Maidens over there behind the wine shops. Orthaios tells me that — " But before I could finish, the butt of Pharos' spear cracked me hard over the shoulder, and I fell instantly silent, aware that I had pressed ahead one step too far.

In the morning, we were on our feet before dawn. We moved

off toward the beach, jogging quickly down Percote's long streets, past the food stalls and the wine shops, and the Quarter of the Maidens — I tried like my fellows to penetrate the darkened doorways with my eyes — and then we reached the main gate and passed through it in the wake of an armed company that was moving to relieve the guard. They were big men, those guards, and as we ran behind them, we imitated the motion of their bodies and quickened our pace. This brought something of a twinkle, I noticed, to Pharos' eyes, and as we changed direction, leaving the guard behind, I thought I heard Pharos chuckle.

As soon as we had poured the appropriate libations to the Master of Thunder and Poseidon, Shaker of the Earth, we launched ourselves smartly, scudding out through the surf to find the race, and when we found it, we turned south, hoisting our sail to catch the wind. In three short hours, with the strength of the windy race behind us, we arrived home, beached, and swaggered up the streets of Abydus.

4

ONE MORNING that summer, I awakened well before dawn to voices in an outer room. As I lay listening on my pallet, rubbing the sleep from my eyes, I made out one voice well enough, my uncle's, and then another, Pharos', but there were still others whose sounds were unknown to me. They went away presently, and in the same moment, Pharos came into my room and shook me fully awake.

"Now listen to me, Dymas, for we have little time. Get up and breakfast well on the fish that the mute is frying for you. Then go immediately and collect your boat crew. You are to command this morning, without questions. Agelaos is to act as bow hook and mallet master, and Orthaios will man your lead oar, but the others will dispose themselves according to your orders, and brook no back talk from anyone. You are to wait on the beach, in the lee of that fast Trojan hull which came up last night from Dardanos. Don't skylark or scatter about, for at some time within the next hour, a man will come down to you, and you are to take him wheresoever he wishes to go. You will know the man by a ring he will show you bearing the impression of twin stallions, their manes blowing in the wind." He paused, waiting to be sure I understood him.

"Will you not be going with us?" I asked.

"Not this morning," Pharos said firmly; "another matter

presses, and I must be away at dawn. Do you understand what you are to do?"

Repeating his orders word for word, just as he had issued them to me, I leapt to my feet and felt a thrill of excitement course through my veins.

"Keep a cool head," Pharos said firmly, as he turned toward the door. "And Dymas, all of you are to carry your darts." And then he was gone.

I ate my breakfast on the move that morning, as I ran from our door into the darkened streets of Abydus, gulping fried fish fillets from one hand, carrying my dart in the other. I remember going first to Agelaos' house and leaning through a window to prod his snoring cheeks with the butt of my dart. As soon as he was up, I threw him one of my fillets and gave him short orders, sending him off to raise Peiros, Knos, and Noemon while I hustled away in the opposite direction to wake hard-sleeping Orthaios and send him in turn for Alkandros and the blue-eyed Thalpios. Within less time than it takes Helios to harness his team, we were gathered on the beach, in the shadow of a high-beaked war hull, our bronzed darts in our hands, and then the questions came fast and furious.

"Where are we headed?"

"Who is the man?"

"Upon whose order do we sail?"

"This had better be important, or I'm — "

And from Orthaios, whose hard muscles were well hidden beneath a plump layer of fat, "Who is supplying the provisions?"

To all and each I answered that I did not know, and immediately Noemon, contentious beneath black brows but still half asleep, charged me with trying to steal the boat and urged the others not to go with me, warning them that they would all be whipped for complicity in an act of pillage against the state, and in the same second that slow-thinking Knos started to agree with him, I struck both with the butt of my dart, knocking the wind from their diaphragms. That dropped them instantly to the ground, where they writhed to catch their breath. They recovered quickly enough, sucking great gulps of air, and by the time they regained their wind, both were fully awake.

"Let there be no doubt," I said, trying to sound as firm and hard as Pharos, "about who commands this voyage. You know the rules, all of you, so do not make me enforce them again. Now make all preparations for getting under way."

There were no more objections and no more idle questions; immediately, all hands sprang to their appointed tasks, stowing their darts, making ready the oar thongs, the long pine oars, the mast, and the sail. And then, in the dim light of dawn, each of us stood by his assigned post, ready to launch the craft and get under way.

As Aurora's first blush deepened, a low, rolling fog suddenly floated up from the Hellespont, obscuring our sight and separating us irrevocably from the blue walls of Abydus-by-the-sea, and then, without warning, a man came striding toward us through the mist, the corner of his fog-gray cloak thrown back over his left shoulder to reveal that he was wearing the short tunic covered by a light leather cuirass. He wore no helm, this man — his dark hair blew freely in the breeze — but he carried a long ash spear and, at his side, the short sword of a Trojan officer. He seemed neither young nor old, and at the time, I remember judging his age at about forty; now, I think it may have been closer to thirty, but I was no judge of a man's age in those days, and the face I saw before me that morning looked older and much weathered by the sea, and the thin scar that crossed the right cheek beneath those black eyes gave the man's face a gravity it might not otherwise have had in the clear light of day.

"Dymas?" The voice was low but clear.

"Yes, my lord," I answered, trying to lower the pitch of my own thin sound.

"Launch and put to sea," the man said firmly.

I hesitated then, looking up to examine an expression that was hard, without emotion, and serious, without indecision, but still I held back.

"Not . . . not until I have seen the ring," I stuttered, fearful about what my uncle and Pharos might say or do to me if I made a mistake and put to sea with the wrong man.

Immediately, the ring was produced, showing the bearer to be, indeed, the man I had been told to expect. As soon as I saw the twin stallions flashing from the seal, I turned to my crew, and we launched our tiny hull, wading out through the surf and climbing swiftly aboard on my command, and then all hands pulled away together with a smooth stroke. Up forward, holding the boat hook well extended in order to fend off any obstacles that might unexpectedly appear from the mist, Agelaos positioned his squat body above the prow's eyes, acting as lookout, while I manned the steering oar and Orthaios — at my urging — called out the rhythm of the stroke. Wrapped in his cloak, without uttering so much as a word, our passenger sat before me on the rim of a thwart, his keen eyes peering into the mists through which we made our way. That he was unsure of our competence — and of my competence, in particular — there could be no doubt, for he remained alert to my every move and kept his ears well tuned to the orders I gave to my crew. Soon, I knew, we would strike the race, and in that dim mist the current would drive us swiftly south. Before that moment came, I wanted to know precisely where we were going so that I could envision our course and make my compensations for the set and drift that were sure to follow. I waited until what I thought was the last possible moment, the moment when I first felt the pull of the race against the helm; our passenger was still not forthcoming, and I asked him our destination.

"Sestus," he said in a low, guttural tone. "Make sail for Sestus, and take me straight into the harbor."

I had waited a moment too long. Directly across the neck of the Hellespont from Abydus-by-the-sea, no more than three thousand yards away, Sestus was a most difficult port to make, because there, at the neck, the race ran immeasurably swift. The best approach, always, was to sail northeast from Abydus, as though making for holy Arisbe, and then, some two miles up the channel, turn, catch the race on the port quarter, and steer back down the channel, making for the opposite shore; but already we were too late, for we had entered the race. Immediately, I did the only thing I could do, altering course to the east and pointing the bow up the channel toward Arisbe. I raised the sail and, calling for Agelaos to come back and take the helm, I hurriedly climbed the mast, locking my toes in the sheets to hold myself steady. At the top, my head and shoulders rose just above the mist, and in the distance, clearly, I could see the Thynian coast and, broadly before us, the hard black walls of Sestus and the Thracian citadel that my father had captured in the First Thracian War.

We moved ahead, then, under both sail and oar, my crew of six straining behind their long pine shafts while Agelaos labored at the helm to follow such steering instructions as I shouted down from aloft. It was hard going for my crew, I know — the result of my own mistake and one that I resolved, then and there, never to make again — but we were saved from failure by the breath of Zephyr. Responding, perhaps, to the generous libation I had poured out to him on the beach, he came up strong about the time we reached midchannel; then he gave us a stiff breeze from the heights of lower Thynia, and in the end, it proved strong enough to correct our slide, allowing us to make for the harbor's light with the barest margin of safety.

The mists had thinned by the time we beached along the steep Thynian shore, but they had not blown away entirely, for the dark streets of Sestus remained well protected from Zephyr's breath by a sickle-shaped bank of hills that enclosed the coastal plain. That plain, which rose steadily from the moment it left the sea until it backed against those steep Thynian hills, could only be called — at best — shallow; and perched along the shore, fronting the entire panorama, its black walls glistening beneath a clinging damp, stood the citadel of Sestus.

It reminded me of a hook-beaked vulture devouring carrion beneath its feet. Cattle were raised there, I knew, and some grain. Sestus itself served as administrative center for all of Thynian Thrace, housing some five thousand citizens but acting as barracks and market town for many thousands more who inhabited the remainder of the peninsula. Some slave trading continued there, I think, but after my father's wars, the bulk of the slave trade had moved offshore, to Myrina on the isle of Lemnos, yet vestiges of the trade remained. But insofar as Troy was concerned, Sestus' prime importance was strategic, for it controlled access to the tin and copper deposits located in the hills beyond, and those few deposits supplied all Thrace and Dardania with the raw materials for bronze. We kept a garrison there, as a result, of some five hundred warriors — elements of the Hawk — and the King of Thynia, acting as Priam's surrogate, had under his command some one thousand topknotted Thracians with two or three thousand more who could be called up as reserves. And yet, after all that — after my father's victories and the treaties and the sworn oaths — still, as Pharos explained to me, Thynia in particular and Thrace in general remained wounded serpents licking the injuries we had given them in the shadows of their dens. In short, only a scant three thousand yards across the Hellespont from Abydus-by-the-sea, Sestus was the frontier, and her streets and fields could prove more than dangerous in the event that she ever decided to emerge from her den and strike. Just how, when, or why that might happen, no one could guess. For those of us living along the Dardanian shore, the problem remained all but immaterial, for only Trojan hulls were allowed to move in and out of Sestus. As a part of our treaty, you see, the King of Thynia had given up all pretense to a naval posture, allowing nothing larger to be built along his coasts than rafts, ferries, and small cargo hulls designed for local commerce only. Even so, one went into Thynia armed, and on that damp early morning, so did we all.

*

Our passenger went over the side almost as soon as we touched the shore, and then, as each of us leapt over in turn, pushing our hull high up onto the sand, he drew me quickly aside, giving me clear instructions.

"Follow me at thirty paces, Dymas, and guard my back. Pick one other boy — Agelaos, I think, for his eye is keen — to follow you at the same distance and guard your own. We are going to work a draw," he said in low, measured tones. "I am to be the bait, and you are my only protection. If the unexpected happens, give me as much warning as you can, and if you can't, by the hand of Zeus, your spear cast had better be true."

Leaving Orthaios in charge of the others, I set off after the proper interval in the wake of our passenger, who never turned back once to see if I was following, showing me only the broad width of his shoulders as he shoved up the street, spear in hand, through the moving, milling crowd. Agelaos, I hoped, followed in my wake, but fearful of losing sight of my stranger, I never turned to look, relying, instead, on a combination of faith and friendship for my security in those streets.

And those streets were difficult going. Aurora had blushed hard by that time, paled, and disappeared; already, the sun chariot had started to climb. The narrow streets crawled with movement; herds of goats seemed to be issuing from some gate or other around every corner, with herdsmen and small boys driving them quickly up to pasture in the hills. Here and there, stalls were going up, fishermen were moving down toward the beach with their long nets over their shoulders, and graceful, almond-eyed women slipped to and from their homes, carrying water jugs or laundry or freshly baked barley cakes that scented the morning air with an odor of honey. Warriors began to appear, tall, top-knotted Thracians with gold and silver wrist guards who carried black spears with sharp bronze heads and square, ox-hide shields bearing white clan marks in their centers. I saw Trojans, too, singly or in pairs, obvious to me by the sharp cut of their hair and the roundness of their shields. And then I noticed that the streets had narrowed and were narrowing still, and as the press of the crowd increased, I looked ahead and saw that we were approaching the base of the citadel. The gradual narrowing of the streets was part of Sestus' defense, a skillful design that reduced any invader's fighting front to the thinness of a two- or three-man wedge, something that could be dealt with by a small number of defenders. It occurred to me that Sestus must be laid out like a chariot wheel, with the citadel as hub and each street converging on it like a narrowing spoke.

Up in front of me, I could still see the back of my passenger's head, rising above the press of the crowd, but as the street ran suddenly against the hub base of the citadel and turned, so did my passenger, and I, stung by the surprise, lost sight of him altogether. The moment I realized what had happened, my every muscle tightened, and I sprinted forward, dashing quickly between two Thracian warriors and up through a crowd of idlers into the midst of a herd of goats. As I kicked one goat after another from my path, the goatherd put up an angry protest, threatening me with his crook, but just as quickly, I showed him the point of my dart and thrust ahead, rounding the corner at last, only to find myself wedged between the rolling flesh of a vegetable vendor and her at once angry customer. As though they were striking a fly, their fleshy hands swatted me hard, and I was driven instantly through the gap between them and into a long, rectangular square beyond.

Indifferent to what might be taking place behind me, I took in the whole scene at a glance. The square was busy with activity; a horse market appeared to be in progress at the opposite end, but where I stood, the port side of the square seemed to be lined by house fronts and wine shops, while the starboard side held vending stalls of various kinds that backed onto the base of the citadel. At first, I saw nothing of my passenger and grew tense with apprehension, but then, about fifty paces distant, I spotted him passing a potter's stall, his cloak thrown back, revealing to the full his cuirass and arms, and immediately I made ready to rush forward and close the distance between us.

I had no more than taken my first step when, inexplicably, some god must have tickled my nose, and I sneezed and sneezed again. As I cleared my head and made a propitiatory sign to Zeus, something curious caught my eye near the edge of the square, a Phrygian who had stepped in haste from a wine shop. My curiosity became aroused not so much by the Phrygian's appearance as by instinct; I had seen Phrygians in Abydus, in holy Arisbe, and on the beach before Percote, and all of my instincts told me that this Phrygian was not Phrygian at all, and yet I could not say why. He bore a Phrygian shield, certainly, and his hair and tunic were both worn according to Phrygian clan fashions, but there in the square, something seemed amiss, and my nerves instantly quickened.

Yet I held back. By that time, you see, I understood enough of the game to know that I had to be sure. If I made a mistake, alerting my passenger too soon to the wrong man, the game would end with the draw lost. I waited, a rime of sweat breaking across my brow, hoping beyond reason that the Phrygian would unmask himself and give the game away. But he merely moved out across the paving stones and through the crowd in the same general direction as my passenger, and at a safe interval, I followed him.

By that time, my man was far out ahead, already striding past the horse market, and my fear of making a mistake and failing in my responsibility grew sharper with every step he took. Then I really did begin to sweat, for suddenly, from the dark doorway of a low house, a second Phrygian joined the first, this one carrying both spear and shield.

Unaware of either man, my passenger walked swiftly ahead, leaving the horse market and its fly-encrusted dung piles to port while moving briskly toward the end of the square. Opposite a long stone ramp that inclined gradually toward the citadel's main gate, he abruptly disappeared down a side street leading back toward the beach, and in that moment I had the proof that I had been waiting for. My passenger, you see, had remained in plain view all the way across the square, but then, in no more time than it takes an eagle to blink, he was gone. Surprised by such an unexpected move, the Phrygians lunged forward, quickening their pace in order to round the corner behind him, and by doing so, they gave themselves away.

In that second, I knew what was expected of me and dashed forward, my dart at the ready, and as I whipped around the market's edge, brushing the flank of a horse when I leapt over a dung pile, I turned quickly down the narrow side street to find that the scene before me removed all lingering doubt. Sixty yards beyond the point where I had rounded the corner, my passenger still moved ahead at a brisk pace, but midway between us, sprinting silently forward on their bare soles, both Phrygians had elevated their weapons and were preparing to cast.

Mindless of the consequence and having forgotten altogether about Agelaos, I roared the Trojan war cry at the top of my lungs and hurled my dart. After that, I recall, things happened with great rapidity. My dart, thrown true but without sufficient force, missed the vitals and sank, instead, through the leading Phrygian's thigh. Even so, I was close enough to bring him down, and did, in the same instant that my passenger, now alerted, turned to ready himself for battle. Faced so suddenly and unexpectedly with a plan gone wrong, with enemies on either side of him, the remaining Phrygian sized up his predicament and charged instantly in my direction, snorting like a bull from the wine-dark sea and screaming with rage, the vents of his nose flaring far back toward his cheekbones.

In that moment, on that morning, there on that narrow street in Sestus, I felt for the first time the cold hand of death and stood petrified by its touch. I couldn't move; I could barely think. And all I could see was that enraged Phrygian hurtling toward me with a sword in his hands like a Fury straight from the chambers of decay. I sank back, but before I could utter so much as a sound, it was over, the Phrygian — his contorted face registering both terror and pain — crashing to the ground before me in a clatter of arms, my passenger's long ash spear embedded in the assassin's back. Blood squirted in every direction, and as my passenger hurried forward, quickly disarming the other Phrygian, whose agonized screams had filled the air, I dropped to my knees and vomited. Then I rose again, wiping my mouth beneath the gaze of my passenger.

"They're not . . . not Phrygians," I stammered as he moved up beside me, placing one foot firmly against the dead man's spine and forcibly withdrawing his spear.

"How do you know that?" he asked, giving me a penetrating look.

"I don't know," I said, wiping my mouth with the corner of my cloak; "I just *know.*"

By that time, he was cleaning his spear on the dead man's cloak, but when he turned the body over and I had a clear view of the popping, horrified eyes, I thought I was going to be sick again, and put my head between my knees.

"You are right," my passenger said, making me turn and look again; "these are Mysian dogs who go into battle on the bare pads of their feet, believing that their strength as warriors comes directly from Gaia, the Earth Mother."

I looked then, and the source of my suspicion became clear. Phrygians — the Phrygians I had seen — wore sandals with long rawhide thongs.

At the top of the street, bleeding from the nose and the top of the ear, Agelaos suddenly rounded the corner and came charging forward like a sprinter near the end of his distance.

"The goatherd?" I asked him, perceiving the source of his injury.

"And one of the Thracians," Agelaos blurted out, as the sight before him suddenly paralyzed his tongue. Then, before we could get another word out of him, he too became sick, for by that time the street was awash with Mysian blood.

Within seconds, the goatherd and two very angry Thracian warriors came round the corner in search of Agelaos, but as soon as they saw the carnage before them, all three drew up short. My passenger showed the imperial ring, speaking a single, sharp command in the Thracians' direction. Instantly, they melted away into the market square, returning only moments later with members of our own Dardanian guard, Hawks all. By that time we had seen to the wounded man, whose hands and feet we bound before pulling my dart from his thigh; he too streamed dark blood onto the stones of the street. For a while, the man screamed abuse at all of us together, but as his blood flowed, he weakened, and then my passenger removed a length of linen from his wallet and bound the wound so that it bled no more. By that time, the guard had arrived, and the bearded Hawk commanding them gave my passenger an immediate sign of submission.

"He is to be carried down to the six-oared hull on the beach," my passenger ordered, pointing to the Mysian. He turned his gaze on us. "These young men will show you the way, and they are to be well treated, for they have served today like warriors beyond their years."

At that, the commander of the guard smiled; immediately, my passenger admonished him, and all smiles stopped together. But insofar as Agelaos and I were concerned, our combined nausea flattened any sense of pride we might have felt that morning, and in Agelaos' case, he suffered a throbbing headache where the butt of a Thracian spear had bounced above his ear. We were not very alert by then, and as our tensions slacked, our exhaustion seemed nearly to overwhelm us. In short, neither of us cared whether the captain of the guard smiled or not.

I was not allowed to wallow long in my release, for as soon as he gave the guard their instructions, my passenger turned to me.

"I go now to the citadel," he said sharply. "I have given the captain of the guard instructions to go down to the beach with you, keeping the prisoner under close watch until I return, but you must show him the way, Dymas. I should finish my business before Helios strikes his zenith, and then we return directly to Abydus. Do you have any money?"

"No, my lord," I replied.

"Here is a coin," he said, dropping a silver in my hand. "See that your crew is well fed. They have put in a hard morning in the service of the state, and they deserve their fare."

Without another word, he was away up the street, heading toward the square and the long, fortified ramp that wound its way toward the citadel's main gate.

On the beach, the silver my passenger had given me fed both my crew and the Dardanian guards on hot black bread and a quarter of mutton fresh from the spit. The guards ate in turns, two overseeing the prisoner while the other two helped themselves to slices of meat cut steaming from the flank of the bone. We boys ate eagerly, all at once, and over and over again Agelaos and I were forced to retell the events of the morning. Thus revived, we were accurate with all facts, but neglected, as I recall, to say anything whatsoever about having been sick in the street. There was endless speculation, of course, about what it all meant, the guards even going so far as to suggest that the Mysians were Greek agents plotting a commercial encroachment upon Priam's monopoly in the straits. Actually, the truth proved far more insidious, but we did not hear it until the middle of the afternoon, when we were well on our way home.

Good as his word, my passenger returned to the beach not long after the sun's chariot had reached the peak of its journey. Without hesitation, he ordered the Mysian tied down in the sail well, and then we launched our craft swiftly into the Hellespont and pulled away together. The morning mist had long since burned

off, and across the channel, the blue walls of Abydus-by-the-sea
shone brilliantly beneath the sun. Nevertheless, we did not steer
directly toward them; instead, to relieve the strain on my crew,
I beat up the Thynian coast, running northeast before the wind,
just outside the main strength of the current. When I became
certain that a turn south into the race would set us straight back
to Abydus, I came about, shipped oars, and treated my crew to
smooth sailing, receiving their cheers for my pains.

My passenger came up beside me, where I stood manning the
steering oar, and with no more than a slight inclination of his
head, he pointed to our captive.

"You are wondering, I suppose, what this is all about," he said,
a great weight seeming to lift from his shoulders.

I was. I had put a spear through a man's leg that day, and I
wanted above all things to know why.

"I will tell you just enough to make the case clear, and no
more," my passenger said quietly. Throwing back his cloak
across the helmsman's bench, he sat down beside me and leaned
against the keel. When he did, his head must have been about a
foot behind my right ear.

"As Pharos would say," he began in a low, weary voice, "the
Mysian serpent has emerged from its den and prepared to
strike." He paused then, allowing the full weight of his words to
have their effect. "At the moment," he said at last, "the snake's
full length still lies dangerously coiled beneath a bush, but this
one," and he pointed to the Mysian groaning in our sail well,
"and the one I killed this morning are part of its poison. Know
you, Dymas, that the Mysian king covets our prosperity, that hard
Mysian armies are already massing on the south slope of Ida,
their black forges hot with fire as their armorers and smiths ready
them for war."

Suddenly, a gust of wind struck us across the port beam, and
in response, I gave immediate orders to shorten sail before a
growing pressure on our canvas blew us completely off course.

Behind me, my passenger adjusted his position to compensate
for the yawing of our hull, and waited, and when I had corrected
for our drift and trimmed sail, he continued.

"Nine days ago," he said, "I was in Mysian Pitane, acting as
aide to our chief diplomatist. Pitane is an ugly place, fit only for
Mysians. One sees nothing there of cut stone or fitted blocks; the
entire city is built of the crudest mud brick, laid without skill and
left unfinished, and the streets are so darkly narrow as to give the
whole city the confused haphazardness of a warren. Commerce
there was brisk enough and the streets as busy and congested as
anthills when they are disturbed in the fields by passing cattle or
men, but not long after our arrival, we began to notice a curious
change. Low, dark, and dirty like their streets — their faces
grimed, their black hair coated with and smelling of grease —
women, old men, and snot-nosed whelps were everywhere in
evidence, but as the days passed, we saw fewer and fewer of the
swart, fierce warriors who man their Mysian commands. It was
then, you see, that we realized something was afoot, so on the
quiet, I began turning over every log and stone, trying to find out
what it was."

Again my hands moved to make a slight course correction with
the steering oar, but my ears remained fixed to my passenger.

"I had my first piece of information from a Lydian salt vendor,"
he was saying. "The man had just come south from Chrysa. He
had gone there in company with two Carians, intending to sell
both his salt and a quantity of grain, but even before they had
made port, a Mysian naval vessel had stopped them at sea and
ordered them to return to Pitane or face immediate seizure and
imprisonment. Chrysa, as you know, lies close to our borders, at
the foot of Ida's reverse slope, so the Lydian's story, by itself,
gave me enough information to believe that Mysia was preparing
for war. Nevertheless, I wanted proof, and I had it, finally, a few
hours later, from a Phrygian.

"The Phrygian, who was also a merchant, had been traveling
for some weeks from the depths of his homeland, and his route

was such that he had bypassed Chrysa in the night, only days before, somehow skirting both the city and its outlying guard posts. Thus, he escaped a prohibition that he seemed to know nothing about. What he did tell me, however, was that beyond the northern reaches of the city, far in the distance, he had seen what he thought to be hundreds of Mysian campfires twinkling like stars from the slopes of Ida. That told me almost as much as I needed to know, and thereafter I acted swiftly. Clearing my intentions with my chief, I found and bribed a minor court official who made known to us the specific details of what I had already gleaned."

He paused, drew some figs from his wallet, and, after passing them down to my crew, went on with his narration.

"It may seem strange," he said, "and it is certainly vile, but it is also entirely Mysian: for three bars of silver and the mere promise of a safe passage to Lemnos, that sniveling little dog betrayed their whole enterprise. In short, the Mysians were indeed preparing for war and had already massed more than twelve thousand warriors across the wooded foothills of Ida. But as yet, their preparations remained incomplete, because Mysian ambassadors were still afield, in both Caria and Greece, attempting to negotiate military alliances that would combine all three powers against us. Those, we thought, would probably come to naught, for the Mysians had tried the same stratagem during the First Mysian War and met with rebuff from both quarters. The Greeks, it seemed, had always found Carians both uncouth and vulgar, and from what our agents had been able to tell us, they liked the Mysians even less, so on that score at least, we felt reasonably secure. But then the treasonous whelp dropped one more piece of information before us, and it is that morsel which has had such disastrous effects for the Mysian in the sail well and his fellow in Sestus."

My eyes darted immediately forward to the man I had nearly killed that morning. That he was much in pain, there could be no doubt, for his face was ashen, and even beneath the sea breeze, his forehead was awash with sweat. Someone — Agelaos, I believe — had given him a thickness of line to grind between his teeth, and with it, the Mysian was biting back his fear of death, as well as he might. None of us, I noticed, seemed very much to mind.

"Those two," my passenger said, "were agents of the Mysian crown, sent north into Thynia for the express purpose of subverting Trojan control there. They had been given instructions, you see, to lure Thynian nobles with sums of gold and the bright promise of war spoils in Troy and, by so doing, bring them quickly but quietly over into the Mysian camp. Then, as soon as the Thynians had gathered enough strength, they were to initiate open revolt, murder or depose their king, place a Mysian puppet on his throne, and hover over the Hellespont like a bronze spear pointed straight at our backs. The Trojans garrisoned at Sestus and along the lower peninsula were to be either captured or annihilated, and it was the Mysian hope that all Thrace — after seeing the Trojan garrison easily and ingloriously defeated — might ignite against us. Had that happened, Dymas, we would have found ourselves in an impossible strategic position, fighting a war on two or three fronts, with all of our copper and tin — our life-giving bronze — cut off and in the hands of the enemy."

Along the ridge of my spine, I felt a sudden chill and gripped my oar more tightly.

"You and I prevented that this morning," my passenger went on, "and Dymas, only you and I could have done it."

And then I realized that my body had begun to shake, that in some way the morning's shock was being played out.

"By the time we learned their plans," he said, "both Mysians had already departed — well disguised, we felt sure — but by what route they intended to penetrate Thynia, we had no idea. In the back room of an obscure harbor inn, we applied strong pressure to the traitor, and among the last things he told us were these men's names. I knew both; they were Mysian court officials whom I had often seen at Pitane during my comings and goings on my lord's business. I knew the men, then, but had no means of discovering how they would disguise themselves. I expected, of course, that they might make straight for Sestus, where the largest concentration of Thynian nobles is to be found, and resolved, with my chief's approval, to go there myself at the best possible speed.

"The moment I made that decision, I placed myself straight in harm's way, with the security of the state riding very high on my shoulders. You see, Dymas, I knew both Mysians, certainly, but my not knowing how they had disguised themselves gave them a considerable edge, because they also knew me. They knew who I was, where I was supposed to be — in Pitane, conducting official diplomatic business — and what it would mean if I appeared suddenly anywhere along their route. Such an appearance could mean only one thing: that I had somehow gotten onto them. There could be no other explanation, and given the risks, they would have had to kill me on sight or die trying. Knowing as much and knowing, too, that I had to pull their fangs, as quickly and quietly as possible, avoiding all public disclosure and anything like a search of the city, I came up with the idea of a draw, with myself as bait and someone competent but inconspicuous to spring the trap. At Pharos' urging, your esteemed uncle recommended you, and you have not disappointed me. Now, call your crew to their oars, and let us make the beach before Abydus like a fleet-winged war hull."

Blinded, perhaps, by a touch of pride and by a deeper exhaustion than I had recognized, I had not noticed how the beach seethed with activity. When I did, finally, at my passenger's prompting, my cheeks burned with shame for not having remained more alert.

No more than three hundred yards out by that time, we looked ahead toward a beach that was much changed from what we had left behind us in the early morning fog. Gone were the stacks of cargo and gone, too, were the broad-beamed merchant hulls. In their place, I counted as many as thirty high-beaked naval hulls, come up from Dardanos, bristling with fully armed warriors. Armed parties of men, hard Abydian Mustangs and a few Boars, dotted every part of the shore, all the way from the water's edge to the walls of the city, and atop the keep, we could see beacon fires being laid and archers marking off the range with their arrows. In a matter of hours, it seemed, Abydus-by-the-sea had undergone a complete metamorphosis, transforming itself from the sleepy merchant harbor we had left at dawn into an armed camp ready for war.

In that moment, my passenger stood up and rested one broad hand reassuringly on the bones of my shoulder.

"When the time comes, Dymas," he said to me, "and you will know the time when Pharos tells you that it is right, come to me on Tenedos, and I will make you my runner."

I thrilled with pride in that moment and a feeling not unlike joy, for I took his words as a sure sign that I had carried out my duties to the state's satisfaction. But then I experienced a flush of confusion. In that last moment, as we hurtled in toward shore, I realized that I did not even know my passenger's name.

"My lord, how am I to know you?" I blurted out. "By what name are you called? If I do not know it, I may be unable to find you, for I am told that Tenedos is wide, stretching from eye to eye."

I heard him laugh for the first time, and the joy of that long gone moment still rings in my ears. At last, he looked down at me, his flint eyes shining. "I am Polydamas, son of Panthous," he said. "Pharos and your uncle know me well, and they will certainly know where to find me when the time is ripe for you and for any other member of this crew."

All conversation ended there, for the beach was closing fast. I gave command to ship oars, and as we rode high onto the sand and leapt ashore, I saw Pharos and my uncle hurrying toward us across the beach, each of them wearing full armor and carrying a spear. And thus began the Second Mysian War.

5

Like its predecessor, the Second Mysian War did not last long
and ended, inconclusively, after only a few moons, both sides
contenting themselves with hostile gestures pushed reluctantly
forward across Ida's eastern slopes. As I recall, no major battles
were fought, so land combat was generally limited to company-
sized actions, although some of those were bitterly contested and
costly. Negotiations to end the war began almost immediately
and then dragged on, as they are prone to do, while both sides
maneuvered for advantage. The Mysians, rebuffed by both
Greeks and Carians, and disappointed in their Thynian adven-
ture, found little advantage in continuing the war, so after some
tentative, initial thrusts, they failed to press their attack and went
over to the defensive, letting out for political consumption the
idea that they had opened the war for no other purpose than
self-defense in the face of aggressive Trojan intentions. They
stopped even before they reached the headwaters of Scamander,
massed their army, and stood — holding their ground — like a
sterile orchard of sharp, pointed spears.

Such an impasse might have continued indefinitely, both parties glaring at each other across a distance, but in the end we
forced the issue, and again, flint-eyed Polydamas acted a deciding
role. I first learned about it beneath the sharp chill of a November
evening when Pharos and I returned from the hills after an unsuc-

cessful hunt. Angry with ourselves for having missed our chance for a bit of fresh meat, we had no more than stepped inside and crossed to the fire when my uncle burst through the door behind us, his shaggy beard wet from the evening mist.

"Have you heard?" he asked at once, his deep voice thundering across the room as he stamped toward the hearth.

"No," said Pharos, suddenly becoming expectant. "Is it over?"

"Yes." My uncle beamed.

"In the way we expected?"

"Yes again," said my uncle, his broad smile spreading.

"What?" I was already demanding. "What is it? What has happened? Is — "

With the flat of his palm, Pharos motioned for me to be silent and wait for my uncle to finish. "Where?" he said.

My uncle had drawn close to the fire by that time and stood rubbing his hands together over the heat of the flame.

"Before Pitane," he said, his eyes matching the embers. "Before Pitane, with only ten ships. He caught them coming out. He'd lain up all night there, behind the point, in a light mist, and the Mysians had never detected him. As soon as he sighted their dawn departure, he made way with all possible speed, caught them coming out, rammed, and succeeded in shearing the oars from at least nine of their hulls — "

"Who?" I cried, making a little leap in my exasperation. "What are you talking about?"

Pharos' knuckles popped straight down on the top of my head. "Your Lord Polydamas," he said swiftly, "has won a naval battle off the Gulf of Pitane. The war is over. Now, for the love of thunder, Dymas, keep quiet and let your uncle finish!"

While Pharos rapped out his correction across the top of my skull, my uncle remained silent. After my performance at Sestus, he had become convinced, I think, of the efficacy of Pharos' methods and never again interfered with them, regardless of my transgressions. He waited, then, while Pharos administered my rebuke and continued only after I had shut my mouth and dropped my eyes in respect.

"As I was saying," my uncle went on, "Polydamas struck them at dawn. It was a grain convoy bound for Chrysa to replenish their army, and catching them unaware, he swept down on their naval escort like a sharp-beaked eagle. It was those nine hulls which he left dead in the water with half their oars floating broken on the surface of the sea. Their crews took a terrific beating. Went in on the port side, he did. Struck them straight out of the fog. Mysians never knew what hit them, nine of our hulls swinging in like that all at once against nine of theirs. Snapped their oars like twigs. Mysians thrown everywhere — over the side, even into the rigging, so great was the force of our blow. Large numbers of dead. Left all nine war hulls dead in the water. Then he went straight down the line, setting fire to their grain ships, all sixteen of them. Sank seven right there at the entrance to the gulf. Saw six more founder and go down along the coast. The other three got away and beached. Sharp fighting, good victory. He's fulfilled his promise. As far as I'm concerned, on the strength of this victory alone, Priam ought to make him a general."

I had never before seen my uncle quite so excited. Polydamas' victory seemed to thrill him, and in a singular moment, he gave way to his feelings, striking his fist against his palm with a resounding clap.

Pharos remained slightly more restrained. "That is true," he said quickly, "but let us remember as well that Polydamas enjoyed some counsel in this enterprise, counsel that is hardly likely to endear him to his masters."

"Nonsense," my uncle snapped, his ears reddening. "The plan was his. And a bold plan it was, too. We merely helped to work out . . . a few details."

"As you say," said Pharos, a degree of circumspection creeping into his voice.

"Merely a few points of clarification," said my uncle. "Had nothing to do with the operational concept or the execution."

"Humph," Pharos responded. "Talent is being wasted, and you know it. How long can we afford it?"

"Pity they can't see as much in Ilium," my uncle rejoined, seeming to accept the point.

"What are you talking about?" I ventured.

"Politics," Pharos said acidly, and that was as much as I was able to get from either of them.

On the strength of his victory before Pitane, Polydamas was indeed promoted to general, and when the news reached us, our enthusiasm was genuine. And then the war came to an end, our naval victory off Pitane having been just costly enough to the Mysians to tip the balance in Troy's favor. In its wake, within a matter of weeks, Mysia agreed to conclude a peace on our terms. Owing to the generally inconclusive nature of the broader contest, the terms Priam demanded proved to be light: in return for a slightly more favorable rate of cargo transport across Dardania — a face-saving device worked out by Priam's Grand Council — the Mysians agreed to cede us a belt of territory some three leagues in depth along the eastern slopes of Ida and to withdraw their army from its encampments along our border.

"It is a draw," Pharos told me. "The land is worthless, fit only for sheep and goats, and Mysian promises are ever as empty as lean winter wolves. Priam should have pressed his advantage. And don't delude yourself about the peace; we have merely driven the serpent back beneath its bush. It is still there; it is still coiled and ready to strike, and it still retains its venom. In the end, we shall have to kill it."

Life returned to normal, or to as much normality as I had ever known, and the land fell silent beneath stiff Borean blasts that blew incessantly from the heights of Thrace. Pharos had spoken, but as far as I was concerned, the Mysian Wars were behind us, finished and won, and as weeks gave way to months and months to years, my education and training went forward as though they had never begun, until, slowly, I completed my fourteenth year and realized that I was becoming a man.

Each day, it seemed, I could feel my muscles growing and hardening, and on Ares' Field, Pharos matched me against bigger and bigger opponents, and not infrequently I came away victorious. By that time, I had grown larger and stronger than the others in my crew, and I attributed this to Pharos' ideas about diet and exercise, but a certain amount of my growth, no doubt, had also to be attributed to the parents I had never known, or so my uncle and Pharos both told me, and I found no reason for disputing their words. My crew, I remember, accepted me as their natural leader, particularly after Sestus, and on Ares' Field, when we at last took up our practice with spear and shield, moving quickly beyond the rudiments of individual and into general combat, we invariably fought as a unit and came away from our practices without ever losing an engagement against boys of our size.

Once, after a month of elimination combats that we carried forward over frozen February snows, the battle master called out a party of sixteen-year-olds, who had already been in barracks for two years, and pitted four of them against all eight of us for exhibition. We gave a good account of ourselves but lost, even at the odds — Knos suffering a cracked rib, and Noemon came away with a broken nose. We trained with growing determination, looking forward like our peers to the day when we would go off to our appointed barracks and at last be called men.

Winter that year was long, and a hard crust of snow blanketed the earth for many months. But at last the heights of Thynia began to lighten, and gradually Boreas blew with less and less strength, and as the days passed I realized that Helios was spending more and more time crossing the sky and knew that Zephyr would soon blow in spring. Finally, winter died and the snow melted, and from Ares' Field, where we labored at our training in ankle-deep mud, we could look up beyond Abydian rooftops to see the Dardanian Hills quickly breaking forth into a sea of blue and white flowers. I looked at the countryside that year with eyes that seemed both sharp and new to me, eyes that didn't miss a detail, and my heart leapt up. For the first time, you see, for reasons that surpass my powers of speech, I saw my country clearly and recognized her beauty. But if I was smitten in that hour, the emotion only grew and matured, for during the weeks that followed, I came to know her fully and knew that I loved her deeply and forever.

"The time has come for him to know Ilium," my uncle said one night after the coming of spring.

We were eating, and not too pleasantly either, from the hind quarter of an old boar I had killed in the late afternoon. The meat was tough and full of gristle, and we were so fully intent on grinding it between our teeth that my uncle's remark seemed to have come straight out of the blue. When my mind finally grasped what he had said, I gave up chewing altogether and sat gaping across the table.

"And its environs as well," Pharos was saying, washing down another hunk of the boar with a quantity of wine.

"Exactly," my uncle said.

"Tomorrow?" said Pharos, pushing his bowl away while viewing the meat with a jaundiced eye.

Slowly, my uncle nodded. "Tomorrow. And with thoroughness."

"Agreed. He must know the terrain."

"And you must carry a message for me to the Lord Antenor. He will put you up, I think, for as long as you wish to stay, but avoid overstaying your welcome. You . . ." He hesitated, but only for a moment. "You know the reasons without my telling you," he said flatly. "And I don't want *him* coming home soft, either. He's destined for the barracks, and that's the way of it, and I — "

"And who should know better than I," Pharos interrupted, giving my uncle a hard, flint-eyed look. Then he saw me gaping and rapped me across the ear. "That sort of wide-eyed wonder is much frowned upon where you are going," he said to me hotly, "so never let me see you do that again; it is most unworldly to allow flies to graze in your mouth." He looked back across the table toward my uncle. "Rest assured," he said sharply, and my uncle nodded.

On the following morning, we rose before dawn, as always, but for one of the few times since Pharos came to us, we did not take our morning run. Instead, we breakfasted hastily on the remains of the evening meal, finding it not much more tender even after long hours of simmering under the mute's watchful eye.

"Let's leave it," I suggested, eager to be on the way.

"No man marches far on an empty stomach," Pharos said, giving the oft-repeated phrase his usual aphoristic turn, "so grind it down, boy, and then go and pack your wallet: one fresh tunic, your spare sandals, and the coppers that you were given on your birthday. And then come out here, and the mute will give you a ration of barley flour to carry and some remnants of last year's raisins.

"Not yet," he said as I started to move; "not before you finish your meat. And let this boar be a lesson to you, Dymas, never to kill anything so old again: age never makes for tenderness."

We struck out in the glow of Aurora's first blush, after pouring libations to the gods and taking leave of my uncle, and moved south at an easy pace, with our wallets across our backs and our long spears held firmly in our hands like walking staffs. The morning was crisp but not cold, and as we climbed the hills behind Abydus and fell in on the main trunk road where it moved down along a ridge toward Dardanos, our spirits rose like the sea breezes that blew in across our right hands from the wine-dark Hellespont. My immediate inclination was to step out smartly and move like the wind. Troy beckoned to me like the ultimate unknown, and my every desire drew me to make haste.

Pharos must have divined my intentions, because we had not been on the road for more than a quarter of an hour before he pulled me up short with a jerk on my tunic. "Make haste slowly,

Dymas. By the paths we follow, the walls of holy Ilium are more than fifty miles distant. Not even the royal heralds run that far in a day. Patience. The walls of Troy will not crumble, I think, before you see them on the morrow." And so saying, he struck a more leisurely pace, one that we stuck to throughout the remainder of our journey.

For a while, we seemed the only travelers on the road, but as Helios rose slowly amidst a burning, eastern gold, that broad, wide way sprang to life, as if — to my mind, at least — it had an existence of its own. The first persons we saw were smiths, moving north by cart, carrying all of their tools with them in order to expand Percote's armory. They were large men, all of them, and traveled in company with a small party of royal officials, to whom we made our marks of respect; then we had to leave the road briefly so as to avoid a cowherd who trailed not far behind them, driving his beasts toward the market in Abydus. And after that, the whole panorama of Dardanian life seemed to unfold along the road. We saw, in fact, everything from an itinerant apple vendor, who carried his entire inventory on his back, to a noble whose decorated litter was borne forward over the road by eight Carian slaves and twelve armed retainers. Twice, we passed military formations, elements of the permanent patrol that covered each stretch of the road several times daily between the citadel at Dardanos and our own Abydian outposts, and once we even saw a minstrel, his lyre covered by white sailcloth, eating a joint of meat beneath the shadow of a pistachio tree. From time to time — almost at hourly intervals, it seemed — everything on the road moved aside to allow for the passage of one or another of the pack trains coming up overland from Besika Bay, heading for Abydus or holy Arisbe or pretty Percote, the final destinations of the cargoes they were carrying as they skirted the dangers of the sea.

Off the road, farms, hamlets, estates, and villages were everywhere apparent, and as we moved forward, Pharos made me study their configurations, learning their names and purposes.

And not all could be considered alike. Killa, for example, located midway between Dardanos and Abydus, seemed to consist of nothing more than a series of low, log huts that gave the appearance of a military encampment.

"Slave quarters," said Pharos, pointing to a whole row of them, "for housing the repair crews who service the road. The huts behind the trees are where their officers are quartered."

Killa looked bleak to me, but not far beyond, we passed suddenly between two immense stone outcroppings, rounded a shallow curve, and found ourselves at one end of a single, busy street. The moment we appeared, it seemed, food vendors began to hawk their wares at the tops of their lungs, coming right out into the street and pressing against us with the edges of trays that were piled high with every description of food and drink: roasted nuts, raisins and barley cakes, olives, cheeses, whole fowls, and joints of mutton or pork, steaming hot. And every variety of wine that I had ever known.

"This is Sataspes," Pharos said waspishly, threatening several of the hawkers with the butt of his spear. "It looks good, but the meat, you will find, is often tainted, and the whole flavor of the place is unsavory."

I seldom doubted Pharos about anything, but as I looked around me there — along Sataspes' single open street — and saw it teeming with hawkers and travelers and off-duty garrison troops from Dardanos, the whole place seemed to take on an atmosphere of festival or holiday. People streamed into or out of the inns, wine shops, and houses that bordered our way, and as we pushed through the crowds, I looked up more often than I should have to the upper windows of the inns to see the almond eyes gazing down on me from behind long black lashes. I felt my member stiffen, and I blushed bright red even in the middle of the street.

Some moments passed before Pharos took note of my . . . glance, but when he did, his rebuke was sharp.

"Keep your eyes in the boat," he snapped, rapping me above

the ear, "and no skylarking. And while you are about it, try to learn the difference between a pure woman and a whore! Those" — he pointed the head of his spear toward the inns — "are whores; they are as bloated and diseased as the fish that float belly up along the borders of the sea."

How he could have expected me, at that time in my life, to know the difference between a pure woman and a whore, I have no earthly idea. In those days, I had seldom so much as seen a girl my own age; certainly, I had never been in company with one. Amongst ourselves, we boys talked about them often enough, intimating what we would do when finally presented with an opportunity to be with one, but such an opportunity was never forthcoming, because all unmarried women in Abydus and all girls were kept from sight, and it was instant death to touch a married woman or to interfere in any way with her progress through the streets. This was more than a custom; it was Trojan law, and my uncle, in his capacity as Master of the Harbor, saw it rigidly enforced. No matter. Pharos knew all of that as well as I did, and yet he still took for granted that I knew or should have known everything there was to know about women and acted accordingly, so when my eyes strayed again only seconds later, I was rapped on the noggin with the butt of his spear and departed from Sataspes with a slight swelling over my ear.

During the late afternoon, we passed the crossroads that led down toward the fishhook harbor at Dardanos. Several companies of infantry were encamped there, training across fields on either side of the road, and for the first time, there in company with Pharos, who lectured me about each evolution, I watched first-line Trojan units perfecting their tactics in massed practice.

"Those are men of the Boar," Pharos said as he pointed toward warriors carrying black shields. "They fought with your father and your uncle in Thynia, and beyond them, on the hill, those in the leathern skullcaps — they are the Kite; they gave an altogether satisfying account of themselves during the First Mysian War. They also served under your father's command."

There must have been more than four thousand warriors massed across the fields that day, barely a quarter of the force known to garrison Dardanos, and yet as far as my eye could see, they seemed to fill up the horizon. The Boar, Pharos explained, was massing for a mock attack on a long, low ridge that the Kite seemed bent on defending, but before the Boar had covered half the distance between the start point and the base of the ridge, most of the Kite had melted away down the reverse slope. The Boar attack lost momentum then, faltering slightly while the unit threw out flanking formations on either side of its main body; and when it resumed its advance, its front had narrowed, weakening its main assault by the removal of so many men to protect its flanks. In that moment, the entire formation of the Kite reappeared suddenly on the summit of the ridge, and the men swept down to the attack. Having redeployed to repel an expected flank attack when the Kite first melted away, the Boar was unprepared for this surprise to its front and gave ground; even so, the front ranks were unable to withstand the Kite's weight, so when the ram's horn blew announcing the end of the exercise, the Boar had been driven in and the formation split. Needless to say, the military judges awarded the day to the Kite.

"Who commands there?" I was quick to ask Pharos.

In that moment, I recall, Pharos became grave. "New men," he said tightly, leaning on his spear, "and young by the look of it. Since the end of winter, the Kite is commanded by Aeneas, son of Anchises. The Boar is led by Priam's noble son Hector, who has just come up from holy Ilium. Both men only begin their training for command, and it shows. Their assaults were slow." Then, as though suddenly amused by the thought, he threw me a quick wink. "Polydamas would have routed them both," he said, "and with half the force."

"And does my Lord Polydamas also command at Dardanos now?" I asked.

Again, Pharos' eyes narrowed. "No," he said bluntly, "but he should. Instead, he commands the Shark on Tenedos. The warriors of the Shark are quick, fierce fighters, and Polydamas handles them well, but their regiment is only half as large as either of these."

I wanted to know why.

"Politics" came the immediate sharp reply, but before I could utter another word, Pharos indicated that he had said as much as he intended to about the matter. We turned our backs on the training grounds of Dardanos then and left the main road, Pharos electing to take the more direct but less traveled military route, which led up through the high, dark hills ahead and down into the valley of white-watered Simoeis before moving across the Plain toward holy Ilium. In fact, as I was later to learn, we were never far from the main road itself, but after watching the Boar and the Kite at their scrimmage, Pharos seemed to want to distance himself from the masses, and along the path he chose, we passed only a few royal couriers making their swift way north.

We camped that night in a copse beside a spring of clear water, supping on the flesh of a fowl that I had brought down with my sling. To the east, the vastness of Phrygia stood broadly before us, rising tier upon tier until it disappeared into a mystery of purple heights.

"Beyond those mountains," Pharos said, pointing inland, "and through them, a distance of thirty days' hard running, live a people called the Hatti. They are civilized men like ourselves but command far more territory, holding control of all inland centers beyond the limits of our borders. Still, a very great distance separates us, and in between, naught abides save mountains, forests, and glades. The men you have seen in your youth and called Phrygian are merely a variety of barbarians who owe their ultimate allegiance to the Hatti. We count them our friends, so see that in your life path it shall always remain so, for friendship between neighbors is better than the sword."

We did not talk long that night. Tired from our journey, we wrapped ourselves soon enough in our cloaks and bedded down soundly on the bosom of Gaia, Mother Earth; by the time Artemis rose, we were already fast asleep.

With the dawn, we were up and moving, shaking away the stiffness that comes with sleeping on the ground and using our cloaks to hold back the morning chill. As on the evening before, we met few travelers on the trail and nothing of Trojan commerce save a herdsman or two, one of whom gave us goat's cheese and milk in exchange for a second fowl that I was able to bring down with my sling.

By midmorning, we had crossed the summit of the complex range that separates the Hellespont from the narrow valley of the Simoeis, and then we found ourselves working swiftly down into the valley itself along the edges of a quick-running tributary. Overhead, tall pines rustled in the breeze, and more than once I heard a fleet-winged eagle's cry and made the sign of Zeus. And then, negotiating a sharp turn around a massive boulder, we found ourselves overlooking white-watered Simoeis itself where it crashed through a valley no wider than a good cast of a spear. Even so, we found small farms along the banks and close-planted fields of rye bounded by stone walls that had been topped with plated nettles or thorn vines. In all of these fields, strong-backed Trojan men and their women worked side by side beneath the warmth of the sun.

We forded there, and gradually the valley widened, and as it did, the farms increased in number, their size reflecting their prosperity.

"Along the banks of mighty Scamander, it is much the same," Pharos told me; "high, white headwaters that broaden and slow as they work down out of the mountains, unfolding their wide blue ribbons across the Plain. They are the blessings of the gods, these rivers, allowing us to grow strong in horseflesh and grain.''

By the time Helios had reached his zenith, we found that the valley had widened enough to support a manor house or two, and then, as we rounded a bend, I spotted a watchtower in the distance, and in fairly short order we came up on a white stone keep and a barracks, where we had to identify ourselves and state our reasons for approaching the Plain. There, for the first time, I saw members of the Imperial Guard wearing full armor, from the tips of their silver greaves to the tops of the blue horsehair plumes that rose from the crests of their helmets. I had never seen bronze armor so carefully wrought, and my eyes were wide with wonder, and on that day, in the same hour, I resolved that, come what might, I would one day join their ranks, for I thought I had never seen anything so impressive.

We were through the barriers soon enough, Pharos having said something to one of the guards, which made him instantly stand back to let us pass, and within a quarter of a mile we rounded yet another bend and found ourselves approaching the main road. To our right, across the swift white face of Simoeis, the main trunk road descended onto the valley's floor between two low ridges; immediately after, it crossed a low stone bridge and ran straight against the base of a fortified keep on the river's south bank. All traffic coming into Troy had to pass in narrow file immediately beneath fighting platforms on the seaward side of the keep, while all traffic moving north passed through narrow confines around the landward side of the structure. In short, nothing could move in either direction without consent of the Imperial Guard, and the bridge could easily be closed and defended.

"Do you see the principle of the bridge's defense?" Pharos asked me.

Even at that age, I recognized the structure for a brilliant piece of fortification and said so.

Pharos beamed. "So it is," he said, "even if I do say so myself."

"Did you have a hand in building it?" I asked, prompted by sudden intuition.

"As a rule," Pharos said, "the hand is supplied by a slave, the idea by a Trojan."

I said that I had meant as much.

"Then you must say what you mean, Dymas. Good commanders do not confuse their hearers."

"Were you a pioneer?" I immediately wanted to know.

"After a fashion," Pharos said, his eyes sparking fire. "In my day, you might say, I sometimes served Troy as a . . . conceptual pioneer. Now, enough; let us move along smartly. Helios has passed his zenith and the day wanes, and my intention is that we should enter the city before sundown."

We fell in behind a farmer's cart drawn by two shaggy horses. The farmer seemed to be carrying bundles of hay toward Troy, and on their backs, I remember, there perched a small boy, who, from time to time, pulled pinches of straw from the tufts and amused himself by scattering them into the wind.

"Like the seed of Tros," said Pharos, not without a chuckle.

I did not know what he meant and so said, repeating his aphorism about not confusing one's hearers. And for that, I drew a box on the ear.

"I make allusion," Pharos snapped, "to the Dardanian prophecies, as I have heard them from the priestess of Athene who serves about the sacred Palladium. It is said that the seeds of Tros are to scatter across the face of the earth like new-plucked Trojan hay, blowing before the wind."

"Did you say prophecies or poetries?" I asked.

Pharos' eyes narrowed. "What could possibly be the difference?" he asked me. "Truth is truth."

The farmer's cart with the boy on top crept forward at a slow pace, so we soon passed it by and passed, too, a herd of mottled cattle that were being driven before it by the farmer's eldest sons. Then we overtook another drover and another before finally clearing their herds and moving out into the open space in front of them. In the distance, leaving us quickly behind, was a platoon of the Imperial Guard marching swiftly in column.

By that time, the valley of the River Simoeis had broadened to nearly half a mile, and on either side of us, farms and sky-blue manor houses dotted the adjacent terrain. The fields there were green, and the orchards were all in bloom, showing pink and white blossoms, while across the Dardanian hillsides, bright like new wounds, blood-red poppies burst into flower.

We moved on at a steady pace. Ahead, Helios already declined in the west but not so far yet as to create shadows, so the air remained still and warm. Suddenly, where the river cut through the base of a low hill, we found ourselves rising with the road above the river, and as we strengthened our stride to compensate for the incline, I felt my blood quicken and pressed myself forward toward the crest. By the time we reached the summit, Pharos was already pointing forward with the tip of his spear.

"Stand and behold," he said to me, "the Plain of Ilium!"

I felt my ears tingle and my hair stiffen, and hastened ahead the last few feet toward the crest of the hill, and then I saw it and stopped dead in my tracks. Spreading out before me like a wavering sea of grass, the long, broad Plain stood silent and vast. Never, I thought, had I seen anything so grand; never, I knew, anything so immense. To the north, five, perhaps six miles from where we stood, I saw the wine-dark sliver of the Hellespont rolling its way toward the sea athwart a long beach that gleamed a brilliant, flashing white beneath the glare of the sun. Immediately up from the beach, rising inland with the shallowest of slopes, bright green fields of barley, wheat, and rye danced beneath the breezes blowing in from the sea.

"There," said Pharos, sweeping the horizon with the tip of his spear so as to show me a glittering silver ribbon in the distance, "there, the mighty Scamander, heaven-fed river of Troy, and beyond, the Walls of Heracles, whose low brown heights border the sea. And there . . ."

But my eyes had already turned, my head snapping over with an eagle's speed, and then, with suddenness so shocking that I felt myself struck dumb, I gazed at last on the high white towers of Ilium and believed that they had pierced the sky.

". . . holy Ilium," Pharos exclaimed, "blessed by the gods! In all the wide world, she has no rival for beauty or power."

The white walls of Troy were a magnificent sight, wholly overpowering, and I shall never forget standing there that afternoon and seeing them for the first time in the breathless wonder of my youth. I shuddered, I remember, in the face of such beauty, and as I now recall it, I shudder still. I had seen towers and keeps and citadels aplenty by that time in my young life, but where Ilium stood on its heights, commanding the length and breadth of the Plain, I saw for the first time a city made regal by its massive halls and towers, a city made divine by the serene beauty of its walls. She was the heart and soul of the Troad, and like a hopeless lover, the moment I saw her, I knew that I would love her passionately and forever.

Breathless, my heart pumping, I hastened forward to follow Pharos, who already descended toward the Plain. As I caught up to him, Troy loomed larger and larger with each stride we took, filling the eye and mind, blotting out all trace of the remainder of the world. Horse herds coursed the fields around us, their black manes fluttering in the breeze, but I barely noticed them, and once or twice, I think, Pharos may have tried to direct my attention to other points of interest along the path of our approach, but in truth, I barely heard him. Only the city held my attention, and like an eagle on the wing, its every sense bent and molded to the hunt, I concentrated on Troy with such a single-minded purpose that by the time we climbed the long ramp and entered by the Scaean Gate, her walls had become my world, and I was her only citizen.

6

INSIDE THE GATES Troy's full promise unfolded, and again I felt smitten, stopping where I stood to stare at the wide streets and high blue houses that lined their sides, but my halt was cut short by the butt of Pharos' spear, which came up quickly against my shin and left me hopping forward to catch up with him.

"I warned you," he said. "On the streets of Troy, don't stare. People will think you are fit only for letting fleas nest on your head."

We moved hastily forward along a street wide enough to accommodate two chariots side by side. Ahead and well above us, the palace and royal citadel loomed cloudlike where they hovered on the heights overlooking the city.

"Are we going there?" I wanted to know. "Is that where we are going?"

"Have you an invitation from the royal family?" Pharos countered, looking expectant.

"No," I said shortly.

"Well, neither do I, so I think not. Learn patience, Dymas; some think it a virtue, or had you forgotten?"

I knew that we were going to the Lord Antenor's house, for I had heard my uncle say so. Pharos knew that I knew as much, so in the face of his rebuke, I put the question more directly.

"I know we go to my Lord Antenor's," I said, "but where does he live?"

"Right where he lived the last time I visited Troy," Pharos quipped, enjoying both his joke and my continuing suspense.

"Very precise," I said, catching his tone. "I'm sure I must offer you no limit of thanks."

He laughed, his long gray beard shaking beneath his chin. "Look up there," he said, pointing directly ahead, "to that second tier of houses around the citadel's base, the structures that are just below the royal compounds. The broad house with the white door belongs to Lord Antenor."

About a quarter of a mile distant, beneath the shadow of the citadel but well above the level of the street, I saw it, a white speck that stood out against the muted twilight blues of the hill like a bright night star.

"We will be there soon enough," said Pharos, "so take a good look about you as we go, and let us arrive there when we arrive."

He was right, of course; there was much to see, and I had never seen any of it before. I gave myself over, then, to a visual feast: tumblers and jugglers and fire eaters, and a man who led a great Thracian bear to dance on the end of a chain, and honey vendors, who bore their pots before them on short, wheeled barrows, and wine sellers, who carried their wares in goatskins, bearing pottery cups before them as though they were preparing libations for the gods. We moved carefully enough, although swiftly, holding to the wall, for fleet-wheeled chariots coursed the streets like the wind, no doubt pressing forward on imperial business. On the walls, most of which were blue, one saw paintings in rich reds and yellows and deep-seated blacks, and beside almost every window above the ground floor, one saw perforated pots blossoming with flowers or closely seeded household herbs. Where the streets intersected, on one corner or another, depressions were built into the masonry, and there, gushing fountains supplied the populace with a steady supply of fresh water.

"The water is brought down to us from as far away as Thymbra by clay pipes that are planted in the earth, end to end, like rows of fallen wheat. Thus," Pharos told me, "the water supply is ensured, even in the event of a siege, and always clear."

Unlike home, where each household was responsible for its own food, here were greengrocers and bakers and butchers, who suspended their meats — freshly killed and cut — outside their shops on the ends of poles while they bargained with passersby, and here too were tin- and coppersmiths beating out their wares on time-worn anvils, working by torchlight in the space before their shops. Whole families appeared together on the streets, the women sometimes going veiled, the men strolling easily beside them without spear, sword, or shield, and the children who followed in their wake, boys and girls alike, skipping freely over the paving stones, filling the air with their cries and laughter. About the whole, even under the watchful eye of the Imperial Guard, there seemed an easy air of freedom nurtured by a complete absence of danger. I had never before experienced such a liberated atmosphere, and there on the streets of Ilium, I suddenly felt almost guilty to be carrying my dart. At that moment, you see, for the first time in my life, I began to realize just how close to the frontier Abydus lay, just how primitive and precarious my former life had been, just how far I had come away from it when Pharos had brought me down to the Plain across the white-running waters of Simoeis. Struck by such reflection, I was on the verge of stopping, I think, to consider the point when Pharos pulled me up short.

"Look sharp, Dymas," he commanded in a low voice. "We have arrived."

And we had, while I had drifted, comparing Troy with home.

"Step forward to the door," he told me, "and strike three times with the butt of your spear."

I did as I was told, and the white door flew instantly open to reveal a grizzled porter wearing a homespun tunic. He gave me, I'm afraid, a very hard face and seemed on the verge of cursing me until he looked up and saw Pharos standing behind me. Then, recognition played about his face, and we were admitted immediately with warm welcome.

"Pharos? Praise Zeus! The boy? Enter, enter!"

"Present a coin," Pharos thundered, giving me a nudge, "as a mark of respect, for Skalmos is gate guard to the Lord Antenor, and long ago in his youth, he wielded a mighty spear in the service of Ilium."

Bent nearly double, Skalmos did not look to me as if he had ever wielded anything mightier than a broom or a spit, but, observing the amenities, I went into my wallet and fetched forth a copper. Then, when I stepped forward to hand him my token and saw the number of his scars where they rose in weals across his forearms and legs, I became ashamed of my thoughts and made him firm marks of respect, and I could see that Pharos was pleased.

Immediately, the old warrior spun on his heel and showed us into an inner apartment opening on a courtyard, and there he left us, disappearing into the recesses of the house, and we waited beneath the low light of a votive lamp, for Helios was well down and the evening had grown rapidly into night. Even beneath the lamplight, the furnishings in that room were so grand and lavish as to make my uncle's house seem mean, but I was hardly prepared for what came next, because Skalmos returned almost immediately, and without further ceremony, he led us quickly across the courtyard, through a massive wooden door, and into a brilliantly lighted hall beyond, and there, I stopped short, hearing the old warrior announce our names.

We had entered the dining room, you see, and teetering on my toes, I was amazed to see both men and women taking food and drink together around the surface of a polished table. No three-legged stools there. Delicate thrones, rather, of sandalwood and ebony, and sitting in them, attended by servants and household slaves, a heavy, black-bearded man, whom I took to be the Lord Antenor, three younger men wearing military tunics, their beautiful wives, an older more serene woman whose perfectly sculptured features made me think of ox-eyed Hera, consort to Zeus, and two younger women — girls, really — whose firm breasts rose and fell and whose eyes flashed fire. I started to gape, I'm afraid, but remembered Pharos' warning, closed my mouth, and assumed a rigid posture like a warrior on parade. Even so, I had given myself away, and smiles appeared, particularly on the faces of the beautiful wives, all three of whom masked their amusement by lowering their lashes and attending to their plates; but it was not so with the two girls, who immediately broke into suppressed giggles, glanced at each other, and with perfect abandon, erupted into lilting laughter, only to be silenced, perfectly and finally, by a single sharp glance from the ox-eyed queen of Antenor's table.

The Lord Antenor himself seemed to miss most of this, for the moment Skalmos announced us, he rose to his feet and was already well advanced around the table to greet us, which he did with warm enthusiasm, his great hand clasping Pharos' in a moment of genuine human affection.

"And this is the boy?" he was saying as I made my mark of respect, his words coming thickly from between a broken row of teeth.

"The same," said Pharos, indicating that I was to hand my dart and wallet to Skalmos, who bore them from the room.

Antenor looked at me, his black, penetrating eyes sharp but not untouched by kindness.

"Be you welcome, son of Kalitor," he said plainly, giving me the hard, rough hand of a warrior. Then he introduced me to the table, first to my Lady Dia, the beauty of the sculptured features and his wife, then to his sons and their exquisitely beautiful wives, and finally to the girls, whose eyes flashed in the lamplight. "Let me present," he said, "the Lady Atalante, daughter of right royal Priam, whose manners are beyond reproach, and our own daughter, Ariadne, who would do well to emulate the Graces, practicing demure hospitality in the presence of guests."

The rebuke was mild enough, I thought, nothing at all like the butt of Pharos' spear, but it had much the same effect, for both girls paled briefly, dropped their eyes, and ceased laughing at me, and in that instant Lady Dia offered her husband and me a slight bow.

"Pharos," she said in beautifully articulated accents, "please seat yourself here, beside me, where you, my lord, and my sons may converse freely about the character of the world. And Dymas, son of Kalitor," she said, her dark lashes fluttering softly, "please you to seat yourself there, across from our two young . . . *ladies* of Troy, where each may entertain you with pleasantries."

I had missed it, you understand, but the "two young ladies" had not; somehow, beneath the wholly lyrical lilt of those gracious vowels and consonants, my Lady Dia had shown both girls the full measure of her displeasure with them. Later, I had cause to think about her admonition, but at the time, I was given little moment to consider her words, for they were no sooner spoken than I felt Pharos' palm on the back of my neck and found myself offering the entire table my marks of respect. Then we took our places.

At the head of the table, rapid conversation began immediately among Pharos, lordly Antenor, and one of his sons. What they talked about, I can only guess, for in truth, I do not know, but at the time I believed their words had to do with the fortification of Proconnesos, a pet project of my uncle's and one he never tired of discussing with Pharos or anyone else of their station. But as I say, I don't really know what they talked about; I intended to listen, certainly, but I never had the chance, because the moment I took my place at the table, both of those girls forgot all previous rebukes and attacked me like a pair of lionesses when, in a lean winter's night, they find themselves suddenly confronted with an unguarded sheep.

"Let us entertain him with some *pleasantries*," whispered

Priam's royal daughter, mockingly but musically, her brown eyes flashing fierce.

At first, the Lady Ariadne remained silent, looking toward the head of the table in anticipation of trouble, but her attention was swiftly diverted again when Atalante pinched her wrist. "Let's," she said hesitantly, wincing beneath her pain.

They looked enough alike, I thought, to have passed for sisters. They had the same full cherry-red lips, the same rich brown hair piled high above their heads, the same flawless complexions, and the same well-developed breasts that rose and fell with considerable allure beneath gowns of the smoothest fabric I had ever seen. They were even the same height, but their eyes differed slightly, for while Atalante's seemed deep to the point of smoldering, Ariadne's now seemed more like her mother's, wide and soft. No matter: their teeth were equally sharp, as I immediately learned.

"Why are your ears so terribly, terribly long?" demanded the royal princess. She nudged the other.

"And . . . your nose so terribly, terribly . . . *hooked?*" said Ariadne.

"I shall have to speak to my father," Atalante whispered impatiently. "Perhaps he can have them docked, like the tails of our mules."

"It would improve his appearance immensely," said the daughter of Antenor, responding to a second nudge, "just *immensely.*"

"Oh, wouldn't it *just,*" said the princess, flashing me an instant smile that carried all the warmth of an eagle's talon. "Do you know, I *do* believe they eat dog in the provinces."

"And toads?" said the other.

"Oh, yes, fat ones! With great protruding eyes!"

"Raw!"

"Most certainly raw!"

"Without doubt."

"Tell us, boy, *do* you eat dog?"

"And toads?"

"*Raw?*" they chorused together under their breath.

"Do tell, *boy,*" commanded the princess.

"Yes, *boy,* do," said Ariadne, snatching a glance at the upper end of the table.

Having recently passed my fifteenth year, the word *boy* nettled me more than anything you can imagine, particularly coming from those two vixens, who were at best only a year or two my senior. In that moment, I think, stung to the quick by their taunts and insults, I summoned up every bold thought I had ever had about the subjugation of women and prepared to master the two before me.

"My name is Dymas," I said sternly, "and I have long since left off being a boy."

"It talks!" gasped the princess, feigning surprise. "*It talks!*"

"Oh, indeed it does," whispered the other. "Let us coax it; perhaps it will say something amusing."

"It said its name was *Dimness.*"

"Dimness, indeed!"

"And Dimness *implied* that he was a man."

"Oh, now, that is amusing. How in the world do you suppose that he ever arrived at that conclusion?"

"Dimness must have been with a woman."

"He . . . must have."

"Let's ask him."

The Lady Ariadne shot a furtive glance in her mother's direction. "All right, let's," she whispered.

"Well, Dimness," asked the princess, "have you slept with a woman?"

"I don't think . . ." said the Lady Ariadne.

"No, no, dear," said the princess, patting her friend on the wrist, "wrong question. The question is, how many women has he slept with? *That* is the question."

"More than one?" said Ariadne.

"Such looseness!"

"Such lasciviousness!"

"It is unfair!" whispered the princess. "I demand that you reveal their names!"

"Or their ranks," Ariadne hastened to say, the skin over her cheekbones going suddenly pale.

"What perfumes did they use?"

"How did they . . . arrange their hair?"

"Were their limbs as smooth as ours?" said the princess, touching delicate fingers to the flesh of her arm.

"Dimness is very quiet," said Ariadne.

"*I* know: Dimness has never been with a woman or Dimness would have said so."

Ariadne said nothing, merely casting another furtive glance toward the head of the table.

"Perhaps with a whore?"

"Now there's a thought," said the Lady Ariadne, blushing suddenly.

"Tell us, Dimness, do you frequent whores?"

I refused to take the bait.

"Just hoards and hoards of whores, don't you think? Why, I would wager my bracelet that the name of Dimness is carved over every lintel in Sataspes."

They doubled up with laughter over that one, and immediately started again with tongues that were as swift, sharp, and relentless as a flight of Mysian arrows.

"Really, Dimness must have *great* knowledge of whores," purred the royal princess, her eyes smoking like coals.

"Indeed, an intimate knowledge of great whores," returned the Lady Ariadne, "most of it carnal."

"Tell us," demanded the princess, "what differences do you find between a lady and a whore? Look sharp, Dimness; we're waiting! Come to us with an answer."

I had reddened steadily beneath each of their volleys, but in that moment, as their girlish laughter broke in rills over the foot of the table, I felt my member suddenly stiffen, and for the last time in my life blushed blood red all the way up to the roots of my hair. I expected, in that instant, that they would finish me off, but instead, my utter confusion merely stimulated them, and in the minutes that followed, they continued to toy with me like two cats in undisputed possession of a mouse. And if such a thing were possible, I reddened even more.

"Oh," purred royal Atalante, breathlessly moistening her lips with the point of her tongue, "you don't suppose, do you, that he is a . . . ?"

"Can it be?" said the other.

It was — or rather, I was — and they both knew it, showing me no mercy, but as they readied themselves to pounce again, both, I noticed, looked slightly flushed, and if the princess's eyes seemed to have caught fire, the Lady Ariadne's shone like bright stars.

"He *is,*" Ariadne suddenly said.

Immediately, they conducted a private conference, establishing in general that unmarried women were often secluded in the provinces but disagreeing about how far the custom might be observed in Abydus. This seemed very important to them, so much so that they finally turned the full power of their flashing eyes straight onto me and asked me point-blank.

"Are women secluded in Abydus?" both blurted at once.

It seemed the first civil question they had asked me, so I replied accordingly. "Abydus is a garrison town," I said, "so our women are protected."

"*Our* women?" said the princess, enjoying no little mirth at my expense.

"Speak the truth, Dimness. Have you ever even spoken to a woman before?"

"My name is Dymas," I said emphatically in a final attempt to assert my manhood, "and the answer is no."

I would have said more. I certainly intended to, for by that time my anger had made me forget completely every rule I had ever learned about speaking to the nobility, but as events fell out, I never had the chance. As soon as those two learned the truth about my unintentional virginity, they simply went wild with delight and set about trying to arouse me in every way they could think of with subtle movements of their bodies. That they succeeded, I cannot deny, for my member turned to stone, leaving me in great physical discomfort in the same moment that I was trying to ward off the darts from their tongues. And then, all ended with a sudden, involuntary jump, for beneath the cover of the table, one or the other of those two had touched the inside of my thigh with the tip of her toe, and the mere sensation had driven me absolutely crazy, so much so, I'm afraid, that my entire body had broken into a sweat.

The Lady Dia, although I am quite certain she did not know precisely what was going on, did divine that something unusual was afoot at the lower end of the table and chose that moment to rise, showing us the full graciousness of her bearing.

"My lords," she said, taking everyone in, even me, "the evening quickens, and the Lady Artemis calls upon our devotions. If you ladies will join me, we will take our separate leave and go to perform her rites."

In that moment, I saw Pharos, his brows knit, looking quizzically at me from the head of the table, and I pretended not to see him.

With the grace of a swan, the Lady Dia floated from the room, leaving a faint hint of rosewater in her wake, and one by one, the younger women rose and followed her, and at last my tormentors.

"It *is* unfair," said royal Atalante, tossing her head.

"And just when we were having such fun," said Ariadne.

And with a rustle of fabric, both girls fairly slithered from the room, having turned their slender, silken backs on me with sudden indifference. The strap on Atalante's sandal, I noticed, had become untied, the only imperfect thing about either's appearance.

With the ladies gone from the room, my tensions relaxed, and looking at my plate, I realized that I had eaten nothing during my trial, and fell to. That was when I first noticed that the plate before me was gold and the food unlike anything that I had ever before seen or tasted: gull's eggs stuffed with a mixture of sausage and olives, and tiny fowls, also stuffed with nuts, raisins, and honey, fresh cauliflower garnished with onions and salted, and a savory made of sliced pears floating in a bowl of thick whipped cream. It was a far cry from the overbaked barley cakes and wild fowl that I had eaten the night before in the mountains above Simoeis, and I put my food away with haste and relish before at last looking up to find Pharos glaring at me from the head of the table. I slowed down then, finishing the remains of my meal with far more reserve, a factor, I hoped, that might to some degree soften my master's eye.

My hunger satisfied, I began to lend an ear to what was being said at the head of the table, where conversation, since the departure of the women, seemed to become both serious and intense.

"In the end," Antenor was saying, "we shall have to do something, for things cannot continue long as they are."

"No," Pharos said, releasing a grave sigh; "no, they cannot."

"As you may know," said the second son, "I am just returned from the lands of the Cicones — from windswept Zone, to be precise — and venerable Ceas, who still rules those wide climes, begins to feel threatened."

"The same is so in Caria," said the eldest son, a tall man whose black wavy hair was tied back in a Trojan knot. "At Miletus, I often spoke with Nastes, who will soon be king. He is most disturbed, and not without good cause: *their* naval units put in readily both at Cos and Rhodes — regardless of Carian protests —

and among the offshore islands, their merchant shipping is fiercely competitive and becoming even more so."

I had first thought that they were discussing the Mysian threat, but I knew then that they were not, that they were fuming over the Greeks. Mysian vessels seldom ventured far south, and their naval craft never put in at Cos or Rhodes, because both islands had belonged to the Achaian camp since the days of Laomedon.

"I have heard a rumor," Pharos said, "that they are fortifying Scyros."

"I have heard it too," said Antenor, nodding slowly. "If the rumor is true, they will soon be in a good strategic position to control all access to the central Aegean."

"And that will threaten us," added Tyro, Antenor's youngest son, a man who struck me as unusually circumspect.

"He speaks true," said the eldest. "Scyros controls the approaches to Lemnos and Lesbos, and both control the approaches to Troy."

"But both are free ports," protested the second son.

"But still capable of being influenced," said Tyro, his brow furrowing, "or occupied and conquered by hard assault."

"The question as I see it," said the eldest, "is to determine first whether the rumor is true."

"So it is," said lordly Antenor, motioning for his wine steward to step forward and refill our cups. "The matter is already being debated by the Grand Council."

For a moment or two, the table fell silent. In the distance, from somewhere within the depths of the house, I thought I heard the women chanting their orisons before the votive lamps of the household gods.

"They may debate," Pharos said slowly, "as much as they like, but in the end, they will have to send in a man, and . . ."

"Agreed," said Antenor, with a thoughtful nod.

". . . and he had better be a well-schooled master of reconnaissance and accurate with his eye."

"Also agreed. Whom do you recommend?"

"Has the matter not already been decided?" said Pharos, his thick brows rising in question.

"The nomination already lights on Polydamas," said Tyro.

"The best choice," said Pharos, his eyes brightening.

"Agreed," said Antenor, "but there are those on the council who oppose him, and — "

"They are fools," Pharos snapped.

" — would send the leader of the Boar or of the Kite in his place."

"That would be a mistake," Pharos said hotly. "Each is competent enough with an individual spear, but I saw both of them training on the field last night, and I was not impressed. In time, with experience, each will be good enough at command. They aren't yet, mind you, not by half, but they will be; the raw material is there. But this thing at Scyros is another matter altogether. It requires a good eye and plenty of experience, and the council must know that, so I can hardly think that either Anchises or Priam will long support the candidacy of his son. Not on this issue, surely; it is far too crucial to our survival. There is simply no place on this mission for novices, and surely they must know as much."

Again the table fell silent, and again it remained so for several seconds. Finally, lordly Antenor broke the silence.

"My friend," he said, looking Pharos clearly in the eye, "all that you say is true, all of it. Nevertheless, there is division in the council. Know you, my Pharos, that many years have flown since last you lived amongst us, and the wings of change have beat swiftly. Lord Anchises is ambitious for his son, certainly — what man is not? I know that I am ambitious for mine. Still, most of us see reason and act accordingly, and in this case, Anchises might, given the proper stimulus, but royal Priam is another matter. He favors his sons, Pharos — indeed, all of his children: witness the spoiled Atalante — too much in too many things, allowing his heart to control his head. Why else should Lord Hector — who is a fine man, a *fine* man, a friend to my sons, but young, Pharos, young and still untried — be given command of a formation the size of the Boar while a general of Polydamas' mind and proven capability sits becalmed and immobile on Tenedos? Answer that question and you will know the secret of our weakness. Answer that question and you will know why Priam's nephew, Hector's noble cousin, who is equally untried, commands the Kite. Answer as much, and you will know why, even after the victory off Pitane, this boy's uncle still languishes in Abydus and why you, at the height of your powers, are being wasted. Where, here, is reason? Where the order of merit?"

Pharos remained silent, staring into his wine.

"This is no time to be politic," Antenor continued. "Tomorrow, at first light, you must go up with me to the citadel and speak your mind to the elders. I myself will place the staff in your hand, so no man will prevent you from speaking."

"And the boy?" Tyro observed. "What about the boy?"

Suddenly, all eyes turned sharply in my direction.

"We cast his lot with Polydamas the moment we sent him into Sestus," Pharos said flatly. "If Polydamas wins tomorrow, so does the boy."

"And if not?" said Tyro.

"Nothing," said Pharos. "He will be no worse off. His course is already set." He turned back to Antenor. "Done," he said. "I will speak."

"Excellent," replied Antenor. "You have been too long silent, and your clear mind is much needed here. Noble Laocoön will second you, and I will call for the vote immediately after."

"Then with your permission," said Pharos, "I would like to call an end to conversation for tonight, for I have much to think over and too few hours in which to formulate the most persuasive arguments."

We stood, then, as my Lord Antenor stood, but before anyone

had the chance to move, he held up his hand and looked down the table toward me.

"Son of Kalitor," he said, "your lot has been cast with good men, and as a result, Troy is already in your debt for your services at Sestus beside the vigilant Polydamas. On behalf of the state and the royal House of Priam, I commend you. Know that in this house — indeed, in all of holy Ilium — you have the respect of men, and the respect of men is a fine thing, for it is the only deathless thing. Excellence, son of Kalitor, is a gift from the gods. Like life, it is fleeting, but immortal esteem is accorded only by men, so consider your reputation well won and well begun."

At that time, I did not understand, I think, more than half of what he had said to me. Nevertheless, I made my marks of respect, noticing as I did so that Pharos beamed with pleasure, and *that* made me feel particularly good, possibly better than I felt about anything my Lord Antenor had said. I had taken some hard looks from Pharos during the meal, and what I saw in that broad smile of his was a possible reprieve from punishment for my errors. I came up beaming myself, then, which seemed just the right note for ending my repast, and indeed, it proved so, for at the sound of a gong, Skalmos appeared with a lamp to light our way into our sleeping quarters.

"Not for us," said lordly Antenor. "Pharos and I remain here for a time, for we have much to do."

He bade good night to his sons and to me, and each son went off to his private apartments while I, heeding a nod from Pharos, followed Antenor's crippled gate guard slowly down a series of narrow passages, which eventually opened onto a second, smaller courtyard and the guest quarters surrounding it.

High above our heads, the Master of Thunder suddenly loosed one of his bolts, and it rent the black night like a tongue of silver flame, streaking and crackling to earth somewhere out on the Plain. Just as quickly, drops of rain began to fall and then more and more until thin silver rills flashed from the roof vents onto the courtyard below. Instantly, the air cooled, and as it did, a clean smell rose from the earth like a new bloom.

"Smells good," said Skalmos. "Dusty on the road. Dirty. Must be tired. Wash if you want. No one about. Do it myself, some-times. Strip down to your string. Stand under the spout. Relaxes the muscles. Feels good. Gives you a proper night's sleep."

Holding the lamp before him, he showed me into a narrow apartment furnished with a single bed and chest. Hanging the lamp from a peg, he opened the chest and removed several heavy fleeces, which he spread over the bed frame.

"Let you arrange 'em the way you like," he said. "Water's in the courtyard. Pure and safe. Change it myself every day." He stopped then, turned, and stepped forward, squinting hard into my face by the glow of the lamp. "Hmm," he grunted, "even look like him. Served in Thrace; knew your father. Good man. Troy's best hope. Gone now. Up to you. All praise to Zeus."

And with more speed than I would have thought possible, he was gone, leaving the lamp behind and disappearing down a side passage that led even farther back into the compound. I wanted to ask him more about my father, but there had not been time.

Skalmos was right about my being tired; I felt exhausted, but I also felt dirty, so I took his advice. I stripped down to my string, walked outside, and stood directly under one of the spouts, let-ting the heaven-sent water gush over my head and down my tired limbs. It *was* relaxing but cold, the falling water pumping and pounding my muscles with varying force, and after my tensions dissolved and the dust and grime of the road washed away from me, I turned, re-entered my room, and went straight to sleep atop the fleeces.

I do not know how long I slept, but I slept hard and came awake only slowly, and when I did, I became aware that the lamp had gone out and that someone was in the room.

"Pharos?" I said, still half asleep.

Giggles followed, and my every sense went instantly on the alert. I reached for my dart, remembering too late that it had been taken from me, and with a sinking feeling, I knew myself to be cornered. Then the Lady Ariadne lighted the lamp while royal Atalante, her dark brown tresses falling loosely over her breasts, seated herself on the edge of my bed and began touching smooth fingers to the inside of my thigh.

Aroused but nevertheless seized by fear, I instantly drew back. Everywhere in Ilium, it was death to touch an unmarried woman, and I made no hesitation in saying so while protesting the sanctity of the laws of hospitality. Atalante burst immediately into laughter over this, pressing her nails painfully into my flesh and thus stopping all my further attempts to evade her.

"That," she said tartly, her deep eyes smoldering, "is what makes this so very, very delicious."

"For *us,*" Ariadne added from the shadows. "My brothers tell us that you are a man who is to be much respected, Dimness — a genuine hero." As she spoke, I thought her hesitant, for a throaty breathlessness seemed to have crept into her voice.

"Old Antenor says that Troy even is in your debt," said the other, an even greater breathlessness having affected her own whispered sounds.

In response, without being able to prevent myself, I became fully aroused.

"Mmmm," purred the princess, treating me to a practiced flutter of her lashes while pressing her nails even more firmly into my thigh, "he stiffens! I think, Ari, that *we* must pay Troy's debt."

I struggled then, attempting to push the princess from my bed, but the moment she began to feel the strength in my limbs, she seemed to reach a frenzy of desire, and in that second, her eyes flashing, royal Atalante seized my member, threatening to pierce it with the sharpened points of her nails. Instantly, my resistance died.

"Foolish *boy,*" said Atalante as she began caressing my member, "you have only to lie still. We are the priestesses of Aphrodite's delights, and what we intend to show you is the splendor of her mystery."

With a smooth motion, she rose to her feet, unclasped her gown, and let it fall to the floor about her feet. That I was dazzled by the luster of her body, I do not deny. Her skin was beautifully toned, and her breasts were firmly erect in their youthful bloom. She calculated the effect she was having on me — I could see her watching me like a cormorant watching a minnow — and in the precise instant that I reached the peak of desire, she plunged suddenly down on top of me while I exploded into fire.

It was finished, then, almost before it began, and in the next moment she was up, standing beside the bed frame, sneering over my limp body. Her intense satisfaction over what she had done to me betrayed fully the degree of superiority she felt, for it seemed in no way physical but, rather, mental. She had not mounted me long enough to feel much, and insofar as I could tell, her immense pleasure came strictly from the rapidity with which she had been able to reduce my strength. In that moment, I sensed that it was sheer power that Atalante valued, not sexual excitement, not physical pleasure, not affection, and certainly not love — only power.

With a haughty toss of her head, Atalante turned away from me. "Now," she snapped at Ariadne as she disappeared from the room, "*you* do him!"

The second "priestess of Aphrodite" proved thoroughly unlike the first. The moment that she heard royal Atalante's footsteps fade away into the main house, the Lady Ariadne simply backed herself into the nearest corner and broke into tears.

My initial response, I remember, was a compound of bewildered humiliation and fury, and in the instant, I thought to cast her from the room, but as her distressed sobs increased, I realized that her emotion was genuine, and I became seized with confusion, unable to explain to myself what was going on before me, in what new way I was about to become the victim of these women. Fearing that we might be discovered and knowing well the consequences, I spoke words of comfort, and that one small sign of human warmth caused her to hasten across the room and throw her arms around me, a response that merely heightened my incomprehension.

Clearly, I understood nothing. Throughout the evening, from the moment I had first fallen into their clutches, the way they had humiliated me had made me loathe both with an intensity bordering on hatred. And then, without a word of explanation, I suddenly found this one crying her eyes out with deep and obvious shame. I did not understand it, and I could not explain it, even to myself, but as she clung to me, trembling and sobbing, I found that I could not help myself, and a wave of tenderness flooded over me, and we remained locked in each other's arms for a long while.

Finally, her sobbing subsided, and then, somewhat pointedly, I asked her, "Why?"

"Oh, Dymas," she said, again burying her head in the cleft of my neck and clinging to me like a sea urchin to a rock when it is hard pressed by the sea, "can you not see? She threatens me."

"In what way?"

At first, she would not tell me, but as I stroked her hair, the story gradually unfolded. Youngest daughter of Hecuba and royal Priam, the Princess Atalante, it seemed, had discovered her sexuality early by watching her older sisters, many of whom, Ariadne told me, were well known to be adept at seducing members of the Household Guard.

"They are not instantly put to death?" I exclaimed.

"This is Ilium, Dymas, not Abydus-by-the-sea. The laws of chastity are as much in place but much less enforced, and besides, no one would dare to approach royal Priam with such reports. Priam's children are the apples of his eye; the bearer of such a tale would surely have to endure immediate banishment or death. No, the open secret has been well kept, and still is."

She went on then, carefully telling her story, her dark hair falling smoothly across her breast. Owing to the closeness in their ages — the princess had passed seventeen winters and Ariadne counted sixteen — owing to such nearness and also, I think, to Antenor's place on the council, the girls had been playmates since childhood, and up to a point, their friendship had been sound.

The point had been reached mere weeks before, quite by accident, when Ariadne had visited the palace in company with the Lady Dia. Upon being received by Hecuba, Ariadne had been sent along, unannounced, to the royal apartments, and there she had happened on two of the princesses — one of whom was Atalante — in an act of fornication with an officer of the Household Guard. Stunned by what she had seen and instantly aware of its significance, Ariadne turned her back on the scene and burst into tears while the guard officer made his departure, and then, rather than betray even the slightest sense of shame, Atalante and her older sister abused Ariadne for having burst in on their pleasures and went on from there to shock her with the details of their other trysts in and about the palace. It was an act of bravura, certainly, for they lay naked on their pillows, painting for her the most vivid picture they could of their mastery of men, but the act in itself revealed their fury by the lewd nature of its details. Both knew that Ariadne had something on them and that if she ever wanted to use it, she could, and according to their natures, they feared her, for to Priam's daughters, power was everything. The moment Ariadne left, those two must have moved heaven and earth, looking for a way to assert their supremacy and recover a degree of their former security, questions of faith and friendship notwithstanding. And apparently I had provided them with a means to their end.

According to Ariadne, I fell into the plot by pure chance, because *she* was Atalante's intended victim. My misfortune had been to appear suddenly in the wrong place at the wrong time. No one had had foreknowledge of my coming; personally, I hardly mattered at all. To royal Atalante, you see, I counted for no more than a body, quick rather than dead. Any male would have suited, because her scheme had been planned and partially executed even before she had come down from the palace on an extended visit, resolving to capture her prey by waiting like a spider for a fly. Then, two days after her arrival, drawing Ariadne off alone, Atalante caught Ariadne in her web. The gist of it was this: either Ariadne would agree to join her in seducing the first unmarried male to enter the household — an act that would place Ariadne in the same debased posture in which she had caught Atalante — or Atalante of the smoldering eyes would rush home to her father and report that Tyro had attempted to rape her in the darkness of her room. That such a report would have been believed and that Tyro's death would have instantly resulted, Ariadne never doubted. Half maddened by her fear, to save her brother's life, Ariadne willingly agreed to sacrifice herself, knowing full well that Atalante intended to carry out the terms of her threat, and that was the atmosphere into which Pharos and I had unwittingly moved when first we had seated ourselves at Antenor's board.

The Lady Ariadne stayed with me throughout the remainder of the night, and I gloried in her touch and in the rich scent of her hair, but I did not enter her body, preserving for Artemis the thing that is hers. And about an hour before dawn, after kissing me once passionately and speaking her love, she was gone, leaving me utterly sleepless, adrift in the fading scent of her body.

After a time, I rose from the bed and walked into the courtyard. A heavy rain still spilled from the sky, and moving forward beneath the spout, I tried as hard as I could to wash all trace of Atalante from my body.

7

W E D I D N O T remain long in Troy, for events there precipitated our departure. At the time, I did not understand them, and I cannot say truthfully that I fully understand them now, but they had to do with the council, the speech Pharos made to it, and a crucial vote, which selected Polydamas — over the Lords Hector and Aeneas — to carry out the reconnaissance of Scyros. After the vote, as Pharos later explained to me, Priam rose majestically from his throne, surveyed his assembled council, and glared down to where Pharos was standing, leaning on the speaker's staff beside Laocoön.

"It has been some time," he said smoothly, "since you last graced us with your eloquence, Pharos. You tutor, I hear — let us not keep you from your obligations, now or in future."

I learned nothing of this until later, of course, after we were already well out across the Plain in the direction of Ida. At the time, I recall, I tried hard to glean details that would give me some sense of what it all meant, but as had become his habit — one that I particularly began to dislike — Pharos merely swept the whole matter away with a single word, *politics,* and I was left abysmally ignorant of facts. By that time, you understand, I think he may have been mildly amused by what had happened to him — at least he seemed so — but he was not at all amused when he first returned to lordly Antenor's house and ordered me to make ready for the road. Then, he had swept into the house with his brows knit deep, Lord Antenor and the venerable Laocoön not far behind him, and gone straight to the table of my Lady Dia to pay his respects.

I happened to be present that morning, having been awakened by Skalmos not long after Aurora's last blush and told in words that left no doubt, "Lady's up. Wants you. Main table in hall. *Now.*" It was not a command, but at the time it seemed one, so with no little fear, I made myself ready to join her. I felt certain, you see, that all had been discovered, that royal Atalante had effected our betrayal, that I would probably be dead within hours for flagrant violations of the laws of Artemis. But I was wrong, for the Lady Dia greeted me with unparalleled graciousness and saw that her serving women heaped my breakfast bowls with the best things in the house. And then, indeed, she entertained me with conversation that I found sublime, for I had never before heard its like. She was so composed, so courteous, so utterly civilized, that my morning moment with her has always seemed a treasure of my youth; even now — here, in the shadow of your dark Greek hulls — I remember well her eloquence and grace.

My lady's daughters-in-law came down some time after I had taken my place at the board, seated themselves, and began adding their own musical expression to the harmony of the conversation, asking me all sorts of questions about myself and Abydus-by-the-sea. All three, I learned, were daughters of holy Ilium, and, having never been allowed to venture far outside the city's walls, they were immensely curious about the world beyond. I answered their questions as well as I could, but at some time, somehow — looking once too often toward the door, no doubt — I gave myself away, for the Lady Ariadne did not join us, and by that time, I hungered for the sight of her with something that approached pure physical pain. As I say, I gave myself away, and my lady's eye must have taken in all at a glance.

"The younger ladies," she said smoothly, "send their regrets.

Both are unable to join us this morning. The Lady Atalante, daughter of royal Priam, who bears the scepter, returned early this morning to the palace for an observance of some ceremonies of state. Ariadne, I fear, is much fatigued after the vivaciousness of the royal visit, and I have ordered her to rest until this evening, when she may rejoin the company to act as your hostess."

I knew well enough the amenities of state that Atalante had gone home to observe, dismissing that piece of news readily and with pleasure, but when I found that Ariadne would not appear, I discovered a longing so intense that it began to gnaw at the very edges of my being, and I thought I could not endure until I saw her again. As I recall, I actually broke into a cold sweat, and at that moment, precisely, Pharos entered the hall with fire in his eye, followed not far behind by Lord Antenor and Laocoön.

My lady rose, as did her daughters-in-law, and Pharos gave them each his mark of respect and in the same instant, catching sight of me, uttered a peremptory order that struck me with as much sharp force as any axe of battle I have ever known: "Take your leave and make you ready for the road!" His eyes, I thought, might actually be on fire, but nevertheless I hesitated, my mouth hanging half open, and then, beneath deeply angered brows, he shot me such a penetrating look that I shuddered.

"Are you ill?" he thundered. "*What* is the matter with you?"

Without ceremony, I leapt for the door. I feared Pharos, certainly, for I had never before seen him so angry, but there, at that moment, my greater terror by far was that I might never see Ariadne again, and I had to know, and I had to know why, and I waited, listening, outside the door.

"Our cause carried," Laocoön was already saying, "but the effort has cost us . . ."

"Dearly, from your looks," I heard my lady respond in a voice that trembled.

"That is true," Antenor admitted, his words sounding both labored and slow. "Pharos spoke eloquently, carrying the entire council with him, but before the gods, he greatly angered our scepter bearer and not a little the Lord Anchises. It is our misfortune that he will have to go."

"Truth," I heard Pharos say sharply, "is ever painful to the royal ears. Thus is the way of the world."

"Oh, my uncle," I heard my Lady Dia say with a sob, "must it always be so?"

I would have heard more, but Skalmos appeared suddenly from the depths of the kitchen passage, handing me two sacks of barley meal and a bag of olives. "For the road. Pack. Time to go." He grunted, turning me smartly by the shoulders and heading me in the direction of the guest quarters. And not long after, with our wallets over our shoulders and our spears in our hands, we made an unceremonious departure, passed rapidly through the streets; exiting by Ilium's high south gate, we moved down again onto the Plain. In the distance, Ida's peaks made love to the clouds, but in my own heart, I found nothing but desolation, for I had not seen Ariadne again and did not believe that I ever would.

We marched hard down the south road, between fields of barley, wheat, and rye, and green pastures where black-maned foals ran with the wind, and all the while, the snowcapped heights of Ida loomed larger and larger before us. Helios rode high in the sky, and the soil, not yet dry after the night's rain, gave off a fresh, pleasant scent. Like its companion to the north, the south road bustled, teeming with traffic, but this time, given the steadiness of our pace, we sought no advantage, being content to move with the flow past farms and manors and military outposts without regard to the world about us because the minds of both of us, I think, remained focused on Troy.

We continued like that for three days, moving steadily across the sun-drenched Plain and then, after striking the banks of divine Xanthus, up the wide, blue-watered valley of Scamander, past the great citadel at Thymbra — guardian of Troy's southern approaches, home barracks to the Leopard, the Eagle, and the Wolf — and on through the tiny villages and hamlets into the vast wooded foothills below Ida, we at last made a stop. By that time, I think, I had made myself all but ill, feverish with a passion that I had never felt before and that I have never felt since; in short, my suffering had become unbearable. By contrast, Pharos was well recovered from his jolt; indeed, as I said earlier, he seemed even mildly amused by his experience, but he was not amused with me, as became readily apparent.

"It is said by the priests of Apollo that a clean breast of things is good for the spirit."

That caught me quick enough, I can tell you, and when I looked up, I found that the power of those penetrating eyes was turned full on me.

"I have watched this go on for several days," he said to me, "and now, I want to know what, precisely, is at the bottom of it. Spare me any details you think unseemly, but remember, with me at least your secrets are safe."

"It is the Lady Ariadne," I said, hanging my head.

"That is abundantly apparent already!" Pharos snapped. "My lady niece spotted you for a lovesick calf the moment you approached her breakfast table, and it is only through her good graces that I have not broached the subject before this time. You show good taste, Dymas, but pathetic judgment, for the Lady Ariadne is noble, while you, as you very well know, are not. Now out with it, and let us have no more skimping."

I told him then and left out nothing, and he paled, I think, when I put in front of him the malignance of Atalante's scheme.

"Three things," he said when I had finished. "First, you must beware in future of the minx Atalante, for she can do you great harm, placed as she is so close to the throne. Second, insofar as reason allows, I commend you for comforting and not taking advantage of my grandniece; that behavior was manly and speaks well for your character. And that brings me to my third point, and it is going to take a man of some character to deal with it, so make up your mind right now to be of firm resolve. As a daughter of Antenor, the Lady Ariadne is destined to marry a royal prince of Ilium, one of Priam's noble sons, and nothing that you or anyone else can say or do is going to change that. She is not for you, Dymas, and that is the way of the world, the hard fact of your life."

I cried that night for the last time in my life, refusing to give up hope, any of my feelings, or the image of my passion, which continued to sear my mind, the memory of her body's warmth firmly pressed against me, and my pain was terrible. Later, Pharos admitted to me that it had also been terrible to watch. "Like watching a dying animal caught in a snare," he said. But at the time, he remained silent and sat staring into the fire until I reached the limit of my misery and could cry no more. Then, when he spoke to me again, the edge had gone from his voice, and in its place I heard something from him that I had never heard before and never heard again — a weariness that seemed to come over him from a very great distance.

"So," he said slowly, in tones so low that I could barely hear him, "that is the way of it, then."

"Yes," I said, "it burns."

"I know," he said after a moment's hesitation.

"You can't," I protested. "It burns like fire."

He took a long breath then and said, "I know."

And I knew that he did and looked up, amazed. I do not think that he even saw me; in that moment, I do not think that he was even there. Instead, his mind had gone out from him somewhere into the depths of that fire, a very long distance away. He remained that way for several long moments, and then he blinked and pulled himself up and stood looking down upon me, leaning on his spear. Carefully, he cleared his throat and swallowed, and the lines on his face became both long and deep, and from those depths he spoke to me again. "Sometimes," he said carefully, slowly, "the heart prevails where the head should control. In such cases — sometimes — all turns out well, but more often than not, suffering results, accompanied by great pain, and then you have no other choice than to endure, for if the heart is allowed to have its way, to dictate terms, chaos will follow in its wake.

"Such would appear to be your case. You began by doing the right thing. As I told you, your behavior regarding the Lady Ariadne was manly. Now, as well, you must practice the way of the warrior, Dymas, which is to endure your pain and suffer in silence, for the facts are not changed: the Lady Ariadne is not for you. Now, no matter what it costs you, the head *must* prevail, or disaster befalls us all. Do you understand as much?"

I heard and I understood his words, but the full measure of what was behind them remained unclear to me, and I said so.

"Has it not occurred to you, even after this experience, that the lives around you seem to lie just beneath the blade's edge of royal displeasure?"

It was beginning to, and looking at me, he saw that I knew as much.

"In time," he said, "in time, you will know what you must. Meanwhile, you must suffer your pain and endure. At the least, it will make you into a man."

In the end, it did. But on that night, there, as we were wrapped in our cloaks at the foot of Ida, what he said to me seemed cold comfort, only a strict, unyielding matter for the head, while the pain at my heart tore deep, and forever.

Throughout the months that followed, we remained on Ida, hunting and reconnoitering, and the daily regimen Pharos set for me left little time for thought. His intention, as he plainly told me, was to show me our southern frontier, to make me know it as clearly and well as the one I had left behind to the north, and in pressing his plan forward, we left no mountain unclimbed, no valley unexplored. I killed my first lion on Ida's western slopes, a young beast that posed considerable danger, for we disturbed it over its kill, but I stood my ground, meeting the beast's charge with the well-thrown point of my dart, and I wore the skin throughout the remainder of the summer. There were dangers, as there always are in the mountains, but on the west slope they were usually animal or natural, and gradually, as the weeks passed, we worked our way up across the mountain's north face, and there things changed.

Across Ida's eastern slopes, we rapidly discovered a ferment of tension, for there, for the first time, we began to bump heavily armed Trojan patrols up from the citadel at Thymbra. As a rule, only men of the Eagle patrolled the eastern slopes, the high Mysian border being their primary responsibility, while the Leopard guarded the whole southwestern sea frontier and the Wolf watched our far eastern borders with Phrygia. That much, as I say, was the normal Trojan practice, but what we found, instead, along those southeastern ridges and vales, was an abnormally high number of Leopards, Eagles, and Wolves patrolling together, reinforcing one another by the weight and assignment of their arms: Leopard sling men backing Eagle infantry, Wolf archers supporting Leopard infantry, and contingents of the Imperial Guard integrated fully with front-rank Eagle spears, all of them nervous, all of them very much on the alert; and the farther east we went, the more we found it so.

"This bears the mark of Skaiko," Pharos said.

"Who?" I wanted to know.

"A contemporary of your father's," he said flatly. "An adequate general, far better in defense than on the attack. He must be in command at Thymbra now, but the question is *why?* I think that we must go and see for ourselves."

And we did but not in the way I expected. Not at all in the way that I expected. Rather than turn north, retracing our steps in the direction of Thymbra or stopping to ask any of the units that we saw in the vicinity, Pharos turned due south, and we began to climb, moving up through woods, vales, and forests toward the distant high summit of Ida's long eastern ridge. Immediately, we ceased to travel by day, laying up during the long hours when Helios guarded the sky, resting and sleeping before rising with the orb of the moon, and moving quietly forward at a hard, fast pace, our spears at the ready.

Ariadne came often to my mind like a pale specter in the light of the moon, but the pain inside me had long since turned from fire to ice, and in place of its burning tongue, I felt only a hard lump that chilled me to the bone. I saw her image, you see, even more clearly than before, and each time I did, that chill buried me like a frozen crust of snow, leaving me cold, dull . . . senseless; whenever Pharos caught me in that condition, he brought me back to life with the butt of his spear.

"You had better be alert," he would say in harsh, low tones, "for the danger here is great!"

And it was. By that time, even beneath the pale orb of the moon, we had seen the bare footprints of Mysian infantry, and a full day before we reached the summit of the ridge, Pharos woke me suddenly in the middle of the afternoon, and then the two of us hugged the face of the earth as a large party of Mysian archers passed in the distance, running fast, well within our borders.

Finally, four days after we started, in the middle of the night, we crossed over the crest of Ida's long eastern rim, descending quickly so as not to expose ourselves against the pale light of the skyline, and went to ground beneath a dark outcropping of rock. It did not take us long to see what we had come to see, for directly below us, stretching far away into the distance, was the shadowed frontier of Mysia, dark and forbidding, a dim series of narrow valleys and ravines; and rising, it seemed, from the depths of every one of them, we saw narrow twists of smoke, the telltale signs of an encamped army.

"That is as much," Pharos quickly whispered, "as we have need to see." He paused then, putting his hand on my shoulder. "It comes too soon," he said, "but a man must follow his fate, and so must you and I and all Trojan men. We start for Tenedos tonight. As soon as we reach there, you join the Shark as runner in the service of Polydamas, and I will make myself useful as I can, for it is about to begin."

It did, for within two days of the night on which we had turned and crossed back over the ridge to the Trojan side, the Mysian army came howling over the summit behind us, vast in their numbers, and we passed battalion after battalion of Leopard, Eagle, and Wolf as well as huge units of the Imperial Guard rushing forward to meet them. Thus began the Third Mysian War, the first war in which I made my way as a warrior.

8

ON TENEDOS, I went immediately into barracks with the Shark, into a block assigned to juniors of my own age, and for some months we saw nothing of the war, our days and nights being taken up with small-unit training of a kind that I had never before experienced. In short, we trained from dawn to dusk, and not infrequently we continued through the night, learning stealth and the arts of reconnaissance beneath the pale light of the moon.

Meanwhile, Pharos, I think, had returned to Abydus-by-the-sea, to the house of my uncle. We had taken more than ten days to reach Tenedos from our starting point on Ida. We had come down swiftly, I remember, across the north face of the mountain, striking the valley of Scamander just west of Thymbra, where the immensity of our mobilization became immediately apparent. From there, we hurried north to Besika Bay, and from there, early on a fall morning, we took ship for Tenedos. Eager for news, lordly Polydamas had greeted us warmly and made good on his promise, for there, in the high citadel well up from the sea, he had administered my oath himself, causing me to swear hard loyalty to the high, white towers of Troy, and in the same instant, with Pharos in attendance before the altar of the Lord Apollo, I had become a Shark, a fierce Trojan raider of the sea, or so at the time I remember thinking, for I was very green. Preparations were made for my assignment to barracks, and while my lord's aides consulted various of their clay tablets, entering my mark on their rolls, Polydamas and Pharos engaged in serious exchange.

"The reconnaissance goes forward," Polydamas said, "and I offer you much thanks for the part you played in bringing it to fruition."

"And it will not be delayed for this?" Pharos asked, making a gesture toward the mainland.

"No," said Polydamas, his eyes glinting. "I have put good men ashore on Scyros. They will bide their time, regardless of how long it takes us to behead this Mysian snake."

"That is good," said Pharos, "for this time it will not end quickly. We have seen for ourselves, you know, that many thousands of them have swarmed across the summits of Ida, where they spread across our slopes like clouds of summer wasps."

"So I am told," said Polydamas, seating himself on a stool and offering another to Pharos while I stood to one side.

"So what are your thoughts?" asked Pharos.

"Skaiko will hold," said the other after a moment's hesitation, "but across the forefront, there will be long and costly attrition."

"Agreed," said Pharos, his flint eyes narrowing, "and most of it will be a senseless slaughter."

"Also agreed," said Polydamas.

"Be patient," said Pharos. "In the end, they must use you; there is no other way."

Polydamas heaved a sigh. "What you say may be true, and I have planned for the contingency, but . . ."

"But?"

"I cannot do it with the Shark alone. No matter how fierce, we are too small a force."

Pharos leaned forward on his stool, supporting himself with his spear, and for a brief moment he seemed almost like my lord's tutor rather than my own. "Think not small," he said flatly, almost rebuking Polydamas.

"Well?" said the other. "I do not see the solution, and you are as aware of how things stand as I am. Neither Chrysa nor Pitane will fall to a thousand men. By my best estimate, I will require four to five times that number, and as you well see for yourself, I have neither the spears nor the ships to carry them."

"Given time," said Pharos, "you may."

"Do you expect them to come from thin air?" Polydamas protested.

"I was thinking," said Pharos, "more in terms of Boar, Kite, or some other northern regiment."

Polydamas seemed stunned. Then he began to laugh. "If you will not mind my saying so," he said at last, "and in view of your . . . ah . . . sudden departure from the royal presence, you still exhibit the guts of an unbroken Trojan mule."

"Perhaps so," Pharos replied quietly, "but war has a strange habit of changing royal views. When the bodies begin to be returned to Ilium in the high numbers that they are sure to be, even Priam may alter somewhat. Then, if we have done our work well, the Shark may be offered an opportunity to expand or its strength may be enhanced by one or more of the upland formations."

"The chances of that seem very slim to me," Polydamas said, shaking his head skeptically while offering Pharos a cup of wine.

"Look ahead and plan accordingly," Pharos said firmly. "Keep one eye to the west, certainly, but for the moment the Greeks, I think, are not our most pressing concern. That they will chip at our edges, I am sure, but mark me, the Greeks will not move but will allow the Mysians to wear us as far down as they can. Until this southern snake is killed and skinned, we must try to ignore them."

"So much is certain," said Polydamas, "but with due respect, I doubt that the rest of your prophecy will come to pass. Even allowing for my lack of political training, I still see clearly that the tide runs against us, and no man can turn the tide, Pharos."

"You must leave the business of tides and turning them to old men like me and to the gods," said Pharos, pouring a generous libation onto the earth. "I will return to the mainland tonight and begin putting politics in motion while Dymas' uncle studies the problem of recruitment." He stood then and turned to me. "I may not see you again for some time," he said shortly, giving me his hand. "Train hard, serve Polydamas well, and make yourself into a Trojan warrior worthy of the name."

I was much moved, and so, I think, was he, for we had been long together, and our hands pressed hard. Moments later, he was gone, the back of his tall frame fading away down the keep's main passage at about the same time that my lord's aides, their preparations complete, came forward to report that I would train with the Shark's Teeth.

"Ah," said lordly Polydamas, "the cutting edge. Look sharp, Dymas; it is the best place to begin."

"And the most difficult," said a swart aide who caught my eye.

"Be that as it may," said Polydamas, "the Teeth are the points of my attack, so train hard. In time, Dymas, you will serve with all of my companies — with the Fins, the Tail, the Nose, and the Body, even with the Eyes — but the Teeth are the most important part of the regiment, so you begin there. Now, off with you, and show the drill masters your mettle."

The Shark's Teeth — numbering three hundred spears, with forty juniors — were, to my mind, the best fighting formation that Troy ever produced. The same might easily be said about the Shark as a regiment, for man to man they could outfight, outdistance, and outlast any other unit on the Plain or in the provinces, even the Imperial and Household Guards, and the guards knew it and so did all of the others. I did not know as much in the beginning, of course, but in time I learned, learning as well the reason for the Shark's superiority. In a word, it was leadership, and in practice, leadership translated into hard training under vigilant, competent command. Daily, all officers commanding took the field at the head of their formations, leading us individually and collectively through all practice at arms, all tactical exercises, and all mock assaults, and the order of precedence was strictly established according to a demonstrated order of merit. Nobles' sons did not automatically command in the Shark; many were on the rolls, but most of them served in the ranks, following commoners appointed to command them and doing it with determined satisfaction. Polydamas commanded the regiment because he was the best amongst us, capable of overcoming any spear in feats of strength, skill, or intellect, and he was much esteemed. No men were flogged in the Shark, as they might have been in the Lion, Boar, the Guards, or any other mainland formation, and yet the Shark was the least slack, most tightly disciplined unit I have ever seen, and the Teeth were, as Polydamas had said, their cutting edge.

Barracks for the Teeth lay back from the beach but well within sight of it and well within sight of the dark stone fortress that guarded it, acting as depot and base for the Whale, a sprawling garrison force of nearly twenty-five hundred men whose ages or past wounds prevented them from serving at the forefront but whose terms of service had yet to expire. These warriors, known to be adequate and solid for stationary defense, also guarded the harbor facilities and manned, when the need arose, the rowing benches of Shark naval hulls. Between the two formations, the Shark and the Whale, there was neither envy nor competition. Each morning as the men of the Shark poured from their barracks blocks and ran naked to the sea for their swim, it was the habit of the Whales to cheer us and rattle their spears wheresoever they trained or stood guard along the beach, and when our swim had ended and we rose bronzed from the waters to make our run back up the hill toward our compounds, we cheered the Whales as we passed and chanted them our sea hymn. They esteemed us, I think, for the warriors that we were, and we respected them for the warriors they had been, for amongst them were some mighty men.

The Teeth were commanded by Koption, whose age, I think, was greater than Polydamas', whose strength was at least equal, but whose analytical powers seemed slightly less, and yet he led splendidly, inspiring each and all to follow in his wake wherever he directed us. As I say, we trained continually in all facets of infantry and naval warfare but mostly in assault — the lightning thrust followed by rapid, fighting withdrawal, and there, for the first time, I took up my sword, learning its manipulation under Koption's masterful eye.

"You must kill," he taught us, "with the first cast of your spear. But then you must rush forward and kill with your sword, for that is the way of the Shark. No body-strength shields here like heavy infantry and no standing firm to receive the enemy's thrust. Instead, we assault, and assault, and assault, and after your first cast, you must rely on your hard bronze sword, for in the heat of battle, when the dust rises so thick as to obscure the sun, you lose all hope of retrieving your spear. Then your sword becomes the pillar of your life, and you must stand or die by its edge."

Day after day, week after endless week, we trained — across the fields before our compounds and across the beaches that led up from the sea — and in time we mastered every facet of warfare: reconnaissance, ambush, assault, stealth, weapons, and command. Oh, yes, each man, no matter how junior, practiced to command, for in the Shark, blind obedience was anathema; each warrior was trained to think for himself. Each man had to be prepared, in the event of a superior's death, to assume command and carry the assault. Initiative was highly prized, even among juniors, who often found themselves at the forefront as runners, dart throwers, or archers.

I trained hard then. I made friends with my mates and with the warriors of the line, and I grew ever stronger in mind and body. By the time of my sixteenth birthday, my weight had reached twelve stone. Agelaos had joined us by that time, and Orthaios, sent down by my uncle from Abydus-by-the-sea, but the remainder of our crew had been drawn as a draft by the Eagle, which had lost many men and not a few juniors in close fighting across the slopes of Ida.

"They train at Thymbra," said Agelaos, scratching his shaggy head on the day of his arrival.

On Tenedos, in barracks, we had heard little of the war's progress, so the news brought forward by recruits was eagerly devoured.

"Enough talk of friends," said Sapses, a bearded senior with a voice like a rasp. "What news of the war?"

Unsure of themselves, Agelaos and Orthaios both looked to me.

"Dymas can't give you the answers," said Sapses with a laugh, "for he has been locked here with us. Now, out with it, both of you!"

That made them jump a little, and both spoke at once until Sapses elected Agelaos to make the tale plain.

"The center still holds," Agelaos said flatly.

"But barely," Orthaios hastened to add.

"That is true," Agelaos continued, once again scratching his head. "The Eagle, we hear, has lost many men, juniors as well as seniors, and units of the guard have moved up from Thymbra to bolster them."

"Household or Imperial?" asked Sapses.

"Imperial," said Agelaos.

"And the flanks?"

"The Leopard is not strongly opposed," said Orthaios, scratching suddenly beneath one of his arms, "but the Wolf's eastern flank has been turned slightly so that now it fights on two fronts — "

"East and south," Agelaos was quick to point out.

"Obviously," Sapses replied. "So who marches to reinforce them?"

"We don't know," Orthaios said, suddenly slapping his thigh.

"Yes, we do," said Agelaos, again scratching behind his ear, "a battalion of Mustang from Abydus-by-the-sea. My father carries the standard."

"But neither Boar nor Kite?" Sapses asked, looking closely at both.

"When we passed Dardanos, both were still in their barracks," said Agelaos, scratching furiously near his groin.

"Both," Orthaios confirmed, running a hand across his chest.

"I see," said Sapses, gathering that he had exhausted their information. "Good report. Now, my fine, brave fellows, tell me quickly the means by which you reached here."

Not a little satisfied by Sapses' apparent commendation, both found the question a trifle absurd and showed as much in their answer. "By ship."

"Naturally," snapped Sapses, indicating that their own answer had been absurd. "Trojan, Carian, or Phoenician?"

"Phoenician," said Agelaos, looking a little downcast.

"A merchant hull," put in Orthaios.

"Carrying a thick cargo of Phoenician lice, by the looks of it!" roared Sapses, stepping one pace back and laughing. "Now, get yourselves down to the sea and make a good, long wash of it, and *thorough,* or you will sleep outside the barracks until the first winter's snow, or for as many nights as it takes you to rid yourselves of those beasts!"

They were away like the wind and did not come into the compound again for five more days, not until our surgeon pronounced both of them medically fit for service and that only after their heads had been shaved and their bodies closely examined.

In the meantime, I thought about what they had told us, for both had always been accurate, and I trusted their word implicitly. By the sound of it, the war went as Pharos and Polydamas had said that it would. Lord Skaiko appeared to be holding the line at Ida's foot, but barely, and bloody stalemate seemed to be in the offing — a miserable state of affairs that would cost us dearly through unrelieved attrition. But if that were the case, I remember thinking, it would cost the Mysians as well, so the question remaining was who would weary of it first. Neither Agelaos nor Orthaios offered any firm sense of time with their reports, so whether their information was fresh or seedy with age, we found difficult to know. In short, beyond a vague notion of events, we had gleaned little hard fact, and I renewed my concentration on my training, realizing that I had only a dim notion of how the war really went.

Winter came in hard that year with penetrating swiftness, and with the first fall of snow, the vast Mysian army quickly disengaged, withdrawing across Ida's newly frozen ridges into the warmth of their winter encampments along the reverse slopes. Reluctant to remain exposed on the ice-encrusted heights, the Leopard, the badly mauled Eagle, and the Wolf pulled back as well, save for isolated reconnaissance patrols, and went into warm winter quarters along the valley of Scamander. Guards units that had seen action on the heights returned to Troy, and the Mustang from Abydus withdrew to the Plain, where the men rested briefly before serving as caravan escorts as they made their way home. This news we had from the Whale, whose ranks swelled by more than four hundred spears following the close of the campaign, and from our own officers, who began repeating to us — on Polydamas' orders — as much news as was thought fitting for us to hear. By and large, reports from both sources agreed, but on some points there were differences, and as early as that winter, I began to hear from newly sworn Whales that Lord Skaiko's generalship was strong in defense but lacking in offensive spirit, exactly what Pharos had predicted. Thus, under the dead hand of winter, the war's first season came to an end with much blood spilled but with nothing settled, without our even knowing much about the actions that had been fought high across the slopes of Ida.

Without regard to the weather, we continued to train, even

when the snow stood knee-deep, having blown hard out of Thrace to freeze instantly over the ground. We wore the leather armor and long sailcloth cloaks that I had come to recognize as the marks of the Shark, and when I did, I realized suddenly that my own white cloak was exactly like the one Pharos had worn on the night, so many years before, when he had first come into my life. I looked for a relationship, then, but found none and continued long to wonder about Pharos' connection with the Shark but could never fathom it.

In all else, however, I made good and steady progress. My capacities with the sword, to my own surprise, proved prodigious for one my age, owing — I think — to quickness of eye and a fine sense of balance. To my own amazement — and owing to the training Pharos had given me early on — I also proved myself an able leader among the juniors, so much so that I was appointed point warrior in a Tooth of ten and gave a strong account of myself by leading it out to victory in mock combats, fought under Koption's watchful eye, against a variety of other junior formations.

But aside from the endless training, nothing more happened that winter until early one morning, no more than a few short hours after we had returned from a bitterly cold night exercise and long before Aurora made even the faintest blush to the east, when we were called suddenly awake by the wrenching sound of the ram's horn and ran, freezing, with full kit to assemble in the lee of the barracks block. There, we swiftly mustered, and then, carrying our round shields across our backs and our long ash spears in our hands, we set off at a trot down the long road to the beach. It was not long before the pale light of the moon showed me that we were not alone on the road, for the Nose and Eyes had taken the way before us; and — as we picked up the pace and raced forward — running down from their upcountry barracks the Fins, the Body, and the Tail joined their parts to ours until we became the whole of the Shark, one thousand warriors strong, trampling the snow beneath our running feet as we hurtled through the night toward the sea.

Like so many ghosts, our sailcloth cloaks floating away from our backs on the wind, we flew out of the hills and down toward the tide-bound shore, and from the dim darkness the assembled Whales cheered us in our might as we passed between them and spilled onto the beach. And there, their dark prows looming high up on the sands, were the broad-beamed outlines of merchant hulls, and I knew at last that we were really going to sea.

Things happened very quickly then as our officers, as though by plan, divided us according to unit, sending each in turn racing across the darkened sands toward an assigned ship. Among the Teeth, juniors were the last to board, and we waited, piqued by excitement, buffeted by the winds, listening alertly as each senior Tooth was called away down to its hull. Suddenly, Koption stood before me, the high horsehair plume of his helmet outlined sharply against the moon.

"Dymas," he shouted, "and ten. To my Lord Polydamas as runners!"

He was gone even before the command sank in, but so was I, my ten following, sprinting across the wave-washed sands and down that long line of prows toward the fleet's center, where I knew I would find my lord's shield hanging from the sheets of his mast, the emblem of his high command. Agelaos was with me there, and fit Orthaios, and as we found our hull and climbed aboard, urged on by the sturdy Whales who manned the rowing benches, we hastened aft into the cargo well, and there beneath the dim light of the moon, I came face to face with Pharos where he stood silently leaning on the butt of his spear.

WE PUT TO SEA quickly with but a single stroke of the oars. Then all sails went up immediately, and as they filled, catching the sharp north wind, Pharos gestured toward the stern, toward the command deck before the helm, and I followed in his wake, leaving Agelaos to settle our men. There were others in the hold as well, contingents of Shark's Teeth and one ten from the Tail, but we passed quickly through them, and there on the quarter I made out the features of Polydamas, who was issuing an order to the Whale manning our steering oar. Ignoring them, Pharos drew me aside and seized my hand.

"You have grown," he said heartily. And even in the darkness, I knew that he was smiling.

"By the weight of two stone," I said. "And I am a hand higher, and I am glad to see you. Do you come from home?"

"Your uncle is in the best of health and sends his greetings," he said quickly, "but I have been absent from Abydus for some weeks. How goes your training? Does your sword arm strengthen? Let me hear you recite the mark of the Shark."

"The Nose smells out the prey, and the Eyes measure its strength," I quickly reported. "The Teeth attack it, and with the Fins propelling the flanks, the Body crushes it."

"And the Tail?"

"And the Tail speeds the Shark away."

"Exactly," Pharos said, "and let such facts not be forgotten."

"No," I said.

"I am told," he went on, "that you excel, that you command your own Tooth."

"That is true," I said, "with Agelaos as my second and fit Orthaios in close support, along with seven other juniors, all of them drawn from our northern frontier."

"With the makings of hard warriors?" he wanted to know.

"The hardest," I assured him; "the best."

He continued to question me like that until we reached the open sea, shipped oars, and made fast our sheets, and then, as we coursed forward, taking up station in the van of a broad-beamed fleet that counted more than twenty dim lanterns on its masts, I could stand the suspense no longer, broke off my answers, and asked him point-blank, "Where are we going?"

And point-blank, he told me. "You are going to see action."

Even as it had in my boyhood, my hair rose stiffly along the back of my neck, a mixed reaction of excitement, courage, and fear, for fear was ever a part of it, even to the end.

I knew then what we were about but, at the same time, knew what I didn't know and pressed for details. Why did we sail at night? Why did we ride broad-beamed merchant hulls rather than fleet-oared naval craft? Where were we to make assault?

"We seek to cast a deception," Pharos said plainly.

Away to the east, suddenly, above the snowcapped Trojan uplands, a dim gray light brought in the dawn.

"Like our own," Pharos continued, speaking in low tones with his back to the wind, "this year's Mysian harvest was light. Most of their able-bodied men were away when the grain was cut, fighting across Ida, leaving their women, children, and old men to bring in the sheaves. In the case of their wheat, they left it too long in the fields, so much of it froze or rotted beneath the first early snow. As a result, Mysian bread is in short supply — not as short as we would have it but short enough — so amidst their winter encampments, their infantry survives on barley cakes, while at Chrysa and Pitane, their people, eating last year's rye, grow thin and gaunt."

"And do we, too, suffer such an ordeal?" I wanted to know, thinking suddenly of doe-eyed Ariadne.

"Hardly," said Pharos, "for we understand the mastery of storage and maintain several years' supply in reserve, but in Mysia, where men live from hand to mouth, as it were, they stare hunger in the face, and flesh-devouring famine threatens the land."

"They will sue for peace," I said confidently.

"That is a little shortsighted," Pharos said quickly. "What they will do is fight harder and try to import grain."

"And we go to prevent them?"

"Precisely," said Pharos, "for know you, Dymas, that they have purchased a cargo of thirty hulls from Egypt for transshipment through Crete. Agents for King Idomeneus conducted the negotiations, going all the way to Pitane in order to settle the terms, and that is how we first learned of the transaction, through an attentive Carian who exchanges information with us for pay. Cretans transported the grain on the first leg of its journey, from the mouth of the Nile to the isle of Dia, but from there, refusing to become embroiled in our war, Idomeneus wisely demanded that Mysian bottoms load and transport their own cargo for the remainder of the way. As I once told your master, the Greeks will chip at our edges, but they will not interfere, preferring to let the Mysians wear us down, without themselves becoming directly involved."

I remembered that conversation and said as much.

"Then what should be our plan?" Pharos said, putting the question to me as an essay in strategy.

"To intercept," I said plainly, "to capture, if possible, the Mysian grain fleet."

"And if capture is impossible?"

"To destroy it."

"What is the degree of difficulty?" he probed.

"High," I replied, "for their naval arm is sure to sail as escort."

"Thus the deception," he said, "for when the morning breaks full, you will see that we are disguised as Phoenicians and have trimmed our hulls accordingly. Now, an option presents itself to the Mysians, so consider. They may sail by two routes for Pitane: west of Chios up the wine-dark Aegean or east of Chios through the narrow passage that stands between the island and the Lydian coast. Remember the charts that I drew for you on the hearth-stones of your youth? Where do we lie in wait?"

It was a difficult question with many answers, made even harder by my attempts to visualize the situation on the basis of some half-forgotten drawings I had once seen in my youth.

"Just out of sight of Pitane," I said finally, "where we are sure that they must pass."

"Sensible enough, I suppose," said Pharos, "but dangerous, very dangerous, for there we are sure to be sighted, and the alarm will be raised against us. No, Dymas, I think we must wait where we are not anticipated and not expected — south of Chios athwart both channels at once. There, long before they believe themselves in danger, our close deception may catch them off guard and give us the edge."

It seemed to me a brilliant plan, and I said so. "Whose is it?" I wanted to know. "The council's?"

"Ah . . . it belongs to Lord Polydamas," said Pharos, not with-out circumspection. "The Military Council, of course, has ap-proved it," he hastened to add.

"But you and my uncle worked out the details," I said at once, thinking that I saw through him, "didn't you? Just as you did the raid on Pitane?"

"A few of them," said Pharos, and I knew he was hedging. "But that is not widely known, and your uncle and I would like the fact to remain obscure for reasons that I am not going to explain to you, so say no more about it, to anyone. Understood?" His tone had hardened, and in the instant I knew that he was adamant on the matter.

"Understood," I replied.

"Good," he said as the dawn broke full, throwing a dim light through the leaden clouds.

With the dawn, the wind stiffened, and as we shortened sail to compensate for the increased force against the mast, I looked to sea, taking in the full strength of our fleet. Off the port quarter, rigged with dirty purple sails so as to disguise themselves as Phoenicians, twenty-two broad-beamed hulls hugged the sea path like a company of dolphins, scudding across the wine-dark waves, running strong before the wind. Few men were in sight — Whales mostly, wearing Phoenician apparel — but in the holds of each hull, upwards of fifty armed Sharks rested in concealment.

"Time for you to go below," Pharos said to me. "We have a long voyage ahead, forty leagues or more, so bed your men down and see that they sleep while they can. And enforce tight water discipline: we carry enough reserve for only five days. Off with you now, and let all matters keep order."

I turned to go, but before my foot had touched the ladder, Pharos pulled at my cloak.

"One more thing," he said briskly. "What of that matter of Troy?"

"It haunts me," I said, "but I endure."

"In silence?"

"In silence."

"All right," he said, giving me a nod of approval. "See to your men."

In the cargo well, I found little to do. Agelaos and fit Orthaios had already made provision for our men, and all were bedded down, wrapped in their cloaks, seeking the land of Morpheus amidst the unpleasant buffeting of the waves. There, I took my place beside them, wrapped my own cloak about my shoulders, stood my spear within easy grasp, sought the same sleep and the same dreams as my fellows, and failed to find either, for instantly a vision of Ariadne flooded over me, even there, surrounded as I was by restless warriors and the greasy odors of cordage and hemp. I saw her soft doe eyes and lustrous hair in that hour, and even beneath a sharp salt spray, I could have sworn I detected her scent. Soon my misery became complete.

Throughout the remainder of the day, the night following, and the full length of the next day and night, I remained in my agony, dozing off, sleeping fitfully, and waking again to the pain of my deprivation, a searing fire that seemed to bore through my flesh like streams of molten bronze. On the morning of the third day, when Pharos ordered me aloft, I was only too eager to climb the mast.

"Your eyes are sharp," Pharos said, "like the all-seeing kite's, so up you go, and when you reach the yard, lash yourself to the mast, for you are to be the eyes of the fleet. Watch to the south; that is the direction from which they must come."

I was up, then, and out of my armor, which Agelaos stowed for me in the shadow of the mast, and I climbed, shinnying up the pine thickness of the mast with a lashing line held tight between my teeth. At the top, the wind blew fierce, its Borean chill driving in sharp with each plume of spray that came shooting up from the prow like a hail of Mysian darts. I gritted my teeth and lashed myself to the mast and, once secure, wrapped my cloak as tight about my shoulders as I could. Then felt I like some high-flying hawk with the vast, windswept sea spread out before me under its whitecaps. Off to port, the shrimp-shaped coast of Chios spread bleakly across the horizon, but all else seemed wine-dark brine whipped white by the force of the wind.

I remained aloft, scanning the distances, until well after Helios had driven his chariot below the western horizon, and I went aloft again on the following day, having organized turns at the watch for myself and for each man in my Tooth, but we sighted no black-rimmed Mysian sails, no grain-laden ships, and earned for our efforts only such frozen limbs that our chattering teeth did not cease to make their noise until long after we had come down to enter again the shelter of the cargo well. We searched hard but found nothing, not even so much as a fishing smack, and on the command platform, where the two of them stood together, I could plainly see that Pharos and Polydamas were worried. We had exhausted our supply of sea biscuits by that time, and our water skins were nearing empty, and with so many men, soon I knew we would have to turn and make course for Tenedos so as to avoid disaster from exposure, hunger, and thirst. But we did not go that night, taking our fitful sleep in great hunger and considerable thirst, and on the following morning, when we were each allowed only a single moist swallow, we remained on station, patrolling east and west in a loose line astern, the snowcapped heights of Chios barely visible to the north. And in the middle of the afternoon, I went up the mast again, my tongue swollen for lack of water, my body aching from both cold and hunger, and in the same instant that I lashed myself to the mast, I saw what seemed to be needles rising one by one from the sea along the southern horizon, and looked again, and when I was sure, when I had seen in the distance the first black-rimmed sail, I gave the alarm at the top of my lungs, alerting the warriors below. Then, even as I descended from my high perch on the mast, we turned quickly south, running out all our long pine oars, and the Whales at our rowing benches, straining behind their shafts, pulled away together, driving us hard over the sea path.

The first thing I saw as I pulled on my leathern armor was my Lord Polydamas beckoning to me from the command platform and holding up three fingers, indicating that he wanted three runners immediately. Still fastening my clasps, I hurried aft, dragging Agelaos with me and a third mate, Thranites from Percote, while shouting to Orthaios to make ready the remainder.

"Hear my orders, Dymas," my lord commanded. "Station four of your juniors the length of the hull to relay my commands in battle. Agelaos and Thranites go over with the senior Teeth to act as runners for their leaders. Assign Orthaios to run for the leader of the Tail, and you and two others return here to me. Go!"

We went then like slivers of sleet, flying down into the cargo well, where with short orders and firm commands, I deployed my men before racing back to the platform with two of my juniors in tow.

By the time I returned, the Mysians were no more than a league distant, and we could already see the blades of their oars. Hulls down beneath the great weight of their cargo, they labored north under full oar and sail. There were not as many as we had expected, no more than twenty-five as I recall, but the naval hulls of their escort brought the full strength of their fleet up to thirty-eight prows, making them larger and more dangerous than anyone had anticipated.

"It is always so," said Pharos from where he stood near the edge of the platform. "And that is why we are called warriors and accorded great respect among our people, for it is our choice in life to pit ourselves against the unknown, and the final unknown is always death. Not for this, the casual cutter of meats or man of the soil, nor the fainthearted merchant whose interest remains in his purse, and all men know as much, according us our measure of esteem, for we are pitted ever against the hollow chambers of decay."

There, then, as we hurtled down across the waves, running full before the wind — in a moment, I suppose, of doubt, I knew for the first time the fear of oblivion, the fear of death, the fear of disappearing forever into the deep, dark chambers of Hades while the world . . . Ariadne, everything . . . continued without me for all the years of the sun. Pharos must have sensed what I was thinking, for in that moment, he thumped me with the butt of his spear.

"Such thoughts are natural enough," he said. "I feel them myself, but no man lives forever; immortality is the province of the gods. Remember that, Dymas, and remember, too, that no man escapes his fate. Fight well, then, for you were born to it, and the men who know you expect you to give a good account of yourself. Now, how do we attack?"

"Hard," I said, feeling the hair stiffen along the back of my neck, "like the Teeth of the Shark!"

"When?"

"When the high prows crash!"

"Where?"

"At the heart of the enemy!"

"Good," he said, pausing to look at me. "You will be all right, but remember, keep your shield up, your head down, and your spear at the ready. Now stand to and prepare yourself."

We bore down like the great blue sharks of the sea. Reluctant to give ourselves away, we had shipped our oars the moment the Whales had brought us fully through our turn south, and now, retaining the momentum of their few bold strokes, we swept down out of the north under full sail, running hard before the wind. The Mysians had sighted us, certainly, but even as we closed, our deception held, for they showed no alarm, still taking us for the Phoenician merchant fleet that we appeared to be.

Out of sight beneath the sail, the Whales made ready their grappling hooks and boarding pikes and such other weapons as they would use to defend the ship, while farther down in the well, my fully armed Shark's Teeth were already poised, ready to leap to the rail on the first clear command. And then I experienced great tension and mind-chilling excitement, because as the range between the two fleets closed — first to one thousand and then to five hundred yards — the Mysians suddenly sensed their danger, stood to arms, and tried to turn away, while at the same time they hurried to ship their oars so as to avoid the disaster we had given them at Pitane. They almost succeeded but not quite, for even as the Mysians loosed their first showers of arrows against us, finding more than one mark amongst our many men, the hard, bronzed edge of our prow struck the first of their ships a glancing blow to port and ground swiftly down the side, snapping their oar stems like twigs, creating havoc along their rowing benches, where their screaming oarsmen and not a few of their archers thought themselves struck down furiously by the hand of Zeus.

"Grapple!" roared my Lord Polydamas, myself, and my runners in quick succession, and a dozen grappling hooks flew instantly into the air, the Whales scrambling to make fast the bitter ends of the attached heaving lines. *"Board!"* Polydamas, myself, and my runners roared again — even while some of our hooks still flew through the air.

With a piercing war cry so sudden, so bloodcurdling that it lacerated the air, the Teeth swarmed up from the hold like the Furies, struck the rail, and leapt into thin air without so much as stopping once to gauge, measure, or calculate the risk. And within less time than it takes the eye to blink, they came down roaring, lunging with sword and spear, right on top of the Mysian rail. It was an act of pure faith, a perfect leap into the last unknown, carried out willingly at my lord's command and borne forward by limitless courage. The moment I saw it, I knew forever the real responsibility of command, for if Polydamas had shouted his order too soon, all twenty men would have leapt straight into the sea and been crushed between the hulls. As it was, the two senior Teeth broke into battle at the Mysian center, turned instantly back to back, and began hacking their way fore and aft across the Mysian rowing benches, while the Shark's Tail, carrying an assortment of boarding pikes, followed in their wake.

By intention, we had struck the foremost Mysian naval hull, believing it to be their command ship, but in that assumption we were disappointed. Nevertheless, we had a hard fight of it; my mate standing next to me was killed almost instantly by a bronzed Mysian arrow, which pierced his neck and sent him howling into the chambers of decay, his warm blood steaming as it spread across the planks of the command platform. I saw my lord and Pharos both cast their spears and strike home, bringing down two Mysian archers from their perches in the prow, and then, on the instant, my lord turned to me and my second.

"Over you go," he shouted. *"Recall and fire!"*

We were away then, our fear rising like ice along the backs of our necks, the penetrating chill boring straight to the bone. I do not remember feeling my feet, not even my legs, but as I do look back, I recall a sensation of weightlessness as I sprang fully armed from our rail and saw a bronze-tipped arrow pass close beneath me as I crashed down hard into the Mysian hull. That the arrow had been intended to kill me, I had no doubt, and from that moment on, curiously, I was all right and sent my companion rushing toward the stern while I pressed forward toward the melee in the bow, shouting *"Recall and fire"* at the top of my lungs. Contorted bodies lay everywhere, most of them Mysian, and the decks were awash and slippery with blood, which smoked where it ran in the Borean air. And then I came upon Agelaos, with a deep gash above his right eye, where he stood his ground just behind the forefront, and gave him my order and turned and took a second arrow so hard against my shield that it pierced the ox hide to slice across my cheek just beneath the bone. I saw the arrow in flight, felt its slice, and in the same instant hurled my dart at the offending Mysian, who had risen from beneath a rowing bench where our initial impact had overlooked him. He was only then coming into the fight, I think, but my blow struck him full on the chest, and as I dashed by, I seized the bow from his hands even as death closed his eyes.

Amidships, men of the Tail, with tinder and flint and quantities of oil, had already fired the hull, and as one after another leapt back to our own hard rail to cover our withdrawal, using their long, bronzed boarding pikes, the Teeth began to disengage. Few Mysians pursued; those who did died, and the remainder, small knots both fore and aft, could do nothing to save themselves but leap from their burning deck into the cold sea.

I made my own leap then and found myself quickly followed by my seniors, our dead and wounded carried over their shoulders like sheaves of grain brought home to a threshing floor.

Even before I could make my way back to the command platform, we were breaking away, our high stern swinging out, away from the flames, the Whales already running out their oars and backing together into a rolling sea.

My cheek ran hot with the flow of my own blood, and I knew then how Pharos had come by so many scars and my uncle not a few, and as I hastened aft, I saw other men binding up their wounds with wraps of linen and a healing ointment provided for us by our surgeon. We lost four dead in the assault, including my mate, and nineteen wounded, including Agelaos and myself, but we killed or wounded nearly the whole Mysian crew in a hard fight and left them burning at sea to sink under the hand of Poseidon.

Meanwhile, as I quickly learned on the command platform, where Pharos plugged my wound with tar, our other hulls had done as much damage, assaulting and burning some nine of the enemy's naval hulls while boarding and capturing fully three quarters of their broader, slower merchant bottoms and seizing their grain cargoes intact. The Mysian command ship, positioned strangely so as to bring up the rear of their fleet — acting, perhaps, as shepherd to stragglers — had apparently gauged the seriousness of the situation in the moment that we struck, and knowing that it would be impossible to beat up to us in time against the stiff northern wind, had turned south instead, drawing away the landward naval escort and five or six of his closest grain ships. By the time we disengaged from our initial assault, these were already disappearing over the southern horizon, running before the wind under full sail and well out of harm's way. Even so, we had brought off a great victory and knew it and felt the full thrill pass quickly through us.

My Lord Polydamas grinned from ear to ear, and Pharos, if my senses served me, barely restrained himself from dancing with delight, but as we came together and began to take stock, the sobering fact of death hit us head on, for in attacking the Mysians as we had, naval hulls first, we suffered no fewer than thirty-six dead and more than two hundred wounded, twenty-nine of them so seriously that they would have to be relegated to the Whales if they saw service again at all.

Then my lord's face creased deep with his grief, as did my own, for one who died was Koption, struck through the eye and throat with bronzed barbs just as he led his Tooth across the Mysian rail, and his body had gone down beneath the waves. Sapses, too, went down, to a Mysian javelin that pierced his chest and pinned him to a Mysian mast, still standing, as he led his Tooth over the side some five ships distant from the hull we had attacked. We did not know as much in the beginning, but as each of our ships began to pass alongside so that their captains could shout their reports, the grim truth flowed over us like winter rain.

"It is ever so," said Pharos, placing his right hand over my lord's shoulder, "for war at sea is costly beyond measure, but thus is the way of the Shark. Even at the odds, we have brought off a great victory, for far more is at stake here than our puny lives. Consider, the success of this action may be enough to bring the dogs again to heel."

Polydamas wept his tears in silence, for in his heart he knew that Pharos spoke true, and eventually he said as much. Then, calling the fleet together by means of fire arrows, he signaled the turn north, and under full oar but shortened sail, we beat up into the wind, setting our course for Tenedos and home. All voices rose together chanting our sea hymn as we sailed darkly into the night.

10

TWO DAYS LATER, following hard buffeting at the hands of Poseidon . . . tired, spent, some of us still bleeding . . . we beat up into the harbor at Tenedos, disgorging onto the sands beneath a Borean chill. New snow had fallen and frozen into a hard crust that sparkled beneath the gray light of the moon, and we broke its surface with spades to bury our dead. Afterward, we chanted our sea hymn over their mounds, planting each man's great oar firmly over his hands so that he might row himself across Lethe in spite of Charon's demands.

Meanwhile, the Mysian grain ships had sailed east toward Besika Bay, my lord's couriers with them, carrying the news of our victory to Troy and the Grand Council of royal Priam. The Mysian merchant crews, however, did not accompany their ships but were disembarked instead before the Whale's keep to be questioned and counted and, afterward, sent in Trojan hulls to the slave markets at Myrina on the isle of Lemnos. They were a ragged herd, looking and smelling like goats after lean fare in a winter pasture, but brought a high enough price in Myrina. The spoil was evenly divided between the Whale and the Shark, each man receiving his share.

I parted from Pharos on the beach after the burials, knowing that I would see him again soon, and went immediately with the Teeth into barracks, where our surgeons examined us, applied their healing ointments, and gave us something to drink that made us sleep the sleep of the dead. And on the following day, we were all administered a purge — to stabilize our cycles, the surgeons told us — and on the third day, we rose early and returned to our training as though we had never been in action. We did not, however, train the full day, for not long after Helios reached his zenith, we were called in from the bitterly cold field, and then, wearing only our short tunics and sea cloaks and carrying our spears, we were marched away upcountry for purification.

The ceremonies were conducted before the high citadel by Apollo's priests and entailed both prayers for the dead and generous libations poured over the snow in honor of mighty Zeus, lordly Poseidon, and the Butcher of Men, he who calls himself Ares, god of war. And then each man stripped naked, immersed himself in the ritual bath, and re-emerged, cleansed before the gods. The water, I remember, was icy cold, but nevertheless I came out exhilarated, and receiving fresh clothing from a priest, I passed on up the ramp into the citadel, where nine mountain boars and a great ox turned before fires on their spits. There at last I saw Pharos sitting at Polydamas' right hand, and answering his summons, I crossed the great hall and took a place on a stool at his side while servers brought round baskets of bread and bowls filled with steaming slices of meat cut fresh from the quarters of a boar.

Pouring a libation from my wine cup, I broke bread there beside my lord and found it white inside and sweet to the taste.

"That is because it has been made," Pharos said, "from Egyptian grain, and there is none better under the sun, not even among the Ethiopians, who live at the edges of the world."

Prizes were awarded then as marks of excellence, *areté*, for prowess in battle, and Colophon of the Shark's Teeth was granted three bronze tripods and promoted to command following the death of blue-eyed Koption. Milas of the short sword, commander of the Body, earned a silver mixing bowl that day for his accomplishments in capturing the Mysian merchant hulls, and Antiphates, of the Tail, was singled out for a bronze axe for having killed two Mysians back to back with a single thrust of his spear. Those of us who were wounded but could still walk, Agelaos and myself included, were awarded bronzed Mysian arrowheads; mine, I noticed, still carried a stain of Trojan blood. And at the conclusion, the men of the Shark rose as one and cheered my Lord Polydamas for the strength of his victory, voting him a tenth of the spoil that was to be borne home from Lemnos by the venerable Whale. Later, as I was to learn, other honors came down from Troy by order of Priam and the Grand Council, but nothing so generous as those accorded to my lord by his Shark.

"Fully half of this is yours," he said to Pharos, "and my lord's."

"Nothing of the kind," Pharos answered. "It can do us no good where we are in Abydus-by-the-sea, and it is not *your* place but the council's to make such matters right. We will have something from them, I warrant you, in spite of royal objections, and in the meantime our satisfaction will be enough."

"It is wrong," Polydamas pronounced strongly.

"Nevertheless," said Pharos, "thus it must be."

They might have said more, but at that moment the ram's horn sounded, and my lord's herald announced Agias of Antissa, and immediately the hall fell silent as a graying ancient was led forward by his boy and seated in our midst on a three-legged stool that had been covered by a warm fleece. That the man was blind, I could see at once, for his lusterless eyes focused nowhere in the space before him.

My Lord Polydamas and Pharos both stood in the ancient's presence, even though the old man did not seem aware of them, and carefully they both went forward, greeting him warmly and with much respect. Afterward, they brought him choice wine, Egyptian bread, and nothing but the most savory cuts of meat taken hot from the spit. Serving him themselves, they stood by quietly until he had finished the delicacies in his bowl, and then, taking it from the boy, Pharos himself placed the lyre in Agias' hands.

"Sing to us, o my Agias, of the long gone wars of Thynia," he pronounced, "and let our hearts rise high with your song."

Without speaking, the bard nodded, and Pharos and my lord returned to their seats, sitting again beside me.

"Attend you, Dymas," Pharos said loudly, so loudly as to be heard across the entire breadth of the hall, "for amongst warriors, the bard is the bringer and the keeper of our immortality, and we live forever only in his song. Esteem the singer before you, for Agias of Antissa is known far and wide for the immortal beauty of his song as he moves men's hearts to tears."

There was silence, then, so perfect a silence that I thought I could hear heartbeats at the opposite end of the hall, and Agias plucked the strings of his instrument and the clear sound of his voice filled the air.

"The might of Kalitor is my theme," he began, and, struck with wonder, I heard for the first time the exploits of my father, heard them live again in the glory of the bard's song, and such was the singer's power, such the intensity of his passion, that every Shark sat spellbound into the night, and in the end, I think I came to know my father intimately for the first time: how in his youth he had strangled a lion with his bare hands, how he had joined the Boar as a junior and risen by sacrifice and endurance to command; how he had foreseen the danger and repelled the Thynians' invasion when they had assaulted in their numbers across the long, sloping beach before Abydus-by-the-sea; how he had raised a fleet, crossed the swift-flowing Hellespont, and laid siege to high-walled Sestus; how he had defeated noble Palmys, King of Thynia, in single combat and then taken his citadel through long days and hard fighting beneath the light of the moon; how he had led the Boar up the land's neck to demonstrate before Thrace; how my deep-thinking uncle, his brother, had wielded power beside him; how the two together had consolidated their gain and given it over to Priam, royal ruler of Troy; and how my father had shown himself great in the glory of his achievement but ever humble before the gods.

Lord Polydamas wept as the song ended and raised his hand to shield his brow, and yet his tears ran freely enough, falling like raindrops onto the edge of his drinking bowl. As much moved as I, Pharos stared hollowly into the fire, then choked down the lump in his throat, and rose, moving forward to award Agias an exquisite silver drinking cup that he had kept concealed in the tight folds of his cloak throughout the bard's performance. The cup, decorated in relief, detailed the exploits of Heracles entering the Garden of the Hesperides, strangling the guardian serpent, and removing the forbidden apples, which the cup's craftsman showed studded with gold.

"For Agias of Antissa," Pharos announced, "for he now is keeper of the tree, guardian of the apples of our immortality."

Agias stood and bowed low, and after Pharos had made him further marks of respect, the boy took the bard's hand and led him from the hall amidst the Shark's cheering applause.

"You see," Pharos said, returning to his place, "the power of song: your father, mighty Kalitor of the long shield, lives again in the hearts of men."

I saw and was much moved, for around me many men still wept.

"Know you, Dymas," he went on, "that death closes all with oblivion, and the chambers of decay are coldly everlasting, dim and dark. Only the Orphic power of the bard can ever bring us back to life and give us again, for a few fleeting moments, the immortality we crave. That is why we fight. Could we be sure of ageless immortality, we might float like gods above the endless vicissitudes of life, but we are men, and men are fated to die, and no man, Dymas, ever escapes his fate. But still — beyond family, hearth, and home, above life itself, each man seeks to leave his mark on the world, and in the end, that urge becomes our reason for being, the single thing that earns us the esteem of all men as we take the field, facing the unknown, eager to win glory for ourselves or, if another's might excels, yield it up to others. The bard, Dymas, is the guardian of our mark; he keeps it ever safe, ever fresh against the drifting mists of time. Esteem him even beyond your sword."

It was a plain lesson that Pharos gave me that day, clearly told, and I have never forgotten his words, which live for me now, here, even as they did so many seasons past, there in the citadel on Tenedos.

Not much more was said that night, for once Agias and his boy had left the hall, the ram's horn blew, and the assembled warriors rose as one man and prepared themselves to return to barracks.

"I may not see you again for some time," Pharos said to me, grasping my hand.

"You depart already?"

"Just so," he replied. "The immediate threat is ended, and in my judgment the serpent has been struck a harsh blow. It will be silent for a while below its bush, but in the end, we must surely kill it, and I go to prepare the way."

He stopped and, looking me over from head to toe, took my full measure. "You begin well," he said; "your uncle and I are proud of you. Keep to the mark, study to lead, and teach men to honor your name. And Dymas," he said as I turned to go, "learn all you can about Greeks."

I left, then, with the Teeth, passing through the high gates onto the hard winter snow, not realizing that years would pass before I saw my tutor again.

11

PHAROS HAD BEEN right, more right than he had reason to know, for the period that came to be known as the Long Truce descended then, and along our borders with Mysia, few men, Mysian or Trojan, went to war. We had hurt the Mysians more than we knew. That Polydamas had won a great victory for Ilium was all too apparent, but how great his victory had actually been did not appear until much later, near the end of that long, bitter winter. Then at last we heard reports of lean famine in Cyme, Pitane, and Chrysa. As events later turned out, these reports, borne to us by Carian agents, were somewhat exaggerated, but all the same, conditions in Mysia were much worse than we had believed them to be. Still, the Mysians held on, refusing either to sue for peace or enter into negotiations, so the war continued but in a state of suspension. For reasons that remained equally unclear, royal Priam elected not to press our advantage, so such a war as did exist consisted of armed but mostly accidental clashes between opposing patrol groups on or around the heights of Ida.

Like leaves blown seaward on the autumn winds, my seasons passed, year after year, until I counted my age at nineteen, and still the uneasy truce prevailed. Following the first winter of the war — my seventeenth on Mother Earth — the spring had come in hard and, following on its heels, a dry, hot summer, and again the harvests had failed, even on the Plain. This weak year had been followed by a third and a fourth. Trojan grain supplies, bolstered by the Egyptian wheat we had captured, kept to reasonable levels, but having been forced to eat much of their seed corn to prevent starvation, the Mysians were long in recovery. At the end of the war's first year, then, they had given up the attack, gone over into a defensive posture, and sent fully half of their spearmen back down to their fields and farms, where for three years they worked frantically, trying to rebuild their grain supplies and establish a reserve. But still they showed no inclination to establish a permanent peace, and as the years passed, it seemed at times as though peace might almost be ready to establish itself by default, everywhere on Ida's heights, everywhere ashore, everywhere — except at sea.

At sea during those years, for the Shark, the fury of the Third Mysian War went unabated. Again and again, we put to sea in all kinds of weather, sailed far south, and struck the Mysian fleet whenever and wherever we found it, and red ran the rolls of our dead and wounded. I did not escape, going down hard in my eighteenth year with a poisoned Mysian arrow through my leg, and long was the period of my recovery. But in the end, the Shark prevailed, so damaging the enemy's naval and merchant activity that their remaining hulls kept closely to port or made lonely, isolated runs at night, thus giving us complete command of the sea.

And yet, as I said, the costs were high. Gradually, as the Shark brought Mysian naval might to heel, steady attrition reduced the regiment's strength to no more than six hundred spears and fewer than eighty juniors. In the event, flint-eyed Polydamas combed the face of the Troad to make good our losses. Juniors were promoted one full year ahead of the norm, and from the north, where my uncle had been appointed Master of Recruitment, we received one hundred new upcountry juniors who went straight into training. Tireless in his efforts, Polydamas also paraded the Whale and, by thoroughly culling its ranks, drew forward some seventy warriors who looked fit enough to take the field again in hard frontal assault, and these he brought into the Shark. One, a former Eagle, a man who had once taken a Mysian mace above the ear, I came to know as Tarsos of Troy. We grew stronger, then, day by day, but by year's end my lord had succeeded in returning the Shark only to eighty percent of its former strength.

My leg continued to heal, slowly — for the Mysian poison ran deep — but surely, and about the time I was near to regaining full strength, one of my lord's couriers reached me on parade, conveyed to me an order, and I found myself detached.

"You join the Nose *this morning,*" the courier said as he ran up beside me in formation. "Gather your gear and make haste to the citadel, for time and tide wait for no man."

I still remember thinking that the courier had been more than a little pompous in offering me that remark. Nevertheless, I gathered up my kit, slung my shield over my shoulder, took up my spear, and made haste upcountry, and there, in the Shark's high citadel, I found my lord, who turned those dark, penetrating eyes of his straight into my own.

"Your leg is not fully healed," he said flatly. "I heard the surgeon's report for myself this morning. Until you recover all of your strength, until the muscles knit fully, you take your place in the Nose as my aide. Do not put your kit down; we leave immediately for Troy."

It would be difficult to describe to you the sensation I felt in that moment, for what man can truly know the frenzy of the wind or the sharp bolt that the Master of Thunder may throw from the sky? I cannot convey such sensations verbally, but that I felt them, there, in my lord's presence, I cannot deny. For months, I had suppressed all thought of the Lady Ariadne, concentrating instead on the war, on my training, on whatever would keep me from thinking about her, and up to a point I had succeeded, and then, with the first mention of my lord's intention, I was stabbed by the thought of her, by a vision of her face and form so clear and direct that I seemed almost on the verge of touching her, and I became lost in reverie. I did not remain so for long, however, because in the same moment that my vision nearly overpowered me, Polydamas took up his spear and moved quickly toward the door, making me bolt to catch up with him.

Our journey up to Troy proved as swift and dangerous as any I have ever made. My lord's own chariot horses descended, I think, from the eagles of Zeus, for as we raced down from the citadel toward the sea, they seemed to leave off running altogether in order to take flight across the open, rocky ground, and thrice I was nearly thrown to certain death on the rubble in their wake. The next thing I knew, we boarded a raiding hull, and regardless of the seas, which were running so high and hard as to throw green water over the bow with every stroke of the oars, we pulled away smartly into a gale of mounting waves, a crew of strong-armed Whales pulling up and over each wine-dark crest, until we attained something like the speed of a sea hawk. The crew maintained that buffeting pace until we beached hard at Besika Bay. There, we took chariot again, my lord at the reins, and sped like the wind across the frosty Plain straight toward the high white towers of Troy.

Polydamas was not uncommunicative, and the briefing he gave me as we raced toward Ilium made our situation on Tenedos abundantly and forever clear.

"Since the end of the First Mysian War," he told me, "since your father, the mighty Kalitor, was killed, royal Priam has steadily refused to take the offensive. He holds your uncle and Pharos and me partially responsible for your father's death — for not being present to lend him adequate support — and for that as well as for other reasons, all three of us have incurred a full measure of royal wrath. Priam never liked your father — in fact, in council and debate, they were bitter enemies, seldom seeing eye to eye, but Kalitor of the long spear was loyal to holy Ilium and to Priam, and Priam trusted that loyalty and your father's fighting capabilities, which never failed the throne. It was no fault of your uncle's that he was unable to support your father. Bear in mind, Dymas, that your uncle suffered horrible wounds in Thrace, that he took a very long time to recover, and that when he did, finally, he could barely walk. His mind, of course, was in no way touched by his wounds, but like your father, your uncle had long opposed royal policy from his place on the Military Council, and in the hour of his most serious disability, Priam seized the opportunity to be rid of him.

"You see, Dymas, to hold a place on the Military Council, a man must either be noble born or hold an active general's rank. Because your family's origins have always remained in doubt — a condition that the royal family has done nothing to clarify and everything to obscure beneath a courteous cloud of professed ignorance — your uncle's early retirement from military service would have meant his immediate removal from the council, and that is precisely what Priam brought about, citing your uncle's extreme medical disability as the reason for his retirement. Then, you see, it was only by means of the most assiduous political pressure that our friends, Lord Antenor in particular, were able to procure him the appointment as Harbor Master at Abydus-by-the-sea, where your uncle has shown himself to be a great administrator but where his considerably greater military talents have largely been wasted."

My Lord Polydamas warmed to his subject, I noticed, the more he worked into it, but an element of bitterness had crept into his voice, and he continued on the edge of anger.

"No matter," he went on, as we negotiated the bridge over Scamander, "that royal Priam — for reasons of pure political expediency — had been instrumental in your uncle's removal. At the moment of your father's death, when the horrifying news struck Troy so suddenly and unexpectedly, Priam laid much of the blame on your uncle and even more on Pharos, who was equally guiltless for reasons that he may one day tell you himself. Priam's contention was that your uncle had weakened great Kalitor's resolve by advising, out of channels and against royal wishes, a sea invasion of Mysia whereas the land-oriented council, and Priam in particular, had demanded an assault over Ida's slopes. Know you, Dymas, that the idea for assault by sea originated with your father; as always, your uncle had merely supported him in the plan's preparation, doing brilliant staff work in organizing the details. Priam, of course, could see your uncle's hand in the plan, even behind the scene, and having consolidated his power to achieve a majority in your uncle's absence from the council, he had overridden your father's party, pressing the land assault against their considered military advice, and it failed, and with the death of the general commanding, your uncle and his friends became convenient scapegoats, all for a faulty royal decision."

Polydamas spat then and cracked his lash once above the horses' heads, and like a roll of thunder, their hooves echoed with the wind.

"If we are ever to succeed in Mysia," he continued, "if we are ever to sever the head from the serpent, we *must* assault by sea and not across the impossible slopes of Ida. Your father's plan remains good, Dymas. Feint across Ida with a strength of two commands, and when the Mysians have been drawn, strike them from the rear at Chrysa or Pitane with a powerful seaborne assault to be led by the Shark."

"Are we in condition?" I wanted to know.

"*No.*" My lord spat again. "This grinding war of attrition weakens us month by month, although we have played the game well and swept them from the seas, but if the plan is ever to be realized, the Shark must have more men, and in the spring we must go on the offensive, striking at their backs like a hard March wind."

I understood him and I understood, too, his frustration, for the war dragged on, bleeding at the edges like a wounded boar struggling beneath his agony.

"In time," he said, "the Mysians are going to regain their strength, and when that day comes — and it could easily come as early as next year, for the harvest promises plenty — they will again seize the initiative and come pouring down from Ida like angry summer wasps. That, Dymas, is why we make this journey. Tomorrow, as Helios passes his zenith, the council gathers, and at my Lord Antenor's bidding, I go to present the plan, the same plan, your father's plan, and argue for its acceptance."

He seemed prone to silence after that, but for me, one important question remained unanswered, and after short hesitation, I asked it.

"With courtesy, my lord, why should *you* have incurred Lord Priam's wrath in the hour of my father's death?"

In the moment, I saw his head snap south, and I watched as his flint-gray eyes scanned the heights of Ida.

"I was your father's subordinate," he said at last, distantly, plainly, but in a low voice. "I commanded the Tusks, the cutting edge of the Boar's attack. On the day your father was killed, he had led the Snout far out ahead of us, to reconnoiter, and when the Mysians struck him so suddenly from ambush, filling his body with their bronze-tipped arrows, I could not make up the distance between us in time to save his life. He died where he stood, Dymas, taking more than thirty of their barbed arrows over all the parts of his body. In the end, he backed himself against the cleft of a rock so that he could not fall, and the ground before him, when we carried him away, ran red with the blood of his enemies, who — seeing that he was beyond hope — made a great effort to finish him with their swords so as to seize his standard. Even as we broke the Mysian line and rushed forward to relieve him, staunch Kalitor died, still striking out with his sword, cleaving the skull of the last Mysian spearman who tried to impale him. He died a warrior, Dymas, but royal Priam has never forgiven me for not bringing so great a general out alive, even though he felt no warmth for Kalitor the man."

"And Pharos?" I said, fighting back the tears I felt welling.

"Only Pharos knows the matter fully," Polydamus replied, "and he will speak of it to you when he will."

By that time, the towers of Troy loomed high and white above us, and he said no more, for as though they had been loosed from Trojan bows, both of our horses bolted suddenly forward up the long ramp that led straight through the Scaean Gate and on, through the deep blue heart of holy Ilium, straight to Antenor's door.

12

"TOO LATE," said Skalmos, bidding us enter by the main door. "Too late by a day. You come too late."

He took us immediately to the main courtyard of the house, and there, walking by himself, we found lordly Antenor, grown slightly grayer, who repeated Skalmos' news in the same thick voice that I remembered from my first visit to Troy. "We have been outmaneuvered politically," he said, making no attempt to hide his anger, "and now this war may drag on for another three years."

The immediate question was how? What had happened? Why had the council met before the appointed time?

"Simple enough," Antenor said. "For you to speak at all, Polydamas, because you are general now to fewer than one thousand spears, I had to submit your name in advance, and with Priam and those other Generals of Defense, that as much as let the fox out of the bag. Priam quickly sent out couriers to the various generals in the vicinity, including both lordly Hector and the noble Aeneas as well as Skaiko and the generals commanding under him along the front, and early this morning, they achieved a quorum and voted it their own way: we remain on the defensive but continue to harry the enemy at sea."

"But my lord," Polydamas protested, showing more than a little exasperation, "there is nothing left to harry!"

"So it would seem," Antenor said, his beard shaking. "But there is a bright side to this, too. Now that the vote has been taken, now that the matter has been decided — for this year, at the least, and probably for the next as well — now that you can no longer spring amongst them and attempt to force the plan by means of reasoned argument in council, *now* they are going to be magnanimous in their triumph and give you your men."

"How many?" Polydamas quickly asked.

"More than six hundred, with fifty additional juniors."

That caught both of us by surprise, for it was far more than anyone could have expected and would raise our strength to nearly fifteen hundred men.

"How soon?"

"Within the moon," Antenor said, throwing back a quick smile. "Know you, however," he said, turning suddenly more serious, "that they will not be Trojans but rather topknotted men of Thrace."

That gave me a start and my Lord Polydamas a moment of hesitation, but he quickly swallowed his pride. "I will make Sharks of all those barbarians," he said confidently.

"That's the spirit," said Antenor. "You must. Train them hard, but keep their barbaric fighting edge, and they may serve us well."

"Exactly," said Polydamas, "I may even give command of some of them to Dymas here."

At the mention of my name, Antenor registered brief amazement and then, as I made my mark of respect upon being presented, seized my hand.

"My profuse apologies," he said graciously. "I did not recognize you for the man you have become. Had Polydamas not spoken your name, I fear I would never have known you for the son of Kalitor whom Pharos brought before us so many years ago."

Such an oversight seemed natural enough, even to me, for by

that time, my height had already topped six feet, I weighed more than fourteen stone, and my beard had grown from fuzz into a black sea shag.

"In this house," Antenor added, "we have heard good report of you. It is said that you have already killed your man and served well your lord in command of juniors."

"And been twice wounded," said Polydamas, giving me a nod of approval. "Dymas fulfills his promise, my lord. In years to come, you may expect to hear great things of him."

"In the years to come," Lord Antenor repeated, "we will expect great things from all of you . . . possibly even sooner than you think."

Both of us, I am certain, caught the change in his voice and turned, alert, for lordly Antenor had dropped the pleasantries and again spoke in earnest.

"Know you," he said, "that during the past moon certain of our Carian agents have reported a new Mysian fleet to be building at Cyme?"

That much, Polydamas already knew and said so.

"Yes," said Antenor, "but do you know, too, that it incorporates the Greek design?"

"How many hulls?" Polydamas said, his shock immediately apparent.

"Thirty," Antenor said thickly.

I knew, even before my lord raised the question, that they would have to be burned, for the Greek hull, sleeker and faster than our own broader design, would give the Mysians an advantage at sea that we could ill afford to let them realize.

"They must be burned!" Polydamas exclaimed.

"Agreed," said Antenor.

"So says the council?"

"The matter has not been under debate."

"Do they not know?" said Polydamas, registering a degree of disbelief.

"They do not," said Antenor. "During the past three years, I have raised the issue of the assault on Chrysa no less than twelve separate times. Each time, those Generals of Defense have voted me down, and as a result, the war has dragged on and on. They are landsmen, Polydamas; they do not understand the sea, nor do they give due deference to wisely deployed sea power. In the case of Cyme, I feel almost certain — as do Pharos and Dymas' uncle — that the council will not approve a raid."

In that moment absolute silence fell over us.

"Have we not full sanction to harry them at sea?" Polydamas finally asked.

"You have," said Antenor.

"It seems to me," Polydamas began, "that an intelligent plan might be — "

"Let me hear no more," Antenor said suddenly but with some satisfaction. "What may be, may be, and what I do not know, I do not know. Now, you and I must visit the citadel, where you can present your reports, learn more about your Thracian draft, and hear clarification of the council's decision. Afterward, we dine at court. Tonight is the feast of Aphrodite; because you are known to be present in the city, it would be fatal not to be seen observing her rites and making the appropriate sacrifices in the precincts of her temple."

"That will mean a long watch," Polydamas protested.

"Nevertheless, you must be *seen* to honor the gods," Antenor responded, "for that is the Trojan way and, at this moment, politic."

Humble before the gods, Polydamas disputed the point no further, and together the three of us took up our spears. Outside the house, we stepped quickly into the afternoon wind that blew up dustily from the Plain, and squinting into it and tasting the grit between our teeth, we made a quick climb to the citadel. There, before the members of Priam's military staff — the very men whom lordly Antenor called Troy's Generals of Defense — I heard Polydamas make his reports about the operations of the Shark. After the reports had been presented and all of the staff's questions had been answered, there began a series of briefings concerning the present state of the war, the details of the Thracian draft that was being raised for the Shark, and general orders for Shark operations during the forthcoming year. I had to be alert, then, for it was my function as aide to memorize all important particulars and be ready to recall them on my lord's command, and this I was asked to do twice before the assembled company as my Lord Polydamas tested in subtle and inconspicuous ways the limits that were being placed upon his actions. And then, with politic marks of respect, the staff conference ended, and I found myself standing in the courtyard outside the main keep, looking up toward the palace.

"I commend you for a job well done," Polydamas said to me. "You may now enjoy what we call leave and liberty until one hour before dawn, when I will expect you to meet me outside the door to Lord Antenor's house, ready to march."

"I will hear none of it," Antenor suddenly said. "Far be it from me to come between a general and his aide, but tonight, son of Kalitor, you dine at my lady's table, accepting the hospitality of my house. If you do not," he said with a laugh, "the Lady Dia will find the three of us much remiss."

"Your hospitality does us much honor, my lord," pronounced Polydamas. He turned to me. "Dymas, commend me to my Lady Dia and bear yourself in all things according to her wishes."

The words had no sooner passed his lips than the fires within me began to rage, for as I took my leave from them, I believed that I must surely see the Lady Ariadne during the hours to come.

My lady's conduct toward me was so gracious as to border on the sublime, and the fare at her board, particularly after my three years in barracks, seemed no less to me than nectar and ambrosia, and yet, in the end, the evening went stale for me because Ariadne did not appear.

My Lady Dia waited patiently until our dinner had ended, and then she conducted me into the courtyard. There, beneath a pale moon, she told me what I feared to hear.

"Ariadne is married," she said simply. "When the snow first fell, she became wife to Antiphos, son of Priam."

Unprepared for such news, I let a groan escape me, even there. Sensing my misery, my lady touched my hand.

"Thus it was always meant to be," she said quietly, "even from the moment of her birth."

She offered me other words of comfort, I know, although what she said to me, I no longer recall, for all was immediately consumed by the conflagration of my grief. As much as possible, I suffered in silence, but those burning fires ate away my insides, leaving little more than bitter ash.

Sensitive, gracious, and very courteous, my lady knew that I wanted to be alone, and summoning Skalmos, she took her leave. Skalmos, with few words and short — "This way. Carefully. Dark passage" — led me once again into the guest quarters, into the very room where I had first held Ariadne in my arms and stroked her hair and comforted her tortured sobs, and then, I think, I felt the full passions of despair. Fire by that time had turned to ice, and frozen by its slivers as they penetrated my chest, I thought that I might actually die. Thus, I was unprepared for what happened next: as I sank to the bed, the door opened, and a blue-veined hag, bearing the mark of a royal slave, slithered in beside me like an ill wind.

For no longer than it takes an eagle to dip and pluck up a fish from the sea, the old slave glanced at me from deep-set eyes, then dropped a ring in my hand. From the raised crest on its surface, I knew instantly that it was Ariadne's virgin band. "My lady wishes to see you," the slave rasped, "now! Behind the green door on the Street of the Nobles."

She removed herself so quickly that even as I leapt toward the door, she was gone, and the ring burned hot in my hand. For a brief moment, I did battle with the Furies, but in the end, they broke me, and snatching up my cloak, I left the house, searching for the Street of the Nobles.

As certainly as I sit here now and sip your bitter Argive wine, I knew then that I made my way toward certain death and remember as well that I no longer cared. Stung half to madness by my passion, emptied by the fires of my youth, I was driven forward beyond all reason by a growing hunger so deep and gnawing that it consumed my being. In the end, the urge so overpowered me that I ran, knowing full well the destruction that awaited me at the end of my race.

The Street of the Nobles, I found soon enough, and the house with the green door, and even before I had once knocked with the butt of my spear, the door opened, and I was drawn into darkness by the same old slave who had brought me the ring. This time, she said nothing, merely turned and disappeared into obscurity, leaving me to follow in her wake, setting my course by her sound. To me, the house seemed a maze, for I remember turning and turning again down one darkened passage after another until she finally led me up a flight of steps, stopped before the outline of the first door on the left, opened it, and motioned me inside.

"Wait here," she commanded.

Inside the room, which was narrow but lavishly appointed, I found only a single lamp flickering, but that nearly blew out when the old slave suddenly disappeared through the door, slamming it against my heels. A few minutes passed, and my eyes began to adjust to the alteration in my circumstances, but even then, I harbored no doubts about why I had come and knew, finally, that I would have answered Ariadne's summons no matter what the cost, even unto facing chaos itself. And in that instant, a curtain parted, and there, across the lamplight, I found myself face to face with a woman grown to raven-haired beauty.

"You!" I gasped, a wave of revulsion sweeping over me.

"Why, Dimness, what a great big man you have become," said royal Atalante, enjoying both my pain and shock.

"You . . . bitch!" I snarled between clenched teeth, my shame at having been thus lured burying my disappointment.

"Your darling little Ariadne would have loved to come, I'm sure," Atalante snipped as she pushed my spearhead aside and moved in close to me, backing me against the door, "but tonight, you see, Aphrodite preens, and right about now, don't you think, my dear brother Antiphos must be already feeding over the pleasures of her body."

I cursed her and with the full force of my arm pushed her angrily away from me. Thus propelled, she struck her hip against the edge of a table and winced with sudden pain. Any other woman would have taken the rejection as final, but as Atalante recovered herself, the whole of her arrogance came sharply into focus.

"Too late; you're too late! She's long gone, and now I've got possession of you, all to myself! You're in royal apartments, Dymas. There's no escape. My guards are everywhere. Without my safe-conduct, you will be killed on sight. The remainder of your life is forever at my pleasure."

Confident that mere threats of power had broken all my resistance, she drew herself up to her full height and sneered at me across that dimly lighted room. Even then she was beautiful, but her mature beauty was cold and as hard as ice.

"I once asked you," she said sharply, "to tell me the difference between a whore and a lady. You couldn't do it; you didn't know. Now, I'm going to teach you. A whore," she said as she slithered toward me, her dark eyes smoking, "performs at the pleasure of a man, but a royal lady takes men at her own pleasure, whenever and wherever she likes." And in that instant, she seized my member. "Now make it firm," she commanded, rubbing her perfumed breasts hard against me, "for I am ready to take *my* pleasure and leave you limp in my wake."

I struck her then with the flat of my hand, with such force that I slammed her hard against the wall. As she cried out with pain, I saw an expression of terror sweep into her eyes, for no one, I think, had ever raised a hand against her, and in that moment, instinctively, I knew what I had to do and seized her hand.

"*You* are the whore," I said, jerking her to her feet, "and tonight, the humiliation is to be all yours, for surely you are the whelp of some mongrel cur that raided the royal bed, and I am going to take you like the bitch that you are."

And in that instant, as she uttered a piercing cry and reached for my eyes with her nails, I gave myself over to my anger, threw her hard across the table, and took her again and again in my fury. In time, her cries ceased but never her struggle, not even when I thrust her down against the hardness of the boards — and then, I think, I must have moved something deep within her, for twice she called out my name, forcing me to realize that pain was her true pleasure. Springing instantly backward, I withdrew from her, but even then I knew that I was too late, that at the height of my wrath, in a moment of supreme unreason, I had indeed awakened the chaos within her, and in the same moment I knew that I would never be rid of her.

Revolted, both by myself and the insatiable body squirming before me, I quickly turned from her, took up my spear, and walked through the door into an empty passageway. There were no guards waiting, no royal appointments, nothing whatsoever to indicate even the slightest danger. I could have walked away from her at any time and done it freely without ever having tried to take my dull revenge. Instead, I had acted the role of the beast, plunging far below the level of men, and — as I later learned to my horror — kindled a conflagration in a woman whom I could only despise. And I had done something else as well, for as I found the street and walked away through that haunting, hollow night, I knew that I had broken faith with my life, with my vision, with myself, and across that broad night sky, even the flickering stars seemed to reflect my shame.

13

WE STRUCK CYME late in the autumn of that year. Not many weeks had passed since my nineteenth birthday, and for the first time, I acted more than a warrior's role in the assault. In fact, I commanded, and by chance, the means by which we brought the operation to success turned on a plan of my own devising.

Understand that I had nothing to do with the objective's selection. When first the Mysians elected to rebuild their fleet, they themselves determined that Cyme would become a target; as soon as we knew that they had laid down Greek keels, our raid against them became a foregone conclusion, and complete destruction of their fleet, before it ever went to sea, an absolute necessity. I did not enter into the planning until later, after my Lord Polydamas and I had returned to Tenedos; even then, my initial contribution was indirect and accidental.

As I look back, my lord was in the chart room, standing before the great ox-hide maps that lined the walls. He was studying the problem of Cyme, and without first seeing him, I walked into the room mumbling something to myself about fools rushing too swiftly to the mark. On my part, the observation was personal. Driven by shame, I was cursing my rash behavior toward Atalante; Cyme was the last thing on my mind.

"Say that again," Polydamas suddenly ordered.

Immediately, I became red-faced and stuttered an apology, but he quickly waved my words away. "No," he said, "never mind *that*. Repeat what you said as you entered the room."

"About the mark?"

"Yes."

"I said that fools rush too swiftly toward it, my lord."

"And so they do," Polydamas said, his eyes lighting up. "Well done, Dymas; I think you have given us an idea for cracking Cyme. How would you like to command the raid yourself?"

What he then presented to me was a completely unlooked-for opportunity, and without hesitation, I seized it. And some months later, when the raid finally went in, I earned my standard.

From the moment the issue became decided, there in the chart room, I worked continually with Polydamas for more than two moons in order to develop a precise operational plan. At the finish, the outline sounded something like this. We were to . . . no, abide; I will repeat my lord's own words, for I still remember them in fair detail, and their substance will be perfectly clear.

"Given," Polydamas began, almost in the way of the geometric proofs that Pharos had once taught me in Abydus, "a new Mysian fleet building at Cyme according to the Greek design. Given that it must be destroyed . . . *now*, on the beach, before it ever puts to sea. I know as much, you know as much, and Antenor knows as much, but the Generals of Defense, landlocked in their wisdom" — and here, he became caustic — "lack all understanding of the threat's immensity. Thus, they tie my hands with an order to *harry the enemy at sea*. Consider, Dymas, that my orders specifically forbid me to set a foot on dry Mysian soil; to exceed or disobey such orders would mean instant demotion from the Shark and sure assignment to some military backwater like Killa or Sataspes, and yet that Greek-prowed Mysian fleet must never reach the sea, for its great strength and speed will give it the power to defeat us. Agreed?"

"Clearly," I replied.

"What, then, am I to do?" he continued, posing a purely rhetorical question, which he immediately began to answer. "It seems to me that I must disobey my orders while still appearing to obey them, so the plan I unlock — one to which you, Dymas, have unwittingly revealed the key — is this. I think I must find myself a capable young commander who can carry the assault forward, a warrior who is old enough to ensure the raid's success but young enough to survive the political tremors that are sure to follow, for know you, Dymas, whoever commands the raid on Cyme is certain to be charged with overzealous opportunism by the members of the Military Council. Even so, the assault must go forward; the consequences will simply have to be endured. The mechanics seem clear enough. We will wait patiently until late autumn when the leaves lie thick across the ground and chill Borean mists cover the sea. Then, with a fleet of some ten or twelve hulls, we will put to sea to make a threatening demonstration before Pitane.

"If we encounter a Mysian or two at sea, so much the better; a sharp engagement will lend credence to my intentions of *harrying the enemy at sea,* but my hidden purpose will be altogether different, for there — before Pitane — somewhere, two or three of my ships must become *lost* in the fog, and when they finally emerge from the mists, they must discover to their surprise that they are arrayed before Cyme. There — without my knowledge and well beyond my power to prevent, control, or direct — an impetuous young commander may not be thought completely mad if he seizes the moment and rashly takes the initiative by attacking the enemy."

It was, I knew, the means to our end, and on the spur of the moment, I made a second useful contribution.

"Fighting crews of Thracian drafts might be thought even less culpable than disciplined Trojan Sharks," I suggested.

"An excellent idea," my lord said, his shrewd eyes twinkling; "the ships so manned might even be designated 'training commands.'"

And so, in the late autumn, under the close cover of a bitterly cold mist, I found myself and Agelaos and Orthaios — each of us leading a "training command" — breaking away, drifting into the fog, losing contact with the main body of my lord's fleet where it demonstrated hard Trojan strength off the shrouded Cape of Pitane.

On my own, I felt confident of my Thracian crews and the account they would give of themselves. During the weeks in which their drafts had first reported to Tenedos, I had culled their ranks, selecting each man who would accompany me for physical strength and quickness of mind. Then, dividing the entire command with Agelaos and fit Orthaios, I put the whole "training formation" through the most intense preparation that I could devise. When the time came, I knew my warriors were ready for action, and following in my lord's wake, we put to sea.

After the breakaway, we drifted south through the fog, effectively blind to all that lay before us. Under the circumstances, I found great difficulty in keeping together even a three-ship formation, for there in the gulf, the low-lying autumn mists were particularly dense and close, and eventually I had to order my runner to climb all the way to the top of our mast. There, where the cloud was less dense, he could just make out the mast tips of our sister ships, and thus I marked their progress. Finally, late in the afternoon, my runner reported landfall, and very carefully we came up on the finger point of land that lies at the head of the Gulf of Cyme. From there, I knew, the beach we sought lay due south, so padding our tholepins with wraps of fleece, we put out eight oars and began to make our slow, silent way into the darkening gulf while my topknotted Thracians girded themselves for battle.

With clear sailing conditions, we might have covered the distance in less than an hour, but given the need for stealth amidst the ever-thickening fog, we required more than four long hours to work across the bay. Throughout, the awesome responsibility of my command fell across my shoulders like the weight of the world pressing down on Atlas, and I broke into a feverish sweat, even beneath the cold weight of my armor, fearful that we would run aground, miss our mark, or otherwise give ourselves away before we ever got into action. Throughout, my runner, a keen-eyed Thracian junior, remained aloft, lashed to the mast, guiding us as well as he could by reading the stars, which at mast height remained dimly visible to his youthful eye. On the command platform, I remember, I could see nothing, so I placed in him my perfect trust, and in the hour of my need, he did not fail me. In the end, we beached suddenly, and unexpectedly hard, no more than a fraction of a league from the point we had sought. Seizing the moment, I ordered all hands over the side and leapt forward to lead the assault.

Phoebus Apollo must have guided my hand on that night, for never again have I achieved such sure success in any endeavor. Once ashore, having taken the situation's measure as I rushed through the surf toward the beach, I made an instinctive decision to deviate from our plan: instead of going immediately forward into a frontal assault, I moved the entire command inland up to a depth of some four hundred paces, turned them north, and then started working them gradually up the line of the beach toward the unsuspecting Mysian shipyards. Thus positioned, we achieved an element of surprise that would never have been possible had we attacked direct from the sea in bold assault.

As it was, rather than pouring up the beach against an alerted beach guard and a strong defense, we simply strolled in amongst the Mysians from the inland side, capturing the entire guard where they rested beside their watch fires. Lulled by the fog, sleepy, inattentive, and overconfident, they hardly noticed our approach, believing our forward elements to be their early morn-ing reliefs come down from the citadel at Cyme; in fact, they did not recognize us for Trojans until it was too late, until we were already in amongst them with our spears at their throats.

We bound each Mysian's hands with rawhide thongs made wet in sea water, and after setting a watch of our own to guard the prisoners — some forty-seven in all — the remainder of the command set about firing the enemy ships. Having brought with us for the purpose large quantities of oil and pitch, we quickly smeared cordage, sailcloth, planking, hull ribs, keels, and shavings, and when all had been prepared, using brands from the Mysians' own fires, we ignited a conflagration at the given signal. Eager to withdraw all of my warriors without delay and without stragglers, I had practiced the maneuver on Tenedos several times in succession, and in the hour of greatest danger, my practiced plan unfolded perfectly.

I waited, you see, only long enough to be sure that each Mysian hull had been irrevocably set on fire; then, by means of fire arrows shot directly out to sea, I signaled recall, and my fine young Thracians ran like the wind toward the beached prows of our ships. I made myself that night the last man in the withdrawal, and as I sprinted down the beach, shepherding the rear guard, I hurtled past one burning hull after another and felt that blazing heat sweep to the edge of the surf like a raging crown fire leaping from ridge to ridge across the towers of Ida's heights. Then I knew that we had achieved our end; then and only then did I begin to glory in the strength of our victory.

No man died that night; no man suffered so much as a wound, and no stragglers were left behind. All of my tall, determined warriors reached our ships in disciplined order, still whole, still ready for battle. Even our captives remained secure; fearful of the punishments they would have to endure if we left them behind, they ran as swiftly toward our ships as their bound hands would allow. Never have men so willingly surrendered themselves to certain slavery as did those men of Cyme, and my Thracian Sharks pulled them quickly aboard. Then, putting out all oars together, we backed sharply into the fog, making straight for the open sea. On the following afternoon, under the lee of Lesbos, where the remainder of my lord's ships rode a hard sea beneath a bitter wind, we rejoined the fleet and set sail for Tenedos.

14

L IKE TREMORS from the Earthshaker, the reverberations of our strike against Cyme were immediate and far-reaching. On the mainland, where the war had dragged on through its fourth spring and summer and dusty fall — costly but static — the raid on Cyme was heralded as a brilliant victory, and lordly Polydamas was much applauded in popular quarters. Under the circumstances, of course, he had to decline all responsibility for the action, but as later events demonstrated, the Generals of Defense were not convinced by his posture and continued, although privately, to hold him directly responsible for the raid. At the same time, publicly, they tended to discount the raid's value, referring to it as a minor naval combat fought too far from the main center of conflict to have any significant effect on the war. But if those Generals of Defense doubted, the Mysians did not, for by the time Ida's ridges were fully covered by the first winter snows, they had sued for peace, instantly accepting the generous terms that Priam offered them.

Thus, the Third Mysian War ended, leaving the Mysian army still intact but withdrawn from the frontier a distance of some eight leagues, almost all the way back to the valley of the Caicus River. The result was that Chrysa became, for a while, almost an open city, and Trojan merchants, particularly our sellers of grain and foodstuffs, were quick to profit amongst a people they found bordering on starvation. Those were the positive reverberations that rolled away from our raid on Cyme, enveloping all of Troy, Mysia, and the surrounding environs, but as weeks passed, the more we heard from Ilium, the more we realized that in our more immediate sphere not all was going to be allowed to pass. At last, when the winter snows lay deep across the Plain, my lord and I were called to account.

"Given the degree of the victory," my lord said sharply, "they ought to have bitten off the matter with a smile and left it alone. I see Skaiko's humorless hand in this and, perhaps, one or two others who, unlike Skaiko, are content to remain at Troy, conducting the war from their backsides." Suddenly he ceased to pace and looked me straight in the eye. "This is the end of all pretense," he said flatly. "The responsibility is mine, and I will take it. I do not permit you to bear it yourself, so rest you easy."

"My lord, *you* did not make the attack," I said, for the first time in my life attempting to deflect a superior's will. "I moved into this with a clear eye, knowing all the risks. I gave my word, and now it is my place to endure the consequences. I knew what I was doing when I went in, and it is Trojan law that the doer must suffer. That makes it my place to shoulder the blame here, for the strike could not have gone forward without me."

"He is right," said Pharos, appearing unexpectedly in the doorway. "Dymas is right. Besides, there is more to this than either of you yet realizes." And so saying, he stepped into the room.

Even as he took our hands, which were warm with greeting, Pharos gave me the full force of one of his most penetrating looks. "I warned you to beware of *her,*" he said sharply. "By the looks of it, you were not."

I knew in the instant what he was talking about, and my heart sank within me. Polydamas started to speak then, but merely by raising his hand, Pharos silenced him.

"There is not much time," Pharos said quickly, "so pay me close attention. A royal barge is already in the harbor with orders to arrest you both and return you to Troy, where you will have to answer charges before the Military Council. I do not know all that has happened, but I do know enough to understand that Dymas must bear responsibility. There are things here, Polydamas, about which you as yet know nothing but about which Dymas, apparently, knows all too much. It is my hope that he will brief you about them — about all of them — as quickly as he can and that you may help him insofar as you are able. My estimate is that the military charges to be brought against you will be serious but well within your joint capacities to handle according to the plan by which you prepared the raid. But then," he said, his beard shaking and the scars over his pate turning a deep purple, "Dymas is going to have to face the remainder of the account on his own, and I can only hope that the reputation he has made in battle will be enough to save him from an instant and painful death."

Much taken aback, Polydamas had no idea what Pharos was talking about, but it was clear enough that he had caught the urgency of the situation, for a grim resolve quickly filled his face.

"Boy, your uncle and I grieve for you," Pharos told me, putting his hand on my shoulder, "but in this, we can do absolutely nothing to help you. You got yourself into this, and you must — "

"Not quite," I said flatly, my anger at royal Atalante rising swiftly to the boil.

"No?" Pharos said sternly. "The doer was someone else, then?"

"No," I said, burying my anger with shame. "No, you are right. This suffering must be mine alone."

"Would that it could," said Pharos, not without the trace of a sigh, "but owing to the bonds that unite us, none can escape the pain of what is happening to you." In the moment, I felt the warmth of his hand firm on my shoulder, and then he stepped back, surveying us both from beneath his gray bushy brows. "The dangers you face are great," he said, "greater, perhaps, than any you have faced before, but you must survive, for Troy rapidly approaches a time when she will not be able to do without either of you. Do what you must then, both of you."

A Whale courier appeared in the same instant, even as Pharos spoke, and the courier's message confirmed the arrival of the royal barge. He reported as well that officers of the Imperial and Household Guards followed closely in his wake. Pharos, I noticed, did not show the courier his face, but the moment the Whale departed, his words came fast and crisp.

"It will not be healthy for either of you to be seen with me just at this moment," he said, gathering his cloak about him. "I had hoped for more time, but the Fates grant only what they will. Remember, *survive*. Bargain according to your need, but survive!" Without so much as another word, he was gone, leaving the both of us speechless in the middle of the room.

I cannot say that we had much time to prepare ourselves, for we did not, the various officers of the Guards entering the room through one door while Pharos left by another, and then, in that ceremonial way that is common to both Guards formations, we were placed under arrest while imperial heralds recited the formal charges against us. In short, the two of us were charged with exceeding our orders, and in my case, the offense was compounded by an accusation of "gross disobedience," which, if proved, carried an immediate death sentence.

We went up to Troy, then, under a dark cloud and under close arrest but with the freedom of the barge, for the Guards officers who had come to fetch us were acquainted with my lord and respectful and — if the truth were known — admired us, I think, for what we had accomplished at Cyme. Almost all of them, you see, had seen action on the Mysian front during one or more of the preceding campaigns, and even in their most circumspect remarks, they were critical of the static battle that had been fought there. To a man, they were glad the war had ended, and clearly they felt themselves in my lord's debt.

We were free to move about the barge as it sailed north toward

Besika Bay, and it was there that I set before my lord the sordid facts about my tryst with royal Atalante. In the face of my revelation, Polydamas turned ash white, nearly becoming ill, and then he sat down hard on an empty rowing bench, staring some moments out to sea before he fully recovered his color.

"I think," he said finally, "that these military charges are a blind. Pharos was right: the true danger here is to you, although what we are going to do about it, I have not the slightest idea. If you are charged with rape — even though I am convinced that the fault was not your own — there is nothing I can do for you."

I had known as much from the beginning and said so. "And no matter how one looks at it," I said, "in the end, the fault *is* mine for having allowed my wrath to dominate my reason."

"In that," my lord said, seeming to recover himself a little, "you show your age, for the mere idea is overly simple — if you will not mind my saying so — and far too abstract to fit the . . . what I can only call perverse circumstances. No, Dymas, shed your guilt and attack."

"Pardon?" I said.

"Attack," said my lord, rising to his feet as we began to take sea spray over the bow. "Be bold. They will expect you to adopt a most abject posture of shame, but do not play into their hands. Attack. In this case, I think, your best defense is unrelenting assault, because that is the last thing under the sun that they have reason to expect from you, from either of us."

And in that moment, I think, he actually warmed to what lay ahead, so much so that he gave me a broad grin and stoutly slapped me on the back.

"We begin with the council," he told me, "and our position is that the Shark is the true victor of the Mysian Wars, the true bringer of peace to holy Ilium. Let them argue with that if they can. We will fight them with the truth, Dymas; I am convinced that it is the only way to beat them."

And so we did, for no more than five hours later when we finally reached Troy and went straight up before the leaders of the Military Council, my lord and I entered the chamber leading, not waiting to be led by, our guards, surveyed the room with imperious looks, and after making only curt acknowledgment of the generals present, launched ourselves boldly into an attack. The fact is, my Lord Polydamas conducted the most of it by himself while I stood stiffly by, my helmet under my arm, and even now, I thrill to the magnificent way he threw caution to the winds, speaking to those assembled nobles as though he were their equal. Lord Antenor was present, and Hicetaon, and the noble Laocoön, and one other known to be well disposed toward us; but Skaiko had been charged with constituting the council for that particular hearing, and in doing so, he had given the defense faction the edge, packing in the commanding generals of the Leopard, Eagle, and Wolf — men known to be loyal to him — as well as my Lords Hector and Aeneas, whom I saw there for the first time, both of them having come down from Dardanos especially to decide the issue at hand. Notwithstanding, Polydamas held nothing back, and the strength of his rhetoric rolled over them like a Thracian wind driven hard by the gods.

"This war," he thundered, "was won at sea, by the Teeth of the Shark. How is it, then, that you — here — dare to bring these charges against us, you Generals of Defense who through four long years of war have succeeded only in soaking Ida's soil with the red blood of our men? It is shameful, I say, shameful! Hear me, o my generals of Troy, for here, now, within the hard stone confines of this chamber, I charge you all with motives of envy and spite, the bane of the warrior, the perversion of our code, and may the scales of Zeus weigh mightily against you for your loathsome aims."

He had been right, of course: his speech — a speech like that — was the last thing that any of them had expected, and they were all of them, even lordly Antenor and our allies in the chamber, much taken aback. Lord Hector gasped, his mouth hanging half open, while Skaiko above the broad spade of his beard turned grotesquely purple. Curiously, the son of Anchises, the noble

Aeneas, showed the least apparent reaction, merely changing his position once where he sat while continuing to take in everything my lord said.

Polydamas continued in that vein for some time, hammering away at them like a champion boxer who has studied his opponent's moves and knows just how to keep him off balance, and then, when Skaiko seemed poised to rise in fury and at last demand the speaker's staff, my lord launched himself swiftly into a recitation of the Shark's victories, paralleling each one of them with a detailed account of Trojan attrition ashore. In precise chronological order, he matched each Shark triumph with the bloody fighting elsewhere across the Mysian front, finishing at last with a vivid review of my strike against Cyme and the firing of the Mysian fleet.

"And *you* charge the son of Kalitor with gross disobedience of orders?" Polydamas roared, his dark eyes suddenly shooting fire like two bursting stars. "Were we not trying to win? Your charge is ludicrous! The warrior Dymas glories all Ilium with this feat of arms! Without cost, his action at Cyme won us the war! Speak plainly, lords, what man among you can claim so much?"

The silence that followed was deafening, long, and empty. No man rose to seize the speaker's staff in opposition, for the issue was altogether clear. Polydamas, more eloquent than I ever imagined, had seized the initiative and laid out every point with such persuasive clarity that even the dullest Thracian recruit could have seen and understood it. In short, he had given them all a lesson in war. In the end, without even rising to speak, Skaiko called straight for the vote, and it went in our favor, the five-to-five tie being taken for acquittal. Lord Antenor had voted for us, and our other three allies, and then, in a move that left me stunned by surprise, the noble Aeneas had risen and cast his vote in our favor.

"The justice of this issue is not in doubt," he said firmly. "Henceforth, the son of Kalitor should be honored amongst us as Victor of Cyme."

Straightforward and just, the moral independence of his gesture nevertheless struck me as magnanimous, for in voting to acquit, he had clearly voted against the royal house with which his interests had always before been so closely allied, both by ties of blood and policy. Judging from the expressions of the council's other members — Lord Antenor, Skaiko, and the great Hector in particular — Aeneas had clearly done the unexpected, possibly the unthinkable, in siding with Polydamas on even as much as a single issue, so if my lord had shocked them with his speech, the noble Aeneas had completely unsettled them, so much so that in the vote's wake, there was great confusion, and we were all but forgotten by the defense faction as they made their departure.

Antenor, Laocoön, and our other allies were profuse in congratulation, but I was not long allowed to enjoy their company, for I had no more than taken Antenor's lordly hand when the commander of the Household Guard himself arrested me again, this time for "insult or insults to a member of the royal house of Priam."

"What is *that* supposed to mean?" protested the noble Laocoön.

Our two other friends were equally indignant at this second charge coming hot on the heels of the first, but with steady calm, my Lords Antenor and Polydamas placed themselves between our friends and the members of the guard, and all protests were quickly quieted before they exceeded allowable limits. It was then that I was forced to recognize that Lord Antenor knew the whole matter of my shame, and the realization brought me much pain, for if Antenor knew, I reasoned, so did my Lady Dia and, through her mother, the Lady Ariadne.

The hour, then, of my exaltation as a warrior seemed to bring with it my irrevocable degradation as a man, for as I marched away, I felt certain that I had lost forever the person I most cherished by making myself despicable to her. In that bitter hour, I felt utterly alone.

15

SURROUNDED BY members of the guard, I hardened myself to my fate, marching between them toward the high hill of Ilium and the royal apartments beyond. By that time, I had calculated my chances for survival, finding them as slender as Clotho's string. I was content, you see, that Atropos should sever my thread, but the thought that Atalante would do it for her made me harder in my anger. When at last we ascended the stairs, entering the precincts of Priam's compound, my face wore an expression as grim and bitter as any I have ever set in battle.

Straightaway, I expected to be taken before Priam and charged, but instead, as we approached the great hall, the guard veered suddenly left, and I found myself being hurried down a passageway that worked deep into the heart of the compound. Servants attired in royal white and slaves wearing sky-blue tunics were everywhere in motion, coming and going in the performance of their duties, and all of them seemed wholly indifferent to me, but shortly afterward, we entered the women's quarters, and there, servants, slaves, and eunuchs seemed to watch my progress through narrowing eyes. Even then, I was unprepared for what awaited me; in my anger, I believed myself being forced once more into the presence of royal Atalante, and in that, I was wrong.

Making a sudden turn, the guard stopped abruptly before two

high bronze doors. Instantly, the commandant of the Household Guard struck each door once with the butt of his spear, and when the entrance gave way like a pair of massive jaws, I was ordered inside. The moment I passed through, those portals slammed shut behind me, leaving me alone, with the uneasy feeling that I had been swallowed by a beast; and yet appearances belied that, for what struck me most was the luxurious nature of the apartment I had entered. Holding my helm beneath my arm, I moved to the center of that spacious room over a floor which seemed to be covered with fleece, through air that seemed to be perfumed. Everywhere, I saw silver, gold, and silk, and in truth, the mere beauty of the room was enough to make the heart hunger, but as I said, my anger, barely under control, burned deep within me, and I did not permit myself to gape. Thus I remained for several minutes, isolated and unattended, but at last beyond my left hand I heard a door open, turned, and found myself facing a regal, green-eyed beauty whose mature features could only be described as striking, for in many ways they reminded me of Atalante — so much so, in fact, that the moment I laid eyes on the woman she set my teeth on edge.

A servant followed the woman into the room, but stopping at a distance to take my measure, the lady dismissed her attendant with little more than the movement of a single, well-manicured finger. Then, with impressive but haughty grace, she seated herself on a delicate throne.

"I am Hecuba, Queen of all Troy," she said majestically, unconsciously arranging the folds of her gown to their best effect, "and you, Dymas, son of Kalitor, are the thorn in my side. I think that I must pluck you from me and cast you onto the wind." And the fury of her eyes belied the gracious smile that shaped her lips.

"That is easily accomplished," I countered, moving as straight to the attack as had my Lord Polydamas in his engagement with the council. "Keep your daughter under lock and key. Send her to take the waters in Thrace. Marry her to a Carian prince. Do anything. But whatever you do, keep her away from me."

With a flash, a brilliant light broke across the queen's eyes, and in the next second, she simply rolled her head back and laughed, deeply and sensually, displaying a perfect row of gleaming white teeth. "I think," she said, recovering herself and showing me a broad grin, "that I had better have you killed, without delay."

"I think," I said, still holding to my plan by mocking her rhythm, "that you have already tried, and failed."

"Oh," she said, scoffing and looking away but arching one eyebrow coyly, as though she were almost pleased that I had found her out, "those fools — my noble son and my nephew included — were almost sure to bungle your case, and in the end, they did. That's what comes from thinking too precisely on the event: one loses the name of action. No, no, young man, had the matter been left to me, I assure you that I would have had the two of you killed outright, on Tenedos, before either of you set a foot on the windy Plain."

"But for military reasons," I hastened to add, "and for public consumption . . ."

"But of course," she said, examining the hard polish on her nails, "the evidence against you, against both of you, was more than strong enough to warrant it — *now*, wasn't it?"

"Apparently not," I said, "or royal Priam would have ordered our executions himself."

"I . . . lack my husband's scruples in these matters," Hecuba said sharply, screwing her well made-up face into a charming smile. "Sometimes, you see, his immense sense of justice is much too fine to suit what is so obviously his own best interest."

"Ah," I said, this time flashing her a smile of my own, "but in this case, *his own best interest,* as you like to call her, was hardly obvious, was she?"

The queen enjoyed a throaty laugh at my expense. "Atalante," she said finally, "is already beginning to show, so *our interest* was obvious enough to me, and had he known what was good for him, my wishes would have been enough for my lord."

"Yes," I said, holding my ground, "but the fact remains that he did not know . . . enough, as you say, did he?"

Somehow — and to this day, I still do not know how — that resourceful woman had contrived, amidst her immense numbers of children, either to keep Atalante altogether from Priam's sight or at the least to keep him blissfully unaware of his daughter's condition. But by the will of Hera, consort to Zeus, she who oversees the joys and pains of childbirth, the hour was near at hand when the truth could no longer remain hidden, when scandal would at last break full over the royal house.

"So you plotted with Skaiko and your royal son," I charged, "to have me — "

"Hector knew and knows nothing about it," she snapped.

" — executed for supposed military crimes, so that later, after the fact, you could declare me guilty of rape, transforming Atalante from willing harlot into an unwilling victim."

"Something like that," said the queen without so much as batting an eyelash.

"It sounds," I said, not bothering to mask my sneer, "just like her."

"Her?" she asked, amused.

"Atalante. The plan was hers, was it not?"

"Most assuredly, it was not." The queen laughed. "Why, the little minx is quite taken with you, Dymas; she could never have found the strength to plot against you. No, the plan was mine, and now that it has failed, I believe after all that I am going to have to tell my noble lord all about you and let him deal with this himself."

For the first time since entering her royal presence, I began to feel a sense of relief. "I do not suppose," I said, "that you will actually do that. Otherwise you would not have gone to all of this trouble. Now, what is it that you really want?"

Her green eyes twinkled then, even as they darkened. "You are quick," she said. "I like that in a man, but I do not care to have it poised against me. Now sit down here beside me and pay me close attention," and when I did, her scent threatened immediately to intoxicate me, but the single finger she placed atop my hand was as cold as ice, and I knew in the second that she was her daughter's mother.

"You have played your game well enough," she said quietly, "but not as deftly as you think. Know you, Dymas, son of Kalitor, that the royal House of Priam never loses anything and never, never, never gives up a prize. In this case, dubious though it seems to me, you are the prize, and my daughter Atalante has won you as surely as though you were a ribbon at the end of a footrace. In that, she will have to rest content, and it is my opinion that she may live to rue the day, for her choice has been very unwise.

"Even so, the matter goes all our own way. Had you been sentenced and executed, your reputation would have passed with you into oblivion, and Atalante as well as the rest of our family would have enjoyed an endless, ennobling expression of public sympathy while at long last, by means of his son's disgrace, Kalitor's name would have collected the rank abuse it has always deserved. Thus I would have liked it, but the Fates would have it otherwise, and still we win, for your exoneration raises you, I understand, to the legend of Victor of Cyme."

"So it would seem," I said flatly.

"Oh, indeed," said the queen. "In the streets, the rabble are much taken with your name, and know you, Dymas, that even as we speak, my heralds proclaim you throughout the city as the hero of our time, as the victor of the last Mysian war. Within a few days' time, your name will be known far and wide throughout the kingdom, and by then, the reputation that *I* will have created for you will almost make you fit to kiss my daughter's royal feet — almost, but not quite. Nevertheless, we will then announce your marriage so that once again the royal family may bask in the reputation we have so graciously created for you."

"No," I said.

"Hear me out," she said in tones of cold command. "After the announcement, your marriage will take place immediately with full ceremony. Then, just as quickly, you will remove my daughter from Troy and carry her upcountry to one of our manors along the banks of wide Scamander, and there, the two of you will remain — until your . . . your *whelp* is born and for as long thereafter as it takes my daughter to become thoroughly sick of you. Let us say sixteen moons — eighteen to be sure — for she will tire of you very quickly, I think. After that, she and the child, if we do not expose it at birth, will return here while you return to the oblivion you so richly deserve and what I hope will be a quick and painful death in the ranks, for I can promise you without fail that no matter how good a warrior you may prove yourself to be, you will never rise above command of the most insignificant units in the most out-of-the-way posts that I can find. In peace, you will inhabit only the lowliest frontier hovels; in the event of war, of course, you will go immediately to the forefront, where some outland barbarian can kill you at will, and may the rage of Ares guide his welcome hand."

For malicious spite, she outdistanced her daughter by the length of a league, and she was harder, too, and far more calculating, but where she really showed her mettle was on the point of style. Had Atalante made me the same speech, she would have been screaming by the time she reached the end, whereas Hecuba never even raised her voice. Instead, she demonstrated such perfect control as she delivered my sentence that, had I not known better, I might have taken the whole for a skilled exhibition of poise. Rhetoric it was, right enough, but rhetoric of a kind that I had never before heard, a freshly sharpened lance thrust forward with a smile. And yet, although in her own mind she felt certain that she had brought me to my knees, she had not, and I knew it.

"And are those all of your terms?" I said, maintaining reasonable control over myself.

"I have not offered you *terms*," she said, again touching the cold point of her nail to the back of my hand. "What I have spoken is the final word, and whatever I decide, insofar as you are concerned, always will be. Now — "

"Now," I said suddenly, seizing her hand, turning it, and folding her fingers up forcibly until the sharp points of her nails pressed painfully into her palm, "now, *I* am going to give *you* a brief lesson in tactics. You are right, up to a point: I am exposed in a dangerous position, but so are you, and you cannot attack me without giving up your advantage; otherwise you stand to lose whatever natural protection your ground gives you. So, we must come to terms, I think, and here is what they will be.

"I will marry your daughter and protect the royal name. I will take her upcountry as you wish, and keep her there until well after the child is born — in all, I will remain with her for a space of twelve moons but no more. At the end of that time, she and the child may return here if she so wishes; but without regard to anything you may say, I will return to the Shark, and you, my queen, and your vixen daughter will never seek to interfere with me again. Otherwise, I myself will make an accounting to royal Priam that will open his eyes. Do I make myself clear?"

And so saying, I closed my fist, forcing the tips of her fingers even more deeply into her flesh until, uttering a low cry of pain, she wrenched her hand free and saw that I had drawn her blood with her finely pointed nails. The look she gave me as she raised her hand to her lips burned with the most perfect hatred I have ever seen, but at the same time, even beneath the makeup she had so artfully applied to her face, her skin had turned a deathly, terrified white.

In the end, facing each other like coiled adders, we struck a bargain. Then, during the three days that followed, I remained virtually under arrest, seeing neither friend nor foe, while Hecuba's preparations went forward. Isolated as I was, I know little, to this day, of what she accomplished save for a few facts that seem, even now, largely unrelated.

For me, she did, as she had said she would, succeed in spreading my so-called fame from one end of the Troad to the other, so when I did emerge and hear the various reports that she had floated about me, I experienced a new and growing shame because of the hypocrisy of their exaggeration. For another, she carefully masked the suddenness of Atalante's wedding by yoking it, as though on impulse, with the weddings of two other of her daughters who were to be married about that time to court nobles on Priam's diplomatic staff. Each of the sisters, said to be "close," was also said to delight in the notion of a triple wedding. Thus, when I was finally presented to Priam, I went before him in the throne room amidst the fully assembled court, beside my future brothers-in-law on the eve of the wedding, and there, everything took place with such regal formality that hardly a personal word passed between anyone.

In short, my "reputation" as Victor of Cyme proved enough of a support to carry me through without fault. What royal Hecuba may actually have told Priam about me, I have no idea, although I am fairly certain that she kept to our bargain. At the time, I know, I found it curious that Priam did not take more of an interest in the proceedings and doubly curious that he did not instantly see through them, but here, too, circumstances aided Hecuba, for as I later learned, of royal Priam's fifty sons and fifty daughters, some twelve of the males and fully seventeen of the females — exclusive of our party — married during that same year. Speaking forthrightly, I can only suppose that the frequency of these weddings produced such a numbing effect on the senses that one wedding must have seemed much like another, and indeed, in seeking to avoid sibling rivalry and remove any hint of favoritism that might have developed, court officials, acting at Priam's behest, saw that each was conducted according to a set form, a form that quickly became rigid in ceremonial ritual. In a manner of speaking, then, Atalante and I merely became one more in the year's collection of thirty-two blissful couples.

On the morning we were married, wintry Boreas blew down hard from Thrace, burying the Plain under a thick blanket of snow, and that, I remember, seemed the most fitting detail of all, for on that day, at long last, even as I held Atalante's hand and repeated the words of the priests inside the sacred precincts of Hera's temple, I saw Ariadne, her soft eyes shining, where she stood silently beside Antiphos, and my heart froze within me.

16

TENDERNESS was never an element in the marriage I made with Atalante. In the beginning, when I took her first up the frozen valley of Scamander to Xanthus' Lair, the manor designated for our retreat, she seemed as much changed as any woman I have ever known. About her beauty, of course, there had never been the slightest doubt: that had always been the most regal thing about her, and during her pregnancy, even that achieved a new and sensuous bloom. Her skin tones, already rich, deepened, and her luxurious dark hair took on its fullest body; without question, she had opened like some flower, although here — now — I would liken that luster to the unfolding of nightshade rather than to the lily or the rose. Still, I cannot say that I was not moved, and the fact that I was must have been apparent, for as I remember, she seemed pleased.

Her pleasure, if that is what it was, remained silent, displayed only in the heightened color of her cheeks, for her eyes showed plainly that she was more than a little afraid of me. We had not seen each other, you see, until we came together before the altar of ox-eyed Hera — not since the night I had forced her against the table and planted my seed deep within her body — so as we rode forward then, mere hours after the marriage ceremony, across the windswept frozen reaches of the Plain, in some way it was as though we were meeting for the first time. Ballad mongers and old women tend to find such moments moist with emotion, positively greasy with tenderness; I do not, and I did not then, nor, I think, did Atalante. By that time, you see, most of my illusions were gone; I had become something of an emotional realist, knew well what I had lost and knew, as well, what I had bargained for, and it was not wedded bliss. Our union, such as it was, had been as violent a yoking together of opposites as the illicit fornications of Ares and Aphrodite, but whereas their tryst had given birth to Harmonia the Uniter, I expected ours to lead only to discord and disharmony. And I believe Atalante shared my views, not on the surface, perhaps, but down deep, certainly, for she was more of a realist than she may have seemed.

Atalante had married me, you see, not for love, as her mother thought — although there was an element of that twisted into her emotions — but for spite. Marriage was the most effective way she could think of for getting even with me. She told me as much later and told me too that what had first infuriated her and set her on her course had been my all too apparent preference for Ariadne, whose beauty, she said, *paled* beside her own. Then, when she had lured me again, expecting an easy conquest, and found herself caught in her own web — physically used, humiliated, impregnated while being abused, assaulted by a common soldier, and finally scorned — her desire for lasting revenge had reached fever pitch, and she had focused all her energies on bringing me swiftly to heel. In the end, she had decided that the most effective way to achieve her ends was through marriage. As I say, she was more of a realist than she seemed, but even so, she had illusions, and most of them centered on the things I have just told you — on her motives for binding me irrevocably to her by what she believed to be an unbreakable slave collar of marriage. Her view, the only one that she ever admitted to, was that all of her motives had been concentrated on her desire for revenge.

Good enough — as I have said before, pain was her amusement, and its prolonged infliction seemed to be one of the great pleasures of her life. But there was a darker side to that as well, for if she liked to inflict pain, physical or mental, she also liked to receive it, and the fact — a fact she would never admit, not even at the height of her passion — is that her appetite for something nearing violent sexual gratification seemed insatiable. This I know. This, in time, I was forced to learn. I had perceived as much at Troy, on the night in which I had strayed from Antenor's house and first taken her like a stallion mounting a mare, but then I had come away from her having only vague notions to inform me about her, whereas later I had certain knowledge. So as I say, tenderness never became an element in our marriage.

I did not know as much on the frigid day when I first drove her down from Ilium, across the snowy Plain, and up beside frozen Scamander to Xanthus' Lair, and beside me, wrapped tightly in her regal, fleece-lined robes, Atalante, beautiful but cold, remained curiously silent. In the royal apartments, she was to tell me later, up to the last moment before she joined me in front of ox-eyed Hera's priests, her resolve had held firm, her motives sharp with the malignance of her intent, but before the altar, when it was already too late, she shrank back from the hand of fate. The deed done, the ceremony performed, she suddenly found herself withdrawn from the protections of the palace, alone on the howling, snowswept Plain, hurtling headlong into the unknown beside a man she had seen only twice before in her life. Then, she said, for the first time, her resolve failed her, for she knew without question that I had hurt her before and that I fully despised her, and in short, she became afraid.

Thus, I think, her silence. Isolated for the first time in her life, frightened, she felt compelled to draw close to me and did so, and that, perhaps, is the most curious fact of all, for in the face of what she perceived as the deadly danger of that wintry Plain, she turned for protection to the one man she most hated, to the one man who despised her, worked herself between the reins, then back between his arms, and pressed herself against him — still looking ahead over the chariot's rim — to protect herself from the Borean blasts rolling down from Thrace. And yet, it was only cold comfort that I was able to afford her, I remember, for I was driving a matched pair of Priam's most undisciplined mares, and I found them every bit as difficult to handle as his wife and daughter had ever been. Still, in the time that I knew her, those few hours together out there on the Plain may well have been the only moments of genuine human contact that we shared, and their quiet silence was as close as we ever came to a warm hearth between us.

This calm or something a little less perfect continued for several months, indeed until my son was born — a fine strapping boy with my nose and my mother's eyes. Atalante immediately named the baby Tros in honor of her ancestor and sent him to a wet nurse, a good woman who for all practical purposes acted as the boy's mother throughout the remainder of his life. During that time, our relations were civil, if not cordial, and in the evenings, sometimes, we sat before our board, where we were waited on — hand and foot, you might say — by royal servants, and that is when she told me the things that I have told to you and when, at last, I began to know her character. The more I knew her, the more I studied her motives, the more I drew back, and yet, as I have already said, I admired her beauty greatly, for in all externals, she continued to blossom. Even as I was repelled, then, I also found myself attracted by her, and harbored somewhere near the core of my being a supressed desire to possess the one thing about her that I did not find utterly forbidding.

On her part, Atalante was quite straightforward in our relations, for she seemed to have learned at an early age the true source of her power over men; and the more her beauty bloomed — the fact of which she was openly and vainly aware — the more supremely confident she became in its power to override all other considerations in her efforts to bind and eventually subdue me.

So confident was she that she told me as much often, showing neither heat nor passion as she fixed me with her smoke-gray eyes across the width of our board.

"I am in possession of Aphrodite's belt," she would say while putting a morsel to her lips or raising a glass of wine, "and like all men, Dymas, you are powerless against it." It was almost as though I were not even at the table, as though she were speaking to the air or the gods or to whoever she communicated with during her private moments, for never once when she said this to me did she make the slightest effort to hold my eye or gauge the effect of her words. That is how confident she was of her powers, and she remained so right through her pregnancy, and in all that time I did not make one move to touch her in any way. And even this she used to her advantage, for according to custom, during the months of our . . . what shall I call it, our conjugal separation . . . during those months when her presence of necessity was scarce and when we met only for the evening meal, she never came before me without first spending several hours of preparation with her maids, so that when she finally did appear, her polished radiance was often breathtaking. But even then, I wished only to be away from her, for every time I looked at her, I thought of Ariadne, and in truth Atalante, beautiful beyond measure, still lost by the comparison.

Although I buried my feelings as deeply as I could, I wonder whether Atalante did not perceive them or at least recognize the possibility that I might be making a comparison, for early on, she began to disparage Ariadne in ways that grew ever more contemptuous, and from this malignance, strangely, I eventually drew a desperate kind of hope. It began simply enough, I remember, with casual remarks at table. "Poor little Ariadne," she said one night not long after we had reached the Lair, "her breasts are not the same size. You never saw them by day, did you Dymas? Lucky you. She *is* a sight. Pity." I had been unprepared for this, and while I do not recall my exact reaction, I suppose that no matter how deeply I thought I had masked my feelings, they must have showed, for as I remember, a certain delight seemed to leap momentarily into her eyes, and in the end, that may have been all she required to generate the whole ugly game.

She said nothing about Ariadne for the remainder of the evening, but the next night, as soon as we sat down to table, she stuck her knife into a pear, lifted it, and examined it in the light. "A little like poor Ariadne," she said, with a short, vulgar laugh. "She has positively the biggest ass I have ever seen on a girl her size." From that time on, at least once each night, Atalante struck, sinking her fangs as deeply into Ariadne and my supposed feelings for her as she could, attacking at one time or another, in one vicious way after another, every part of Ariadne's anatomy, character, and behavior until, one night not long before Tros was born, she looked me straight in the eye and said quite calmly, "She's frigid, you know. Oh, yes, my dear, frigid as stone in winter. Antiphos won't even sleep with her. He's had to import Phrygian concubines, three of them. Good sex *is* such an important pleasure, don't you think? Poor little thing; she'll never know. Oh, but then you, my dear, know all about her already, don't you?" She went on talking, laying out every lurid facet of Ariadne's supposed sexual irregularities that she could think of, calmly and with all the apparent grace of a female eagle folding her wings over her nest, but by that time, I had ceased to listen to her. Instead, I found that I could concentrate only on the grievous public insult Antiphos had dealt his wife by bringing concubines into their quarters so soon after their marriage, and in that hour, as though from Apollo's hand, I conceived a plan. Admittedly, it was born of nothing more than a prolonged desperation on my part, a desperation that was aggravated by the pain Atalante seemed determined to inflict upon me, but nevertheless, in the end, my plan gave me hope.

Clearly, insofar as my life in the Troad could be valued, I had sunk so low that my position, possibly even my life, seemed past recovery. I had dishonored myself with a vile woman, incurred the limit of royal displeasure, betrayed my code, and lost face with my friends. I had, I thought, nothing more to lose, and in that dismal hour, when faced with what I believed to be Ariadne's most abject misery, I made up my mind to wait for the right opportunity and then carry her away with me into the depths of Phrygia or the heartland of Thrace. There, I reasoned, I might hire myself out as a warrior and support the two of us in a life that would be well removed from our pain, a life that might be lived out in relative calm well beyond even Priam's royal reach. As I say, it was a plan born of prolonged desperation; even so, its most fanciful and impractical elements gave me hope, and I spent long hours working out the details.

Meanwhile, Atalante's time came, and Tros was born, and then she went into her quarters for four months while the royal surgeons sent up from Troy hovered everywhere about her to ensure that she quickly recovered her strength.

Spring had come even before Tros was born, and then summer, and I passed my daytime hours much as I always had, training and hunting, working daily to keep myself fit and my body hard. I learned then the upper banks of Scamander in a way that I had never known them before, for I hunted across all their slopes, providing most of the meat for the Lair's various boards, including our own. While I hunted, along with only a single slave as bearer, I thought long on my plan to rescue Ariadne and even longer on how we could escape into whatever life we might find beyond the Trojan frontier. And then one night in late summer, as I came down from the lower slopes of Ida with a stag over my shoulders, I entered the confines of the Lair by the south gate and found Pharos waiting for me beneath Xanthus' sacred oak.

17

"AND YOUR MARRIAGE," he said, as the two of us ate slices of venison that I had broiled before the fire. "It goes well?"

"It goes . . . not well," I said, "nor is it likely to do so, ever."

"Much as I thought," he mused, "but you have only yourself to thank," and he was not kind as he placed my blame.

"Still," I protested, "I am not altogether — "

"Still," he quickly interrupted me, sounding again very like my tutor, "whenever the heart rules the head — and that covers anger as well as the softer passions . . ."

"I know," I said. "You do not have to tell me; I have learned."

"The hardest way, nevertheless. You should have used more imagination, boy; you should have looked a little into the future."

He was right, of course, and I remained silent.

"And the other," he asked, "what of your feelings for her?"

There, he knew, he had struck a nerve, and beneath his beetle brows, his penetrating eyes bored into me.

"For her," I said, "my feelings grow only stronger, for Antiphos insults her, and she lives in much misery."

"That," said Pharos, leaping suddenly to his feet, "is rot! Do you not know that Ariadne has just given birth to a son whom she has named Ilius in honor of her husband's ancestor? She and Antiphos are as happy as two larks twittering in the branches of some freshly leafed oak. Who, in the name of Erigone, pours such poison in your ear?"

Totally unprepared, I felt the blow like the hard hand of Poseidon, he who shakes the earth beneath men's feet. As I sat stunned, unable to move, my mouth half open, all my plans — built like well-made towers to keep and protect my Ariadne — crashed around me into dust, and I learned again the depths of Atalante's treachery. In the end, I told him: "My wife."

"I see," Pharos said. "Not only did you make her pregnant, you made her jealous and angry as well. You had better listen to me, Dymas; jealousy and anger form an altogether dangerous combination, and — "

"We do not choose whom we would love," I shot back.

"Nevertheless," Pharos said, waving away my remark, "it is my advice to you to remedy the situation immediately and make your peace with your wife. Now, what is this other thing you think you are so cleverly concealing from me — and remember, I have raised you and I can read your moves like those of the stags that range these hills around us, so try no slips or feints with me, for I will know them and pursue."

Like a dutiful son, I suppose, but venting on myself my full fury for having permitted Atalante again to dupe me, I revealed to Pharos, in embarrassment and shame, the plan I had so foolishly constructed.

"Romantic, adolescent drivel!" Pharos roared. "Were you still a boy, I would strike you with my spear merely for thinking such nonsense! You? You are Victor of Cyme? It defies all imagination!"

He had never been more angry with me in his life, and for several minutes he paced back and forth, fuming silently, his white beard standing almost straight out from his face where the hard line of his jaw jutted furiously forward.

"All right," he said at last, "cut your losses and let the matter be ended, now and forever more, for as I told you in the beginning, she is not for you, and she *is* happy where she is, and she has all the more reason to be so with the birth of her son and with the respectful love of a husband who honors her. Let be what you cannot change, and give up, once and for all, your foolish obsession. Your future lies elsewhere, and where that is I am going to show you now."

He sat down then, and slowly, carefully, he adjusted his breathing. "Know you, Dymas," he said to me finally, "that once I commanded the Boar. In the beginning, of course, I was a Shark, and once a Shark, always a Shark. I went up amongst them well before my twelfth birthday and learned my craft in the shadow of the Whale's keep, for in those days, know you, that stone-gray keep was the Shark's barracks. I did good service in the ranks, rose to junior command in the Teeth, and in Priam's tenth year on the throne, rose to overall command, well before my thirtieth birthday. For five more years, on Tenedos, I led with a strong hand, making the Shark into what it is today. My merits did not pass without notice, and at royal command, in Priam's fifteenth year, I went up to Dardanos and took command of the Boar, and there I remained for four more years. Both your father and your uncle acted as junior commanders under my supervision during our long campaign in Phrygia and again during our raids on Imbros, and then came the threat of war in Thynia."

He poured himself a cup of wine and for several seconds sat looking into the fire.

"Trusting my capacities," he continued, "royal Priam promoted me to be leader on the Military Council — the position Skaiko holds today, the post your father held near the end of the Thracian conflict and at the beginning of the First Mysian War — and that is when I promoted your father to command the Boar and sent your uncle with him into Thynia. Then came heady days, o my Dymas, when nothing that we did ever seemed to go wrong, and victory after Trojan victory followed each of our efforts like the breath of an unwavering wind. Indeed, all Troy prospered, for as more and more of the tin and copper deposits in Thynia came under our control and more and more of Thrace opened wide to our trade, Troy waxed strong, and the royal treasure rooms of the House of Priam rapidly became the envy of all the world. And yet, Dymas, not everything in holy Ilium was fit and good."

He gave me a penetrating look as he sipped his wine. Then he continued.

"As first wife and consort," he said, "royal Hecuba should have been content with the prosperity of her husband's house, but she was not, Dymas, and therein lies the root of the difficulties that have befallen us, for she has ever had her husband's ear and has turned him against us whenever she could. And in some cases, we have aided her, making our own way harder, as I shall show you. As I say, then, Hecuba should have been content, but she was not. Elevated from the minor nobility by her fortunate marriage, an event that took place in the same year I rose to command the Shark, royal Hecuba became immediately ambitious for her own family, seeking their promotion in a variety of clever ways. Know you, for example, that Skaiko is the queen's half brother?"

I had not known and said as much.

"You have much to learn of politics," he said. "Know you that Skaiko is much promoted by Hecuba, as are other members of her family." And then he quickly listed for me the names of the generals commanding the Leopard, Eagle, Wolf, and Lion — all of them cousins of the queen — as well as four subordinate commanders, men slated for future formation command and each a royal nephew.

"For her sons," he continued, "she is even more ambitious. Hector's early and swift rise is a case in point, but as yet most of her sons are too young to command. Even so, their names now cram the subordinate list, so much so that merit is largely ignored in favor of family or royal influence. Such has not always been the case, Dymas. Certainly it was not so when I ran the Military Council, but, just as certainly, it began then, and in thwarting Hecuba's nominations — most of them cunningly indirect — I frequently ran afoul of her, and in the end, she poisoned my standing with Priam. Quite clearly, she wanted Skaiko to command the Boar and conduct our campaigns in Thynia and later in Thrace, but I managed to block such an appointment, for Skaiko has ever lacked the offensive spirit, and before Priam, I made the matter plain.

"And then, as though adding salt to the wound, I placed your uncle in subordinate command to your father, this time in lieu of the queen's cousin — he who now commands the Lion — and in doing so, I incurred her wrath. Hecuba's candidates for command were inadequate for the roles in which she wanted to cast them. In the end, I think, I was proved right in Thynia and Thrace, and Skaiko's performance during the Mysian Wars has only served to confirm my judgment. Regardless, Antenor, Laocoön, Hicetaon, your father, your uncle, and I — our entire party — had stretched our relationship with the throne almost to the breaking point, for in the moment it became clear to Hecuba that we were all ranged against her, she launched a campaign against us — against me in particular — which lowered us all in Priam's eyes, making government more difficult than ever. And then came the blow that, politically, broke our backs, and that blow, as you can see for yourself, I did not survive."

He stopped, and looked deep into the fire, and in the same moment I saw on his face a look that he had shown me only once before in my life — on Ida, on that night many years before when I had first told him about my passion for Ariadne.

"I had a passion once," he continued, "and it spelled my end. Know you, Dymas, that royal Priam's oldest child is a female. Even as we speak, she passes her fortieth year, yet still the bloom of youth is as much a part of her as it was then, twenty-two years ago when I headed the council. In those days, know you, I was often in or about the royal apartments, and in the natural course of things, I saw her frequently, and even at my age, I was captivated by her. It was her eyes that caught me, held me, and finally swallowed me, for they were uncommonly large and dark and deep — as deep, I think, as the wine-dark sea that surrounds us, so deep, it seemed, that they might have fathomed the very sands of time.

"In truth, Dymas, those dark, deep eyes could see all the way into time, for my Lady Cassandra had been touched in her youth by Apollo, and with divine sight, she always saw the truth. I loved her from the moment I first saw her, from the moment I first heard her liquid voice, from the moment I first felt those deep, dark eyes turned full upon me and saw the sadness there that I would later know to the full. I fought my passion, Dymas, and I lost, and as the hard result, I have endured with pain through every day of my life, for unlike you, I have never been allowed a second chance. Know you, then, that I declared myself in plain voice and sought her hand, and then began my misery. 'I, too, love you, o my Pharos of the Shark,' she said to me in mature tones, 'and it is my misfortune that I will go on loving you even to my own destruction, for know you must that I am courted by a god. Forget me. Absent yourself from Troy, and do not look back, for if you persist in loving me, you will share my fate and die before your time.'

"Those were the last words she spoke to me, the last words that ever passed between us, for on that very night, royal Hecuba — great with child — was frightened by a dream. It was my misfortune, Dymas, and Hecuba's that the passion of my life, my Lady Cassandra, was called to interpret the dream; she had amazing powers, you see, and everyone who knew her also knew her powers and never doubted her word."

He shuddered, as though a sudden chill had blown across his spine, and without needing to — for it was high summer — he moved closer to the fire and warmed his hands.

"Hecuba's dream," he went on, slowly rubbing his hands, "was that she was to be delivered not of a child but of a firebrand. I was present, you see, as were others on the council, for royal dreams are ever matters of state because their augury affects us all and responsive action must be decided by a majority vote. The moment Cassandra heard the dream, she refused to speak and steadfastly continued so for three long days. In the end, the priests of Apollo — acting on orders of both Priam and Hecuba — compelled her to speak on the strength of her vows, and before the high god's image, she dared not refuse. 'The man child my mother bears,' she said in a voice that still haunts my ear, 'will be the destruction of Troy.' "

On the moment, I thought I heard Pharos' voice break. "O my Cassandra," he said falteringly, "how great was your sadness when you read them that omen. I tell you, Dymas, she was devastated by her revelation, so much so that she fainted straightaway and had to be carried from the room while Hecuba and Priam both screamed abuse in her wake. After that, no one in the royal family ever believed a word she said.

"But that was by no means the end of it, for within three days, from the depth of her outrage and by way of revenge, angry Hecuba put forward a lie, a subtle distortion in which she charged that Cassandra had refused the advances of Lord Apollo, who wished to lie with her, and had been struck dumb to the truth as punishment for rejecting so mighty a god. Even before my hapless Cassandra had recovered her senses, she was transported directly from the palace into the precincts of Apollo's temple, and there, by her mother's order, she has remained a virtual prisoner ever since."

Again, the shudder passed quickly up Pharos' spine, and I read on his face a pain that closed his eyes.

"And?" I prodded.

"On one point," he continued, in a voice that sounded drained, "on the point about her man child to be born, Hecuba's lie came too late to prevent the council from taking action, and we did so over her protests and Priam's by voting with great humility before the gods to expose the child at birth and escape the hand of destruction. The vote was close, closer than it should have been, for by that time Hecuba had already succeeded in moving some of her own favorites — Skaiko and one or two relations — onto the General as well as the Military Council, but with Antenor, Laocoön, and four other elders voting with me, we seized the moment, and the voice of reason carried by a single vote, my own. I knew, then, that I had incurred the full measure of the royal wrath, but I had no other choice and voted for Ilium over Priam, Hecuba, and my own well-being."

Once more, Pharos fell silent, and then, slowly, he drew the folds of his cloak close about him and went on.

"In the night, Hecuba was seized with her pains," he said, "and toward morning, the babies were born. The man child was named Alexandros by his father, but even over Priam's protests, even before Aurora's first blush, the Grand Council, all attending, compelled him to hand the child over. The babe was then given to me, and I wrapped him in my cloak and set out on the run for the slopes of Ida. I ran all that day and throughout the following night, never slackening my pace, with the man child, Alexandros, strapped to my back, and in the end, in the throes of my exhaustion, he felt to me like the hard weight of the world, and, like Atlas shouldering his load, I bent to earth beneath him. I left him exposed atop a blue rock slab between two cleft pines as old as the heights of Gargaron and made my long journey home, torn nearly apart by the harsh responsibility that I could not escape.

"I returned to Troy three nights later, and by that time, I had fallen from power in disgrace. During my absence, you see, Hecuba had risen like a Fury from her bed and hatched her hard revenge. In the end, as Cassandra had warned, I shared her fate and died before my time. The means was Hecuba's lie. According to Hecuba, the very things that had turned Cassandra's head and moved her to insult the mighty Apollo were my 'hideous, unnatural attentions.' How effective that lie became may be measured by the readiness with which the rabble accepted it. That, by itself, would have meant little in the council chambers, where cooler heads were wont to prevail, but there, too, Hecuba worked instantly and assiduously against me in my absence, and in the end, by means of threats or bribes or something more insidious, she turned one of my allies against me, and thus I fell into oblivion even before my time, even before I had struck the Plain on my return to holy Ilium."

He fell silent, and this time his silence was sustained, for he seemed to have reached the end of his account, and looked both withered and drawn. But if Pharos felt drained, I did not; my pulse had quickened.

"You said *babies*," I urged.

"What?" he said after a moment, for he had ceased, I think, to pay me any attention, and his mind seemed to be drifting.

"Babies," I said again; "you said *babies*."

"Yes," he said at last, pulling himself together. "Twins."

"And the second child was a female?"

"Yes."

"Who?" I instantly asked. "Who was she? Who is she?"

"She is your wife," he said grimly, stunning me with the revelation. "And that is why you must make your peace with her, Dymas, for she carries within her the seeds of much destruction, and already you see something of their effects. Do not draw the woman's full wrath against you, for the treachery of that family is great; if you draw it in full, it will swallow you, Dymas, as surely and swiftly as it swallowed me — as surely and swiftly as a night owl swallows a mouse — only to spit you up later, withered and desiccated."

"It has done that," I said, "already. I have nothing left to lose but my life."

"But that," said Pharos, rising to his feet, "is still worth more than you think — if not to yourself, then at least to Troy, and in the morning, I will show you what I mean."

Refusing all invitation to spend the night under the royal roof, he retired, to sleep outside the compound while I endured another weary night within.

18

WE ROSE before dawn and, taking our wallets and our spears, set out upcountry along the banks of wide Scamander, and when Aurora blushed, it seemed like old times in the days when we hunted the hills behind Abydus-by-the-sea. The poppies were in bloom, bathing the whole valley in a brilliant blood red, and in the sky above, an eagle dipped its wing, turning slowly toward the sea. For the first time in many months, I think, I felt free.

By noon, we had climbed high into Ida's foothills. Far above us through the mists, Gargaron's snowcapped peak made plain its point, and in the same hour, we found ourselves moving up a stag run that rose steadily higher through thickets, breaks, and pines. Never once did Pharos slacken his pace, so, stopping neither for rest nor water, we continued to climb until midafternoon, and then, quite suddenly, we broke into a clearing and halted before a goatherd's pen that was empty but filled with fresh dung and the fat flies that attended it.

"There," Pharos said, raising the point of his spear, and in the distance, between two cleft pines that overlooked a long blue slab of rock, I saw a hut and, sitting before the hut on a three-legged stool, an ancient graybeard who seemed older than Pharos.

"Twenty years ago," Pharos said grimly, his blue-veined knuckles going white over the shaft of his spear, "when I exposed the infant Alexandros between those overshadowing pines, that hut did not exist. For reasons that you can well imagine, I would never have come here again had it not been for a startling piece of news that I had some fourteen days ago direct from Antenor at Troy. Upon receiving his message, I came here straightaway, finding both pen and hut — and the ancient goatherd, whose name is Thoön — and learned something that you too must know, for it concerns the future of Troy."

He strode forward past the goat pens and on, up the rise, toward the rock slab, and I walked in his shadow until he stopped before the ancient.

"May the blessing of Zeus fall greatly about you, old one. It is I who came before, Pharos the Shark."

"I knew as much by your footfall," said Thoön, and it was then that I saw he was blind. "My hut, poor as it is, opens freely to you with the blessings of hospitality, so come, Pharos the Shark and the young man who walks in your shadow, and let us share together a barley cake and some wine."

We broke bread, then, with ancient Thoön, seating ourselves before him on the ground, and we shared salt, and at last Pharos extracted a skin from his wallet, pouring each of us a full measure of Thracian wine.

"The man who sits beside me," Pharos said plainly, "is Dymas, son of Kalitor, and he must know, Thoön, what you and I know. For the story to retain its credence, he must hear it from your own lips."

Carefully, the ancient poured out a libation, naming golden Apollo. "I have heard of Kalitor," he said, his hairless head tilting back to reveal the empty sockets of his eyes. "Kalitor was a mighty warrior in the service of Troy, and are you, Dymas, also a warrior?"

"Of the Shark," Pharos said.

"That is good," said Thoön, raising his wine cup to his lips, "for the way of the warrior is the pathway of man. Long ago, even before Priam took the throne — in the days of royal Laomedon and my youth — I too carried shield and spear, smiting the Hatti with my strong right hand. Now, my warrior days are long gone and my spear arm grows cold. In Phrygia, fighting the Hatti, I came close to death when copper spears punctured both of my thighs; ever since, I have lived a lame goatherd here on the slopes of Ida."

He leaned back against the wall of his hut, taking the late afternoon sun full against his brow.

"*They* were here," he said quietly, "and they made me blind, the three of them together."

"Who?" I quickly asked. "When?"

"You forget yourself," Pharos rebuked me. "Do Thoön as much honor as you would wish for yourself, and let him offer his words in his own way."

I begged the man's pardon and held my tongue.

"That was not so long ago," Thoön went on, "but Dymas is right. He cannot know the meaning of what I speak without hearing it from the start, so I go back now and begin with the beginning. Know you, then, that I have herded goats across these slopes for seventy long years. In the old days, my hut stood in a glade to the east, where I kept a large herd and lived quietly with my wife, but after fifty winters together, my wife fell to Apollo's arrows, leaving me alone on this mountain beneath the shadow of Gargaron. I had no sooner buried her, it seemed, than an archer sought me beside her grave. His appearance sent me into consternation, for he was a bronzed warrior, larger than life, with locks of golden hair that seemed brighter than the sun. He said that he came from the queen, from Hecuba, and then, without another word of explanation, he brought me here, where we sit, and showed me an infant boy whose hair was also gold and whose tiny lungs screamed loud with hunger.

" 'By order of Hecuba, consort to Priam, you are to raise this boy to a man,' said the bronzed archer. 'Carry him in your wallet as you herd your goats, and call him Paris.' And with that, the archer was gone, gone like a fleet golden arrow loosed from a mighty bow, hurtling down through the pines on the road toward Ilium.

"I asked no questions, of myself or the gods. I was left alone with the boy, and infant that he was, he was near to death from hunger, so I brought down one of my she goats and fed him fresh milk, warm from the teat, and his cries ceased, and almost immediately he fell asleep. It seemed a small matter then to raise this hut about him while he slept, and on the following day, I built the goat pens you see and moved my herd here. And during the seasons that followed, the boy thrived.

"Childless during my life with my wife, I knew nothing of infants, neither the joys nor the sorrows of raising them, so as the boy waxed strong and grew, my days were filled with wonder as I learned his ways and answered his quick, endless questions. He took to herding as though born to it and knew more about goats by the time he was five than most men learn in a life, and he learned as well the craft of the woods, ranging far and wide to hunt with bow and sling. When he became older, I sought to teach him the spear, but, in fine, he refused to learn it, calling the weapon 'stupid' beside his bow, and 'slow.' 'Why should I place myself close to danger,' he asked, 'when I can kill at a distance with sling or bow?' I tried to explain to him the way of the warrior; in the end, he allowed for the spear's use but still declined to learn its craft, saying that it was no weapon for him, and it is my belief that the bow will always remain his weapon of choice.

"That I spoiled him," Thoön continued, taking a second sip of wine and breaking off a corner of a barley cake, "I do not deny, for Paris was my weakness, and I indulged his every whim. Amidst these rustic surroundings, his whims seemed simple enough, and satisfying them caused me no great difficulty . . . except once . . . except once, when the boy craved honey and I found myself incessantly stung in my efforts to get it for him. And then" — he laughed — "when I brought it back to him, Paris ate himself sick through overindulgence and vomited throughout the remainder of the day. I should have learned, then, and taught him that his instant gratification was not always good for him — for either of us, for those bees were very painful — but I did not, and my failure to learn that lesson and teach it to him came home to plague me. Ox-eyed Hera knew well what she was doing, I think, when she gave the rites of child rearing to the young, for only the young seem to have the strength, will, and stamina that are required to regulate a growing child. I say this to you now, in my sorrow, for when Paris was handed over to me, I was already too old and too tired, and I failed to raise him in the ways that should be."

He sank back against the hut, slowly rubbing his forehead with gnarled fingers.

"At seventeen," he went on, "Paris glimpsed a wood nymph hereabouts, gave her chase, caught her, violated her, and carried her home without so much as a moment's hesitation. Oenone was her name, and she was a pretty thing as light as air. The boy had used her roughly; her divinity destroyed, she became immediately and entirely dependent upon us for protection, shelter, and food. Shuddering with fear, I made instant sacrifices, seeking to propitiate the gods in the best way I could, for know you both that I fully expected the archer goddess to strike us dead and send us howling into the chambers of decay. Seeing me frantic with fear sobered the boy enough so that he softened toward Oenone, entered by rustic rite into marriage with her; and for a while, with his conscience thus salved, they were happy together, going out in the mornings to tend our goats and returning at sundown to take their meals and sleep together beneath the stars.

" 'I couldn't help myself' was all he ever said to me. 'She was pretty, and I had to have her.' What could I say? After the fact, rebuke seemed pointless. It was done without my knowledge, on pure impulse, with a wood goddess, and as each moon passed, I continued to live my days in mortal fear as I waited for Hera or Artemis or Zeus himself to make known the full measure of divine displeasure.

"But if I remained frightened, Paris did not and pretty Oenone soon ceased to be, and in time she seemed the light of our life, bubbling about us with the natural music of a brook or the leaves in the tops of the trees, and her breath was fresh with spring. Gradually, my fears dropped away, or I forgot them, and I took great delight in seeing the pair of them together. In the blossom of their youth, Oenone seemed the perfect mate for Paris, gazing ever upon him with eyes that were blue like his own and filled to overflowing with love. And so the spring went and then the summer, but in the autumn of that year, the blow I feared struck hard.

"Oenone was absent in that hour. As I recall, she had gone out alone to pick mushrooms in the shadows of an oak, or watercress beside the brook's edge, so when this clearing filled suddenly with light, she was not here to see it, neither the light nor the three golden chariots that descended here so miraculously from the heights of Ida. In the moment of their landing, glittering goddesses stepped down from those chariots, glided toward us across the clearing, and stopped, side by side, before this long rock slab. In a flash, another god appeared, and I knew him to be Hermes the Guide, for his feet were winged, and in his right hand he carried the wand, the caduceus that is capable of putting even Argus Panoptes into a deep sleep. But in his left hand, held at arm's length from his body, Hermes carried a brilliant gold apple, and this, with a flick of his wrist, he tossed directly onto the stone so that it rolled to rest on the very spot where I had first seen Paris uttering his infant cries. This done, he who bears messages from Zeus stepped back, losing himself beneath the shadows of the trees.

"No sooner had the Guide backed away than one of the three

goddesses stepped forward and spoke, and the sound of her voice made music in the air like the clear, fresh water that falls from Ida in the early spring, and in the moment that she spoke, I knew that she did not speak to me.

" 'Alexandros of Troy,' she said to Paris, who stood dumb before the slab, 'hear the words of Hera, the ox-eyed queen. The lord of heaven charges you with the task of making a judgment. The prize is the golden apple that rests on the womb of your infant stone, and the measure of your judgment is to be this: you are to award this apple to the fairest amongst the three of us who stand here before you,' and as she spoke, the immense power in her dark, round eyes flashed blinding bright. 'Award the apple to me,' she quickly said, 'and I will give you power, power, and more power, power beyond your most ardent dreams, power over the Troad, and the distant dark Black Sea, and over all the wine-dark Aegean through the lingering length of your days.'

"She might have offered him more; she seemed prepared to, but she never had the chance, for the goddess on her right hand suddenly interrupted her, and warm were the words that followed.

" 'Know me, Alexandros of Troy,' said the second, striking her spear against the face of the stone, 'for I am gray-eyed Athene, she who sprang fully formed from the forehead of Zeus. Award the apple to me, and I promise you wisdom enough to make you secure against the most brazen bribes of the powerful,' and so saying, she leveled a scornful glance in ox-eyed Hera's direction. 'Wisdom enough,' she continued, 'to win you military victories of your own over Mysia, Lydia, Caria, Phrygia, even unto the lands of the Hatti, which lie far to the east.'

"Gray-eyed Athene continued, but Paris no longer listened, no longer heard her words, for almost as soon as she had planted her spear and started to speak, the enchanting goddess on the left had revealed to him her lovely breasts and utterly consumed him with her sparkling eyes. 'Give the apple to *me*,' she purred, making a slow, sensual motion with her hips, 'and I will give you the most beautiful woman alive.' Completely seduced, Paris at once seized the apple and tossed it into her hands while golden Aphrodite smothered his body with her scent."

In the distance, an eagle screamed, and Thoön fell silent, finishing his wine and turning his cup upside down on the flat of the slab. "I do not know," he said at last, "what other choice he could have made. Even as I watched the event unfold, even as he made his choice, so instantly, so impulsively, awarding her the prize, even then I knew he was wrong and knew that disaster was sure to follow, and it did. And yet, presented with the same choice myself . . . well, who can say, or even know the heart, for the lure of beauty lies deep within us all, and on that day, before this hut, bright-eyed Aphrodite of the perfumed zone seemed the fairest of them all. Here, now, in the twilight of my years, amidst this darkling wilderness, I know his choice for the act it was, selfish and self-indulgent, and I condemn myself for the failure of his upbringing. Better for all, I think, had he thrown the apple to gray-eyed Athene or the ox-eyed Hera. Best . . . best not to have made the judgment at all — best to have returned the apple to Zeus, for as surely as we are men, only his wisdom could ever have made the choice.

"But Paris chose as he chose, and, the choice made, great was the wrath that the scorned goddesses showed and mighty the fire in their eyes, almost as though the whole of the Troad had gone up in flames. Suddenly, they were gone, their two golden chariots rising in a sharp, fierce blaze of light. To be truthful, I do not think Paris noticed their departure; from the moment he had tossed her the apple, you see, Aphrodite had so locked him in the coils of her embrace that he had eyes for no one else, and so the matter remained for a seeming eternity. Finally, as twilight descended, golden Aphrodite withdrew her intoxicating scent, mounted her chariot, and left in a passionate burst of light. It was some time, I remember, before we, shaking before the stone, recovered ourselves enough to move.

"Oenone returned not long after, carrying bundles of sweet

green herbs from the mountain's hidden vales, singing and dancing, but the moment she saw her Paris, she knew that he was changed, for he gazed right through her as though she no longer existed. I shall never forget the wretchedness that seized her then, for in a single second she knew, and like the herbs, which fell instantly from her arms to the ground, her summer freshness began to wither. She knew she had lost him, but she never knew why.

"Days gave way to weeks, and as each moon passed, Paris grew ever cooler toward her, ever more distant. Pretty Oenone seemed tireless in trying to rekindle his love and unwavering in her own devotion to him, but our little wood nymph was crushed by Aphrodite's power. Gradually, I saw the light disappear from her eyes and the blush fade from her cheek, and early on a winter morning, I saw wrinkles lining her face and realized that she was growing old. I knew, finally, that she would die, and she did — here, before this hut, while Paris gazed away toward Troy — not many weeks ago. Indeed, I could do nothing to save her but hold her in my arms; like a young sapling before the raging fires of the forest, she withered before her lover's new passion and died. That Paris was callous, I do not deny. That his indifference killed her, of that I am certain, but the outcome was not premeditated. He had done with her, and during those last, lingering moons, it was as though she no longer existed for him."

From the center of his being, the old man groaned, and from the dry sockets of his eyes, I could have sworn that tears would flow.

"Her spirit had no more than departed from her body," Thoön said, his words coming ever more thick and slow, "when the archer from Troy, looking not a day older nor a whit different from the first time he came to me, appeared suddenly before us beneath an immense burst of light. 'Alexandros of Troy,' the archer said, 'the time has come for you to make your appearance on the Plain and take your place amongst the highest orders of

Ilium.' Without so much as a word or a look, the two of them were gone, leaving me here before our hut, still weeping, still holding the lifeless Oenone. I made her mound there, beyond the slab, patting the earth with my hands, and my lingering grief has washed the sight from my eyes."

Thus his story ended, and when he finished it, ancient Thoön fell silent and refused to speak another word. Leaving him wine and barley cakes and a quantity of olives, we rose and took our leave, making our way slowly down the mountain toward wide Scamander, where the river spread before us in the dim twilight below.

19

DARK NIGHT had long fallen by the time Pharos and I returned to the Lair, and across the broad sky, the numberless fires of heaven twinkled like burning desire. Even so, the valley of Scamander seemed silent, as though asleep or waiting beneath the high canopy of the sky.

"I will not stop," Pharos told me as we stood before the stone gates of the estate and rested on our spears. "I have told you what I came to tell you and shown you what I came to show you, and now you know the whole of the danger. Make your peace with your wife, Dymas, for if you do not, she may prove the greatest threat against you, and in the times that are sure to come, windswept Ilium is going to need all her fine young sons if she hopes to survive."

No inducement that I could offer him would make Pharos remain the rest of the night on the royal estate, so, taking his leave, he disappeared into darkness, walking swiftly in the direction of the Plain. Seeing him go, I turned away and covered the short way toward the manor, which remained well lighted even beneath the beams of the moon.

Afterward, time passed quickly, and as summer waned, the leaves on the oak and ash turned from green to gold and then to yellow brown and fell fluttering to earth beneath the first Thracian wind, which blew down cold across the Hellespont.

Throughout, Atalante remained secluded, and, according to custom, I did not see her once during the entire interval. But I was allowed to see my son and delighted in the strength of his cries and the sturdiness of his limbs and in the loving attention of the wet nurse, who brought him, wrapped in royal robes, to place him in my hands or sometimes on the floor atop warm fleeces, where soon he rolled or turned or pulled at the polished tusks of a boar that I dangled before him on the end of a sturdy string.

At last, November came, and I completed my twentieth year, and on the very night, as I sat thinking before the fire, turning my wine cup around and around, the great doors opened, and Atalante swept regally into my presence, wearing a gown so sheer, so clinging, so glittering with gold and silver thread that she stunned me. Even against my will, my member so stiffened that I was unable to hide the fact beneath the folds of my tunic. My face, as well, must have betrayed me, for in the same moment, the overpowering force of her mature beauty — the effects of which she had so carefully calculated — struck me harder than an axe in battle, and I saw her cheeks flush high with the color of her success.

I do not think I said a single word to her, and on her part, she seemed content to preen before me, showing herself to the best possible advantage while she tantalized and teased me into pain with her every liquid movement.

"Poor Ariadne could never have offered you *this*," she whispered as she pressed in close to me, brushing my face with her scent, "or this," as she opened her gown, cupping the swelling flesh of her breasts with her long tapering fingers, "or *this!*" as she stepped swiftly away, throwing her gown to the floor and revealing the fine silkiness of her body gleaming freshly with oil.

I could hold myself no longer. Taunted beyond endurance, I had to possess her, and I leapt from my chair while she pounced at me like some ravenous lioness when, after a long hunt, she springs on her kill, uttering a high feline scream, clawing and scratching and biting with all the strength of her being. Such was the passion of Atalante as I took her down beneath me onto the fleeces, entering her body with a yell. And in the end, after a long night of unrestrained passion, she devoured me and rose and walked away, leaving me limp and sore where I lay. As she left, trailing the sheer gold and silver of her gown behind her from the tips of her fingers, I heard her laugh deep and call to me to come to her chambers at midmorning. And then she was gone, the high wooden doors closing silently behind her, and I found myself alone.

I rose and went to the river to bathe, allowing wide Scamander to rush cold over my bones. When I returned, I broke my fast on gulls' eggs and the boiled flesh of a fowl that had been soaked in wine, and I tried to understand what was happening to me, for in that hour, at long last, I knew that Atalante had awakened my fire, and I thought finally that we might make our peace.

I waited then and went to her at midmorning along painted corridors that burned with the hues of the sun, and before her doors, I found the same old crone who had come for me in Lord Antenor's house at Troy, and she with her hag's fingers opened the doors, passing me into Atalante's chambers.

I have no power, my lords, to make known to you the strength of the emotions that next struck me, for what I found when I entered my wife's rooms so shocked me, so angered me, so . . . revolted me that I became ill, instantly vomiting gulls' eggs over the distance between me and the ornate bed where my wife lay, writhing with pleasure under the perverse attentions of not one but three of her young female slaves, who sought eagerly to satisfy her cravings. The degree of degradation I then knew exceeded anything I had ever known before, and worse. Even as the four of them reached a climactic frenzy in their nakedness, imperious Atalante looked across to where I stood, trying to recover myself, and threw me such a chilling look of triumph that it froze me to the bone. As quickly as I could, I removed myself from the room, slamming the great doors on the ecstatic screams behind me.

My first thought was to kill her and her slaves with her, and I ran to my chamber for my sword, but when I returned, I found her great bronzed doors already barred against me, and then I knew for certain that all of it, including this final scene, had been planned. Many things seemed suddenly explained: her coldness, her cruelty, even her rage and revulsion on the night I had first taken her hard against the table, making her pregnant with our son. And with that — knowing even before I knew — I thought of Tros and raced to his room, only to find it empty, my son and his nurse gone.

Half crazed with fear for his life, I ran back swiftly to the great hall, determined to force Atalante's doors, but as I moved to do so, a piercing cackle rent the air, and as the hair rose stiff along the ridge of my spine, I whirled and stopped, and saw that gnarled crone watching me from afar while she warmed her hands above the wreath of the fire. My only thought was to seize her and make her produce my son, and indeed, I would have done so — had already lunged forward, my sharp sword raised, my hard hand reaching for her throat — when she raised a single finger and uttered a cry so darkly piercing that it froze me to the core of my being.

"Raise not your hand to *me*," she screamed, her sharp tongue flickering like a snake's, "for I am Erigone the scorned one, high priestess of Eris, who always brings strife!"

Instantly, I drew back, for the true terror was on me, but even so, somehow, I found the strength to ask for my son.

"Fed to the wolves," she replied, "in the middle of the night, and Ida soon will whiten with his bones!"

I sank back, staggering into the pit of despair — knowing without knowing, seeing without seeing, that Tros, my own son, my only son, had been exposed, set out for the wolves and kites and cold maw of Boreas somewhere on the high slopes of Ida during the very hours in which his mother had unleashed our passions.

When I recovered enough to look up, loathsome Erigone had gone — where or when, I know not. Then, I think, knowing what I knew, I felt myself nothing more than a shade, and thought to end my suffering by the strength of my own right hand. But in the end, I did not. In the end, refusing Atalante her final victory, I rose from my knees, walked blankly into my quarters, took up my spear, and left the manor, heading down toward the Plain. It was a grim day and cold, gray beneath the low leaden clouds that were already blowing down the first spitting snows from the mountain fastness of Thrace, and I was already halfway to Besika Bay when I met a courier and learned that the Fourth Mysian War had commenced.

20

THE FOURTH WAR, as we called it, proved long and bitter. As with the previous war, I spent most of the fourth at sea, commanding a trim hull and fifty Teeth. I fought fiercely then, for in the hollow of my life, I lived utterly without hope, caring not how or when or where grim death might find me, and mighty was the power of my spear.

Throughout the conflict, the Shark pitted itself against a rebuilt Mysian fleet, a fleet constructed according to Greek designs. Owing to its speed, it was vicious in battle, and great grew the numbers of our dead. Even so, I was desperate for action, desperate to turn the tide, and often I thought of repeating my raid, but in each instance, my better judgment prevailed. The council, you see, threatened us all. Its clear aim was to curtail the power of the Shark, keep Polydamas in check, and prevent the unexpected rise of anyone else like the Victor of Cyme. Fearful of retribution against my men, I bowed to the laws of Ilium, sought battle at sea, and found it in sharp, bloody engagements that proved strategically inconclusive.

I was wounded many times, and during the second winter, I went down hard with an arrow through my thigh and remained down through nine moons, waiting for my wound to heal. And as the first Borean snows blew hard out of Thrace, I began my twenty-third year and for the first time felt myself growing war weary and old.

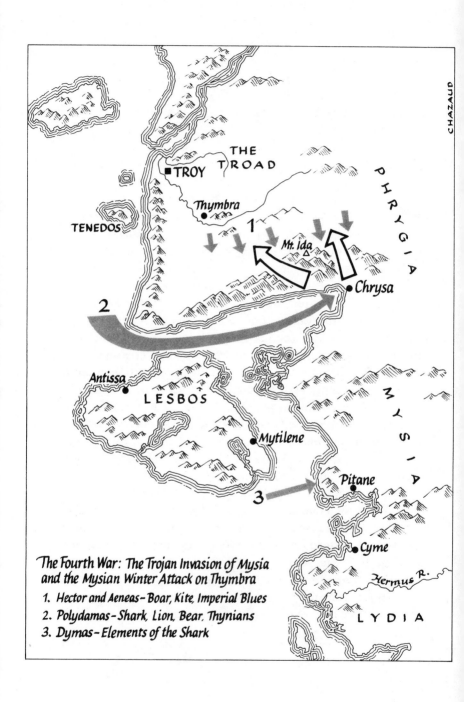

THE TROAD

■TROY

Thymbra

TENEDOS

1

Mt. Ida △

2

Chrysa

PHRYGIA

CHAZAUD

Antissa

LESBOS

Mytilene

3

Pitane

MYSIA

Cyme

Hermus R.

LYDIA

The Fourth War: The Trojan Invasion of Mysia
and the Mysian Winter Attack on Thymbra

1. Hector and Aeneas – Boar, Kite, Imperial Blues
2. Polydamas – Shark, Lion, Bear, Thynians
3. Dymas – Elements of the Shark

I thought much then of blue Abydus-by-the-sea, and of Pharos and my uncle, whose weathered brows I had not seen across many spans, and suddenly I longed to go home. As it seems now, I might have planted my spear on some forgotten mound and disappeared into oblivion, seeking nothing more glorious than an Abydian afternoon. Curiously, I gave no thought to my son, my wife, the Lady Ariadne, or even the high white towers of Troy, but only to Abydus and the long afternoons of my youth, when the brown leaves lay warm and deep across the earth. Such thoughts, I know, were prompted by my wound, but even so, for the first time I saw the potential of peace.

Ashore, the Fourth War became bitterly static. Across Ida, Skaiko and the queen's relations fought dull, unimaginative battles, and the cost in Trojan blood became alarming. First, the Eagle was decimated, then the Wolf and the Leopard, and finally the Bear, which had marched across country from Arisbe to be thrown piecemeal into the battle. So the war had gone, through two long seasons, and during the third, the Mustang had been thrown into the line, and a large portion of the Imperial Guard. And still, the Mysian front remained ravenous, sucking down hard Trojan strength with grinding force. Then, as the first light snows blanketed Ida, the two great armies disengaged, the Mysians at last withdrawing slowly over Gargaron while our own tired formations limped down toward Scamander. So it went, only this time the Mysians outsmarted Skaiko, and the result was catastrophic.

Always, with the coming of winter, the Mysians had withdrawn over Ida into warm quarters on the reverse slope, but this time they did not. Instead, they remained on the heights, waiting for our army to retire, and then, when our line formations were already in disarray, falling back on Thymbra, the entire Mysian army sprang from the heights like a pride of blood-maddened lions. The combined rear guard of the Eagle, Leopard, and Wolf was instantly overrun and annihilated to the last man. On our western flank, the Imperial Guard escaped the main assault, but even so, its rear guard was also hit hard, badly mauled, and scattered. Inland, to the east, the commander of the Mustang found his entire regiment cut off from the Trojan main body, and his response was nothing short of courageous. Refusing to surrender, he struck north, with little water and less food, into the frozen fastness of Dardania. Nine days later, he brought his entire command into the outskirts of Sataspes, and there, with utter contempt for the consequences, he threw open the warehouses and fed his starving warriors on royal provisions.

In the interval, the might of Troy had fallen back on Thymbra, and there, finally, Skaiko organized an effective defense and stopped the Mysians. It was the kind of war at which Skaiko had always been best; to his credit, he performed this single feat with hardheaded competence, and within five days, the Mysian offensive was brought to a halt. Then, leading a counterattack, Skaiko was killed, and the front froze, no more than seven leagues from Troy.

Like flashing thunder when it fires the forests on Ida, the Mysian offensive shocked and terrified Ilium, and then things underwent a swift change. I remember this time vividly, for one morning I was summoned to the citadel, and there, I found Pharos and my uncle, wearing armor and studying an ox-hide chart.

Greetings were warm but swift. My uncle, I remember, seemed shocked by the sight of me — taken aback, he said, by how much I had grown to resemble my father. He intended to say more, but at that moment Polydamas arrived, and my uncle became serious. "We had best begin," he said, giving me a quick look of dismissal.

"Dymas stays," my lord said quickly. "He commands a contingent; if he is to take the risk, he must know the whole of it."

To my amazement, my uncle clapped a hand over my shoulder in a gesture of approval.

"It is done," said Pharos, stepping forward as though taking command. "Like adders, the Mysians have come from beneath their rock; this time we must sever their heads. All Troy is in shock, so all reserves are brought to readiness. Before nightfall, the fleet will come down from Dardanos, bringing the Lion from Percote, the Bear from Arisbe, and one thousand spears of top-knotted infantry commanded by Rhesus, King of Thrace. At last, the great raid goes forward, and you, Polydamas, will command a field army."

Polydamas said nothing, but across his face I detected a hardening resolve, and then I saw a trace of reservation.

"Where?" he asked.

With level gaze, Pharos looked him straight in the eye. "At sea," he said flatly. "The Shark will lead the assault. It was the best that we could do."

For several seconds, no one spoke.

"Hector commands, then?"

"The entire army, yes," my uncle said, "but not the raid. The raid is the key."

"There was no other way," said Pharos. "The Military Council remains under the queen's influence, four to three, even with the Mysians at the gates. Even so, digestion may not prove as sour as you think. In return for his unanimous election to command, Hector has raised you and Aeneas to leading subordinate roles — you at sea, Aeneas at Thymbra — and the raid goes forward as planned."

"The bargain is good," my uncle charged. "It gives you authority over all individual formations, even the Boar and the guard."

"*At sea,*" Pharos said, arching a clear eye in Polydamas' direction.

"Still," my uncle said, "Hector is no fool. He has neither your resourcefulness nor your strategic intuition, but he is more aggressive than Skaiko and is eager to end this war."

"Invade," Pharos ordered, "and in the same hour that you put Chrysa to the torch, Hector's army will move to your support."

I knew then that the days of defense had ended. Hector ap-proved not only of Polydamas' plan but also of an addition that had been proposed by Antenor and, I think, Pharos and my uncle, who did not allow their hands to be seen. Their intention was this: within seven days, the Shark, followed by the Lion, Bear, and topknotted Thynian infantry, would race in on the morning tide to strike and capture Chrysa, seizing the granaries and cutting off all supplies to the exposed Mysian army that was fighting before Thymbra. Meanwhile, the Boar, the Kite, and the Imperial Blues were already on the march, already moving up hidden trails into concealed positions behind Thymbra. There they would remain — hidden, fresh, and ready — until the enemy's starving army began to fall back; then Hector, calling on Aeneas, would pass these fresh regiments through the tired units on the line, sound the ram's horn, and send the Boar, Kite, and Blues howling up Ida in pursuit of the retreating enemy, and great would be our victory.

"By the time they go over to retreat," Pharos said flatly, "they will be so weak with hunger that we will find them easy prey."

"We shall cut them to pieces!" exclaimed my uncle.

What, I wanted to know, of the Mysian garrison at Pitane, which was known to be large? "Will it not march north, against our flank?"

"Certainly the Mysians will try," said Polydamas, "but if you are sharp, Dymas, they will not succeed, for it is my intention that your command — including the companies of Agelaos, Orthaios, and old Tarsos — may so distract them that you will pin them down and hold them in place during the critical hours of our attack. My suggestion is that you intrude yourself between Chrysa and Pitane, and there use whatever tactics you think best."

The assault went exactly as my lords had planned it, on a cold winter's morning, on the strength of a flooding tide, and sharp were the Teeth of the Shark as they leapt to the beach and raced into Chrysa. Caught by surprise, the Mysians reeled, losing more than five hundred dead and as many wounded during the first daylight minutes. Then, as the enemy tried to regroup for defense, the Bear and Lion poured suddenly ashore, and the Mysian line was completely overrun. Rhesus' infantry had been held in reserve, but in good time they too rushed ashore and began rolling up the slopes of Ida, capturing supply trains and granaries and one party of Mysians after another, whose combined function had been to organize logistic support for the hard Mysian army before Thymbra. This supply network proved so vast and so well manned that in the end the Lion also had to be committed in order to dismantle it. Meanwhile, the Shark, the Bear's Paws, and the Lion's Teeth spread south and east to cover Chrysa's inland approaches. In time, all formations saw fierce fighting, and even with Pharos and my uncle to help him, Polydamas was hard pressed, for the Mysian response was stronger than anyone had anticipated and much better organized. Even so, my lord held his ground, winning a considerable victory.

All of this, I heard later from Pharos, Polydamas, and my uncle, for know you, all of you, that I was not present at Chrysa, neither for the assault nor for my lord's prolonged battle to hold the city while destroying the Mysian supply net. Instead, I was fighting for my life north of Pitane.

21

No, we came up from the beach running hard, running inland, running deep into the night, five hundred spears at the ready. The Whales had set us ashore north of Pitane, withdrawing rapidly under cover of darkness, leaving us isolated and alone on the barren Mysian coast, and the moment they departed, we sprinted inland, sounding neither war cry nor battle hymn, racing like antelope for the surrounding cover of the hills, and great was the strength of our wind.

We bumped Pitane shortly before dawn, striking like thunder, delivering a single sharp bolt into the city's rim. We went in from the northwest, masking our numbers beneath the dark of the moon, and caught two companies of the Mysian guard completely by surprise. My men, all fierce hard warriors of Troy, had even removed their sandals, moving silently ahead over the frozen stubble of the fields like so many floating ghosts. Suddenly watch fires appeared in the distance, and around them, stamping their feet to ward off the chill, oblivious of our approach, some two hundred Mysians, the matted tangles of their hair plainly visible against the leaping glow of the firelight. I sounded the signal with my horn, and five hundred Trojan javelins ripped instantly into the air; within seconds, the night was pierced by screams as each bronze blade found its mark. We hurtled forward, finishing the job with our swords, and poured into the outskirts of the city, shouting the Trojan war cry, spreading fire, tumult, and confusion, and killing any Mysian male who dared to appear in the street.

Sharp that night were the Shark's Teeth and mighty the force of their blow, but like the sizzle of lightning when it first flashes bright, then disappears, we struck hard, raining fire and fierce destruction into Pitane and then withdrew, retreating rapidly down the axis of our advance. We remained in Pitane no longer than a few quick minutes, killing whatever crossed our path, firing storage compounds, rooftops, and granaries enough to light up the sky, and then, having made only a shallow penetration into the city, we withdrew, running for our lives, for it did not take long before the Mysians recovered from their shock, and when they did, whole battalions of them took to the field, dogging us in blood-hungry packs. Had I waited a moment longer, had I so much as hesitated once, we might not have survived. Within the hour, you see, fully three thousand enraged Mysians had joined the pursuit, and these were battle-hard veterans, not militia, and bright were the blades of their spears.

With the dawn, gray Borean sleet blew down hard from the mountains to the north, but even before that first faint light made the sleet visible, I had already effected our escape. Feinting to-ward the sea, I ran my command north, putting as much distance as I could between ourselves and our Mysian pursuers, and then, mere minutes before the dawn broke, I altered our line of retreat, swinging east, running my entire battalion up a narrow defile, Agelaos and Orthaios leading the pack while Tarsos brought up the rear, and from that moment on, we hastened east under cover of the draw, distancing ourselves from the sea and the low range of hills from which we had first attacked Pitane.

Our pursuers were completely taken in by my maneuver. Four, perhaps five thousand yards behind us, charging through the last vestiges of night into a dim, gray dawn, a bitter sleet blowing sharp into their eyes, they missed our turn and raced on toward the sea, expecting to run us down and slaughter us on the beach before we could launch our ships and escape across the wave path. They had no way of knowing that our high-beaked hulls were already long gone, far out to sea; and from a distance, near the mouth of the defile where I had gone to ground in order to watch them pass, I had no difficulty in counting their numbers or imagining their enraged frustration when they broke through the hills to find the beach empty, their prey escaped. When the thunder of their footfalls finally became silent, I rose from concealment, took my bearings on the fires in Pitane, and hastened east to rejoin my command.

Before noon, the sleet turned to snow, the wind died, and the earth became blanketed by a thick wet white. We went to ground, then, sheltering on a hillside beneath the snow-laden bows of the pines, and there, wrapped in our sea cloaks, making a cold meal on dried fish and barley cakes, we watched with shivering satisfaction as the leaden clouds slowly buried our trail.

"We are safe," Agelaos said.

"For a while," said Tarsos, sharpening his blade on the flat of a stone.

"Until tonight," I said, "for tonight we must strike again, east of Pitane, somewhere near the road from Cyme. That is the plan; that is what my lord expects. In the morning, before Aurora blushes, he assaults Chrysa with five thousand men. We must hold in place as many Mysians as possible, here, around Pitane, and prevent their moving north to attack his flank. See to the men. Give them what food you can, and insofar as conditions permit, rest them. This is going to be a long campaign."

With the coming of twilight, I uttered a single order and assembled the command. Unrested save for a few nodding moments snatched beneath the trees, hungry, stiff with cold, all my fine brave warriors hobbled from concealment like so many old men, formed into companies, and marched off, dragging their feet through the snow. By that time, the storm had ended, the sky had cleared, and bright stars twinkled in the sky. Not long after, I remember, the snow on the ground froze into a thin, hard crust that crackled sharply with each passing footfall. After a mile, the blood in our bodies had warmed, and after we had covered two miles, the strength in our limbs returned. Then I ordered the men to run, and like hooded owls gliding over the snow pack beneath a bright night sky, they flew through the night, their sea capes fluttering like wings, the points of their spears as sharp as talons.

In the early morning, less than a league east of Pitane, we cut the main road from Cyme and went into ambush, waiting for whatever might come our way. The morning chill, I remember, was bitter beyond despair, and within a short span, all of us were shivering so hard beneath our sea cloaks that the combined chatter of our teeth resembled the noise made by a cloud of cicadas when it settles in trees. That is when I knew that the ambush could not succeed, and that is when I moved.

"Not long remains before Aurora blushes," I said to Tarsos, Agelaos, and Orthaios, summoned by my command. "To remain here is to give ourselves away by the mere clatter of our jaws. Get the men up, and get them running, south by east. We are going over to the attack."

I had no alternative, you see. My battalion had not the strength to strike a Mysian barracks or assault again into the alerted outskirts of Pitane, but strike we must if we were to threaten Pitane, for our objective was to alarm the Mysian king and draw his warriors into the chase. I had hoped to ambush a supply convoy or a Mysian column, there on the road, but when no targets presented themselves, I was forced to seize the initiative in another way, and I did, forming a three-company front and sweeping south along both sides of the road, burning everything in my path. Farms went up that morning, and hamlets, and a stone way station where royal clerks and carriers attempted a sharp but brief defense, and when lordly Helios finally took to the sky, he could mark our progress by the high pillars of smoke that thickened in our wake.

With the coming of daylight, my every sense quickened, for I knew that we were vulnerable, alone, exposed, deep in Mysian territory. We had taken a terrible risk in order to effect a draw, and within that first bitterly cold hour, my worst fears were realized when we were suddenly brought to battle and had to fight for our lives. The blow, when it fell, was not entirely unexpected, for as early as sunrise, far out beyond our flanks, I had seen small parties of Mysian militia racing south across the snow's frozen crust, clearly trying to get out in front of us. Pursuing them would have been pointless, for they seemed few in number and so far distant as to be mere specks on the horizon; yet the moment I saw them, I knew that they might come together, somewhere in the grim distance, and make a concentrated attempt to block our progress. Had it not been for our fight at the way station, they might never have gotten around us, but the brief delay caused us by the station's defenders gave those small parties of militia an opportunity, and in short, they seized it. Looking back, I suppose I should have bypassed the station, leaving clerks and carriers alone, but short of food, we made what I considered a necessary assault, coming away with few wounds but with enough barley meal for two days' rations. And in that small span, I exposed my command to attack.

No more than a league beyond the way station, marching hard down the road toward Cyme, we struck a wood and, without once slackening our pace, emerged to find ourselves confronted by the enemy. Clearly, during our delay, the Mysians on our flanks had moved around us, concentrating a scratch battalion of militia hard in our path. They were assembled on the windswept crest of a rise, and in the instant, shouting his war cry, the enemy commander filled the air with his spears. Then, like hungry winter wolves on the scent of a deer, the entire pack came hurtling toward us, screaming for our blood, their broad bronze axes whirling above their heads. They were a ragged lot without form, discipline, or restraint, and the warrior who commanded them must have been woefully inexperienced or well past his prime, for he had launched his attack too soon, from too great a distance, and most of his spears fell short. Even so, some found their mark, and good men went down hard, pouring bright Trojan blood over the snow.

Silent, motionless, I held my Teeth at the ready, waiting for the enemy to close, and then, when they had halved the distance between us, filling my lungs with air, I barked *"Slings!"* Instantly, all my ready men planted their spears in the snow, and within a heartbeat, the air above our heads whirled with the whistle of thongs. Mindless in their rage, heedless of the danger, utterly fearless, the Mysians raced forward, their matted hair streaming backward into the wind, the whites of their eyes growing ever larger, and when they closed to within forty paces, I roared the sharp order to let fly, and my men released a hail of flint-sharp stones.

The impact was devastating. Along the Mysian line, throughout their entire pack, whole clumps of warriors dropped their weapons and fell, bright blood gushing from their wounds. Howls of Mysian rage became agonized screams as fully half their number fell to their knees or went over dead onto the glittering surface of the snow. At short range, with a single deadly blow, we had shattered their attack, and we went instantly in for the kill, leaping forward from the edge of the wood, pulling up our spears as we ran, and casting them with Trojan might. Then was much killing, and within seconds, the new-frozen snow ran bright with Mysian blood. Some few, I think, escaped, dropping their arms and running for their lives in whatever direction they could, but the main body we destroyed, littering the field with some four hundred of their dead and not a few of our own.

But even before the slaughter was complete, I broke off the action, sounded a recall with the ram's horn, and ordered our withdrawal. Clearly, my morning assault had run its course, the Mysians had been drawn, and, without wanting it, I had stumbled into a battle, coming away with a victory that I owed largely to the enemy's incompetence. Sensing danger on every side, I knew that it was time to leave the road, and did, running my entire command north toward the distant hills. Later that afternoon, I knew my instincts had been right, for while reconnoitering to our rear, I discovered that hard companies of the Mysian Ram were hot in pursuit from Pitane, while to the east, from somewhere along the road to Cyme, battalions of the Mysian Cat were on the march, moving to support the Ram. I had removed from the road in good time, but the Mysians were coming on fast, and, returning to my men, I ran them north, making for the shelter of the hills.

By that time, I felt certain that my lord had made his assault, that Chrysa was in Trojan hands, and up to a point, I had achieved my objective, dealing the enemy two successive blows, raising the alarm, and drawing two large formations away from their bases and into the field, where they would be hard to locate and unavailable to reinforce Chrysa. The trick now would be to elude them and remain alive, and so we ran, for two nights and days, first north into the hills and then east along the ridge crests in the direction of Phrygia, remaining well out in front of our pursuers but leaving them a clear trail while drawing them farther and farther away from the road to Chrysa. The Mysian hills were bitter cold, and Boreas blew sleet constantly into our eyes, but we endured and ran on, for Polydamas and for Troy, like the fox before the hounds. And on the third eve, hard by the Phrygian border, I attacked a way station, replenished my men, and struck south, striking hard into the Mysian plain. For hour after hour, we burned every farm and hamlet through which we passed, and at sunrise I gathered my men.

"You must run now," I commanded, "as you have never run before. As soon as Aurora blushes, the Ram and the Cat will see these fires and come hurtling from the hills, ravenous for our bones. While the Mysians lunge south, I intend to slip west, get on their flank, and withdraw toward the northern passes. Pour your libations here and make your peace with the gods, for we go now to block the way into Chrysa, and hard will be the hours of our war."

We were away, then, like shades, skimming the snow field with the strength of our wind. Soon we struck a watercourse, and instantly I ordered the men in, urging them forward, masking our line of advance beneath the swirling surface of the stream. The water was bitter cold, but I kept my warriors to the task, driving them mercilessly forward, and after an hour, far downstream, I brought them ashore across a windswept ledge and started them north through the scrub shelter of a wood.

By midmorning, we struck the foothills, and there, for the first time, I gave the men pause, turning back myself to reconnoiter. Carefully I made my way to the top of a ridge, concealed myself in the branches of an oak, and surveyed the plain. With the coming of dawn, Boreas had retired, the sleet had died, and the bleak surface of the earth lay white and still beneath low, gray clouds; but far to the south down the axis of our advance, those clouds were darker yet, blackened by the fires in our wake. And in the grim distance, far to the east and packed closely, the massed Mysian regiment of the Cat moved rapidly away from us in the direction of Pitane, with the Ram not far behind. With the aid of the Fates, I had succeeded again in throwing the enemy from our track, and without another second's delay, I plunged from the ridge and put my command in motion.

We were two days working north, and famine dogged our march. No way stations there or farms or hamlets, only a deep snow that often rose to our knees in the barren wilderness of those cold Mysian crags. In the end, hunger ground hard in the bellies of my men, and we survived on boiled acorns and what little wild game we were able to bring down with our slings. And on the third morning, after a long night's march, we struck the road just below the southern entrance to the pass and saw hard evidence of the passage of marching men. Without doubt, some Mysian units had gotten through, marching toward Chrysa to reinforce their men, but I was confident that we had drawn off much of the main Mysian might about Pitane and knew in my bones that we could never have drawn them all. Immediately, I put my scouts into the mouth of the pass, setting my commanders to conduct a reconnaissance, and the moment they returned, I was on my feet.

"Give me your estimates," I charged, drawing all three into immediate council.

"Two regiments through the main pass," Tarsos said bluntly.

"One company by the western trail," said Orthaios. "We counted their fire pits."

"Militia," Agelaos added, "wearing sandals."

"Not in the main pass," said Tarsos, his gaunt jaw set hard. "Those were regulars, running fast and leaving bare footprints. Their tracks froze hard two days past. By now, they must be already engaged before Chrysa."

"And the militia?" said Agelaos.

"A rear guard," I said, drawing my own conclusion, "to hold the pass in case those regulars are forced into retreat. Get up there and knock them out. Don't kill them all; I want some of them to escape north. I want those main-line regiments attacking Polydamas to think that these passes are closed, to think that they have the enemy at their backs. They have no way of measuring our strength, and the threat we pose will shake them; it may give Polydamas the edge."

Agelaos was up on the instant and away, and well before mid-morning he had carried out my instructions, falling hard on the enemy from the rear, catching them by surprise, killing more than one hundred of their number where they warmed themselves about their fires, and driving the remainder — some thirty rag-clad survivors — down onto the plain, where his feigned pursuit sent them running for their lives in the direction of Chrysa.

In the process, he captured some food — barley meal and a few salted fish, no more than enough for half a ration between two men — and on this, when he returned, we feasted like kings and gloried in the hour of his victory.

Throughout the remainder of that morning, I rested my men, but following the meal, during the same hour in which Helios passed his zenith, I assembled my spears, outlined our grim task, and assigned my dispositions. Then, with perfect silence, all my weary men marched forward into the pass to take up their positions. We were worn by that time and thin, for we had marched hard on short rations, but man for man, I would have matched the four hundred warriors I had left with any for the strength of their resolve, and on that last gray afternoon above Pitane, they played their parts well and made themselves into an army.

We had not long to wait for the blow that I knew must fall, and fall it did during the late afternoon. Near the mouth of the pass, high up beneath the lip of a crag, I watched them approach at a fast pace, company after company, battalion after battalion of the quick-moving Mysian Ram. Knowing that they must come, knowing that they would, I had remained motionless throughout the afternoon, shivering beneath the cold hand of Boreas, watching, waiting, focusing all of my concentration on a distant clearing in the direction of Pitane. There, I knew, they must come down from a hillside, break from beneath the cover of the pines, and cross a frozen ford before beginning their long climb into the pass; and so they did, never once slackening their pace, and there, for the first time, I saw them, the sharp points of their spears glinting dully above the ox-hide rounds of their shields. They marched in column, six men abreast, two companies to a battalion, five battalions to the regiment, more than two thousand warriors coming on fast, without flankers and without scouts, feeling themselves entirely secure in the depths of their native land.

That is when I was certain that they were no longer looking for us, that they had indeed given up the chase. Somewhere south in the direction of Pitane, three, four, or five leagues distant, elements of the Cat must have taken responsibility for the hunt and still been looking for us, but the Ram, coming on hard, was clearly marching to war, hurrying north to relieve Chrysa, and the speed of their pace became the instrument of their undoing, for in their haste they had made no provision for dealing with the unexpected.

When I had at last seen the Ram across the frozen surfaces of the ford and knew them to be coming on hard up the road toward the pass, I backed away from my place on the crag, came quickly to my feet, and raised high my pennant of command. Behind me, some two hundred feet below, all of my hard-eyed warriors concealed themselves instantly along the sloping walls of the pass, and there, behind logs, boulders, and trees, wrapped in their sailcloth cloaks, blending with the snow on both sides of the road, they waited, spears at the ready, swords within easy reach.

Then felt I like a kite or hawk or swift-winged eagle in the last moment before it stoops to strike its prey. Below, all was silent, white, still, but in the distance, beyond the mouth of the pass, we began to hear the first, faint sounds of the Mysian war hymn as the leading battalion approached the final turn that led steeply into the gorge. We waited, then, as their chant became louder and louder, until suddenly, the head of the enemy column began snaking into the pass. Below, showing perfect discipline, all of my men remained still and silent as rank after rank of tramping Mysians passed rapidly between them. And when the tail of the column finally entered the pass, I brought down my pennant hard, and on the ground below, Tarsos sounded the ram's horn, and four hundred Trojans broke instantly from cover, making the cold air shriek with the whistle of their spears.

Not all of the enemy went down with that first bold cast, but most did, with bright Trojan bronze penetrating their necks or chests or thighs, and in the last moment before we rushed in to annihilate them, their howls of enraged surprise melted into a single, agonized moan. Then my warriors were in amongst them, hacking and slashing with fury, killing score after score of skin-clad Mysian warriors. Some, who had not been struck down by the first cast, might have organized for a fight, but so swift had been the shock of our blow that all became unmanned, and none got away. To this day, I remember the steam rising from their bodies, filling the late afternoon air with a mist so grisly that it seemed to hover above the floor of the pass like a battalion of shades. When I finally sounded the recall and my warriors leapt to retrieve their spears, returning rapidly to concealment, I estimated nearly four hundred Mysian dead lying hard on the floor of the gorge.

Without fully expecting it, I had brought off, I think — the perfect ambush. Had our cast been made against an isolated company or a single battalion, we would have won, certainly, a great victory; but by attacking the lead element of a regiment, I had merely given away my position and lost forever the element of surprise, and when the second battalion of the Ram pressed into the pass, they were armed to the teeth, forewarned and ready, and we had to fight for our lives in order to hold them at bay.

From my perch on the crag, I watched the engagement develop, directing my men by means of runners, my pennant, and coded blasts of the ram's horn, and in time, I brought up twenty of my men, who made excellent use of their slings, causing the Mysian front rank to retire from the narrow confines of the pass on three successive occasions; but before nightfall, the Ram commander brought forward his archers, and in short order they drove us from our perch and down onto the floor below, and there, across the narrow front, we fought toe to toe with bitter Mysian infantry, pitting spear against spear, holding our ground but losing man after man as the bodies piled up, Mysian and Trojan alike. And as twilight became dark night, the Mysians pulled back, unbeaten and hard, leaving us still in possession of the pass.

"My lord," advised Tarsos as we bound our wounds, "we cannot continue to meet them head to head. We have not the depth. In the morning, they will assault again, meeting us man for man, and eventually overrun us with the strength of their numbers. We must either retire or prepare ourselves to die."

He was right, of course, a veteran of long experience, and he spoke true. With the ambush and throughout the late afternoon, we had struck the Ram hard, killing a quarter of its number, but we had not fought without cost, and our strength — such as it was — numbered fewer than three hundred spears, and not one amongst us moved without his wounds. With three quarters of the Ram remaining intact, we were beaten.

"Polydamas asked me for six good days," I said bitterly, "and we have given him seven. Get the men on their feet and start them moving."

Three days later, footsore and weary, gaunt with hunger, we limped into the outskirts of Chrysa and made contact with the Bear. For us, the Mysian Wars were done.

The enemy collapsed, not with a war cry but with something like a groan. Their army, scattered and starving, limped down from Ida, leaving half its number dead across the frozen slopes. Inland, some few battles remained to be fought with isolated formations like the Ram and the Cat, but within two weeks, all resistance had collapsed, and in a cave outside Pitane, the Blues captured the Mysian king and put an end to his reign. Thus, the Mysian Wars ended, and total was the enemy's defeat.

EPILOGUE

Look about you, my lords. The high white towers of Troy are destroyed, the Plain is in ruins, and all the fine brave Trojans are dead . . . save one. You have been ten years at it. Do you not long to go home, to dandle your sons on your knees, to make love to your wives, to make a stop finally and rest in the warm Greek sun? You do; I can see it in your eyes. Now that the war ends, now that Ilium is ash, lordly Agamemnon longs again to return to Mycenae and sleep with his loving queen, and the same holds true for you, Nestor, and you, Odysseus, and you, and you, and you. And so, once, did I.

With the wars ended, with the Mysians destroyed, I wanted nothing more than to return to my home in blue Abydus-by-the-sea. I had grown war weary by that time, feeling old, even to the marrow of my bones. In truth, I wanted nothing more than release. But the Shark did not move, and slowly, days became weeks, and weeks became months, and, riding the west wind, spring blew in, covering the brown Mysian plain with sunflowers and a kind of thistle that bursts purple before the breeze. Meanwhile, the Boar, the Kite, and the Blues returned to Troy, marching up over Gargaron, their war hymns rising through the pines. Meanwhile, diplomatists consolidated our position, establishing a Trojan governor in Mysia with an astute staff. The Shark trained alongside the Bear, the Lion, and topknotted Thracians, all four regiments remaining in place as an army of occupation. And then, one bright summer's day, Pharos drew me aside from my men, who were taking their noonday meal beneath a long row of sunflowers.

"It has been a long war," he said as the two of us went to ground in the shadow of a milestone.

"That is so," I said, propping my spear against the stone, "and I am ready to go home. The two of us should hunt again in the Abydian hills."

Out across the plain, dust swirls soared above the fields, scattering tiny particles like showers of gold. There, for a moment, both of us searched the sky, but neither of us spoke. In the distance, above a barley field, a butterfly fluttered its wings, but then I blinked, and when I looked again, the butterfly had become an eagle, stooping in pursuit of its prey.

Pharos saw it too but turned away, casting his grim gaze toward the sea. "I too would like to walk the path of peace," he said wearily, "but we are not to have the chance. The Shark sails tonight, to assault the Argive stronghold on Scyros, and mighty must be the strength of our blow."

In shock, I looked not toward the open sea but toward my men. Beneath the drooping sunflowers, they broke their bread in silence, but red were the scars that freshly colored their limbs.

"Why must we fight again so soon?" I demanded.

"The situation demands it," Pharos said quietly, lifting a handful of dust and tossing it onto the wind. "Because we are warriors. Think why the Trojans honor us, Dymas, sending us the best joints of meat, the brightest wine, and the largest measure of salt. Do not these marks of respect oblige us to fling ourselves into battle, in the van? That is our code, boy; that is who we are. I tell you, if now — after this long bitter war — you and I could go home and rest secure, I should never again take my place in the line nor send you forward onto the field. But such is not our way, and when reason fails, we may know the hour by the fires in the sky. Then, death comes for all men; therefore we must go, either to win immortality for ourselves or to yield it to others, and there's an end."

"But we have won," I said. "What in our situation demands it? Where has reason failed?"

"The Achaian Greeks are coiled like an adder," Pharos said, gazing toward the sea, "and these Mysian Wars have already bled us white. Had we been listened to — your father, your uncle, and I — we could have put down these Mysian dogs during the First War. Instead, we fought stupidly — having no choice, because of the queen's influence and Skaiko's designs — and all the while, we should have been repulsing the Greeks, who have made deep thrusts into lands that should obey us. Do you not know that the Fourth War was instigated by the Greeks and directed by several of their generals?"

I did not and said so.

"It was Greeks who helped the Mysians to plan their winter offensive," he said quietly, "and Greek ships that supplied the grain. Even more than the Mysians, the Argive Greeks covet Troy's Plain, and sooner or later they mean to wrest it from us by force, so make no mistake, we are greatly threatened, and this adder is most dangerously fanged."

"We go then to make a punitive strike." I groaned.

"Punitive and pre-emptive," Pharos said, "for the Greek has already prepared his war. For years, the Eyes of the Shark have been closely fixed on Scyros, and what they have seen eliminates all doubt. Scyros has become an immense base, with enough granaries and armories to supply three hundred hulls and up-wards of fifteen thousand spears. Only an attack on Troy could warrant such preparation. If they intended to strike Egypt, they would have marshaled their forces on Crete."

As he went on, pouring out his words, the issue became as clear as the first spring melt.

"And there is one other thing," he said finally, and in the

instant, I saw beads of sweat burst from his forehead. "Priam sends an ambassador to Greece, to the sons of Atreus, to Agamemnon of Mycenae and Menelaus of Sparta. It is to them that our ambassador must go, bearing our terms for treaty, terms to be presented in the wake of our devastating blow to Scyros. Strongly urged, carefully presented, we might yet bring them to heel, but — " And there, suddenly, he broke off.

"What?" I urged.

"The wife of red-haired Menelaus," he said grimly, "lovely Helen, daughter of Zeus, is reputed to be the most staggering beauty in the wide world."

"*Who goes?*" I cried, seized instantly by a premonition of disaster.

"Hecuba's newfound son," said Pharos, his gray brow coming awash with sweat. "Paris of Troy, in whom both Priam and his queen take obsessive joy."

He said no more then, nor did I, and after a long, despondent silence, we rose to our feet beside the milestone, took up our spears, and began our march to the sea, while all my fine bronzed warriors trailed out behind like so many handfuls of dust thrown carelessly onto the wind. And the rest you know.

Names

Places

*A Note on
Military Organization
and the Trojan Order
of Battle*

NAMES

ACAMAS. A Thracian commander assigned to Polydamas for the raid on Scyros

THE ACHAIANS, ARGIVES, DANAANS. Homer's names for the different peoples who unite to fight against Troy (Ilium). The word *Greek* is not used by Homer.

AENEAS. The son of Anchises and the goddess Aphrodite, he is also Hector's cousin and field commander of the Kite. Following Hector's appointment to supreme army command in the Fourth Mysian War, Aeneas becomes field commander of the Boar, Kite, and Imperial Blues.

AEOLUS. The Keeper of the Winds

AGAMEMNON. The King of Mycenae and supreme commander of the Greek expedition against Troy. Agamemnon is overlord of the Argives.

AGELAOS. Boyhood companion of Dymas. Later, he is Dymas' subordinate in the Shark.

AGENOR. An elder of Troy

AGIAS. An ancient singer who remembers the exploits of warriors

ALEXANDROS (PARIS). The youngest son of Priam and Hecuba, originally exposed on Mount Ida and raised humbly; he becomes the abductor of Helen and is the source of much of Troy's trouble.

ANCHISES. Cousin to Priam, he is the father of Aeneas.

ANTENOR. An elder of Troy, he was a boyhood companion to Priam and eventually became the leader of the Grand Council. Although he has lost control of the council, he continues to be a major political force in Troy.

On military matters, he is aligned with Pharos in opposition to Priam's military policy. Throughout his career, he is a proponent of naval warfare. He is also the father of many sons, including Tyro, and one daughter, Ariadne. He is married to the Lady Dia.

ANTIPHATES. A Trojan warrior who commands the Shark's Tail

ANTIPHOS. A son of Priam and Hecuba. He commands a battalion of the Imperial Guard.

APHLASTON. A warrior of the Shark who comes from Abydus

APHRODITE. The daughter of Zeus and Dione, she is the goddess of love and beauty.

APOLLO. Variously the god of music, poetry, arts, medicine, and prophesy. Falling in love with Cassandra, he grants her the gift of divine sight, only to find himself rejected by her. His revenge is to make certain that no one believes her when she foretells the truth. When death comes by disease, the death is attributed to the penetration of Apollo's arrows; Apollo is then called Smintheus. He is the son of Zeus and Leto.

ARES. The god of war

ARIADNE. Daughter of Antenor and Dia

ARTEMIS. Goddess of the moon, the hunt, and chastity

ASIUS. Son of Hyrtaeus, he commands the Lion of Percote

ASSARACUS. Son of Tros, he is brother to Ilus and Ganymede and grandfather of Aeneas.

ATALANTE. One of the daughters of Priam and Hecuba

ATHENE. Having sprung fully formed from the forehead of her father, Zeus, she is the goddess of wisdom.

ATREUS. The father of Agamemnon and Menelaus

AURORA. The goddess of the dawn, she is wife to Tithonus and mother of Memnon, the leader of the Ethiopians, who come to Troy's aid late in the Trojan War.

BOREAS. The north wind

CASSANDRA. A daughter of Priam and Hecuba, she has the divine gift of foresight but bears the curse, bestowed by Apollo, of having no one believe her prophecies.

CEAS. Lord of the Cicones

CHALEDON. A warrior in the Shark who comes from Arisbe

CHARON. The boatman who ferries dead souls across the river Lethe in Hades. The dead are buried with a coin in their mouths in order to pay Charon for their passages.

THE CICONES. The Trojan allies who live in western Thrace beneath the shadow of Mount Ismarus

CLYTIUS. A son of Laomedon and brother to Priam

COLOPHON. A Trojan warrior of the Shark who rises to command a battalion of the Shark's Teeth

CRONOS. Father of Zeus and Hera. He is married to Rhea.

DARDANIANS. The Trojan outlanders who inhabit the northwestern Troad

DARDANOS. A son of Zeus and ancestor of the House of Priam

DIA. Wife of Lord Antenor. Niece to Pharos the Gray

DYMAS. Son of Kalitor, a Trojan warrior

ERICHTHONIUS. Son of Dardanos and father of the first Tros

ERIGONE. High priestess of Eris, goddess of strife

ERIS. The goddess of strife

THE ETHIOPIANS. The people who live at the ends of the world. During the Trojan War, they are Troy's allies.

THE FATES. The three goddesses who determine man's fate by spinning, measuring, and cutting his thread. Clotho spins, Lachesis measures, and Atropos severs the string.

GAIA. The Earth Mother

GANYMEDE. Son of Tros. Prized by Zeus, he is made cupbearer to the gods.

THE HATTI. The Hittites, who rule in central Anatolia. Phrygia falls into their sphere of influence.

HECTOR. A son of Priam and Hecuba, he commands the Boar and is later made field commander of a Trojan army in the Fourth Mysian War.

HECUBA. Daughter of Dymas and Eunoë, she is the wife of Priam and mother of Hector, Alexandros, Cassandra, Atalante, and others. She pursues her self-serving aims for Troy, seeking to promote her family and power at the expense of her enemies.

HELEN. Daughter of Zeus and Leda, Helen is the most beautiful woman in the world. Choosing from among many suitors to marry Menelaus, son of Atreus and younger brother of Agamemnon, she becomes Queen of Sparta. Paris abducts her from Sparta, an act of wife rape that infuriates all of the Argive kings, who have sworn to protect her.

HELENUS. A son of Priam and Hecuba, he is thought to have divine vision.

HELIOS. God of the sun

HERA. Queen of the gods, she is wife and sister to Zeus.

HERMES (THE GUIDE). Messenger of the gods, Hermes also guides dead souls to Hades.

HICETAON. Son of Laomedon and brother to Priam

THE HITTITES (THE HATTI). Lords of Hattusas, they rule a vast empire in the east, in the area known today as central Anatolia.

IASTROS. A Thynian warrior, assigned to the Shark, who is killed on Scyros

IDOMENEUS. The King of Crete whose hard sea warriors open the Trojan War by assaulting Tenedos

ILUS. (1) Son of Tros and father of Laomedon
(2) Son of Antiphos, grandson of Priam

KALITOR. Father of Dymas. After Pharos the Gray, Kalitor is the most accomplished general ever to command in the Trojan army. Because he is promoted ahead of Hecuba's relatives — Skaiko in particular — to command the Trojan armies in the northern wars, he earns Hecuba's enmity. Owing to his many victories, Kalitor is a trusted general who retains Priam's respect and support until late in his life. In time, because of the poison Hecuba pours into Priam's ears, the king grows to dislike Kalitor the man. Obscure rumors suggest that Kalitor and his brother are the bastard sons of Lampus, Priam's brother. The House of Priam denies all knowledge of such a connection, which might give Kalitor and

Dymas a claim to nobility. Kalitor falls to Mysian warriors during the First Mysian War.

KAMAX. A Trojan from Arisbe who is assigned to the Shark

KNOS. A cadet companion of Dymas' youth

KOPTION. A Trojan warrior who commands the Shark's Teeth

LAMPUS. A son of Laomedon, he is also Priam's brother and an elder of Troy. He is possibly Kalitor's father and Dymas' grandfather through an illegitimate liaison with a priestess of Artemis.

LAOCOÖN. A Trojan elder and a priest of Poseidon. He agrees on political and military policy with Antenor, Pharos, and Kalitor.

LAOMEDON. Son of Ilus, he enlarges the boundaries of Dardania and builds the towers of Ilium. He is the father of Tithonus, Priam, Lampus, Clytius, and Hicetaon.

MENELAUS. The injured husband of Helen, and King of Sparta. On his account, his older brother, Agamemnon, leads the Argive expedition against Troy.

MILAS. A Trojan warrior of the Shark

THE MYSIANS. From their towns and citadels south of Mount Ida, the barbarian Mysians look hungrily on the wealth of the Troad, coveting both Priam's lands and treasure. Stimulated by greed and blood lust, they eventually launch a series of attacks on the Troad that lead to four major wars that last more than a score of years. Although Priam's wish is to keep the peace with the Mysians, he is drawn time and again into costly battle with them, and Trojan military strength is sorely weakened. To the west, the Greeks watch and wait, lending secret aid to the Mysians as they tear at Troy's flank. Following Mysia's defeat and political subjugation by Troy, its hard-fighting warriors are made part of the allied Trojan army. Dymas uses some of their archers in his attack on Scyros.

NESTOR. King of Pylos and the oldest and most experienced general in the Argive camp

NOEMON. A cadet and boyhood friend of Dymas

ODYSSEUS. King of Ithaca

OENONE. A wood nymph seduced and deserted by Paris during his sojourn on Mount Ida

OIAX. A Trojan warrior from Percote

ORTHAIOS. A boyhood friend of Dymas; later, he is Dymas' subordinate in the Shark.

PARIS (see Alexandros).

PHAROS (THE GRAY). Tutor to Dymas and, before Dymas, to Polydamas. He was once commander of the Trojan army and chief of the Military Council. At Hecuba's urging, he is disgraced for an alleged involvement with Cassandra.

THE PHOENICIANS. Based on Tyre, the Phoenicians are neutral, trading with all sides in all of the wars in which the Trojans, Mysians, and Greeks engage.

POLYDAMAS. Son of Panthous, he is a commoner who was born on the same day as Hector. Owing to superior skill, he is the first in his generation to gain command of a Trojan regiment, the Shark, and in this capacity he is Dymas' commanding general.

POSEIDON. Brother to Zeus and Hades, he is Lord of the Sea, the Earthshaker.

PRIAM. King of Troy, husband of Hecuba, he is father to Hector, Alexandros, Atalante, Cassandra, and others.

RHESUS. The King of Thrace

SASPES. A Trojan warrior of the Shark

SKAIKO. A contemporary of Kalitor who rises to command at Thymbra. Related to Hecuba, he is chief of the Military Council during the Mysian Wars and head of a party known as the Generals of Defense.

SKALMOS. An old retainer who serves Antenor

SMINTHEUS (see Apollo).

TARSOS. A warrior of the Shark, a subordinate commander to Dymas. Originally a warrior of the Eagle, he is badly wounded in the Third Mysian War and relegated to the Whale, where Polydamas finds him fully recovered and recruits him into the Shark.

THOÖN. An ancient Trojan goatherd who finds and rescues the infant Alexandros

THE THRACIANS. Barbarian warriors of Thynia and Thrace who wear their hair long but tied in thick topknots, the supposed source of their fighting strength.

THRANITES. A Trojan junior in the Shark

THYNIANS (see Thracians).

TITHONUS. A son of Laomedon. He falls in love with and marries Aurora, the goddess of the dawn.

TROPOS. A warrior of the Shark; he is Dymas' subordinate.

TROS. (1) Son of Erichthonius, lord of the Trojans and father of Ilus, Assaracus, and Ganymede
(2) Son of Dymas

TYRO. Antenor's youngest son

ZEPHYR. The west wind

ZEUS. Father of gods and men. Lord of Thunder, the Cloudgatherer, he is also Hera's husband and brother.

PLACES

ABYDUS (ABYDUS-BY-THE-SEA). Blue city by the water's edge, Abydus is located in the "eye of the fishhook," on the coast of the Hellespont due south of the Thynian citadel of Sestus.

ANATOLIA. The east — the domain of the Hittites in Asia Minor

ANTISSA. A port on the northern coast of Lesbos

ARISBE. A Trojan frontier city northeast of Abydus; a staging port for Trojan commerce with the peoples around the dark, black sea. Arisbe is often described as "holy" because of a sacred grave in its precincts.

BESIKA BAY. Southwest of Troy, Besika Bay fronts on the Aegean Sea, looking toward Tenedos. In order to avoid the dangers of the race in the Hellespont, merchant ships unload their cargoes along the beaches at Besika Bay. For a fee, which is paid into Priam's treasure houses, the cargoes are transshipped by horse and mule to the northern ports of Abydus, Arisbe, and Percote, whence they are again carried by ship into the dark, black sea.

CARIA. During the Mysian Wars, Caria remains neutral, but at the time Agamemnon invades the Troad, Caria joins the Trojan alliance. The nation is located in the southwest corner of Asia Minor, immediately north of Rhodes.

CHIOS. A large island situated immediately to the west of Lydia and to the southwest of Mysia

CHRYSA. An important Mysian port, citadel, and supply center located south of Mount Ida on the Mysian coast. Chrysa is the frontier base from which Mysia launches all of its attacks on the Troad.

CILICIA. That part of Asia Minor fronting the Mediterranean Sea directly north of the island of Cyprus. Cilicia backs on the Tarus Mountains.

COLONAE. A Trojan outpost located near wide Propontis on Ilium's northeast frontier

COS. A small Greek island located northwest of Rhodes in the Sporades

CYPRUS. South of Cilicia and west of the Phoenician coast, Cyprus is the largest island in the eastern Mediterranean.

DARDANIA. Troy is the chief city of Dardania, the coastal region north of Mount Ida and the Scamander River, bordered by the Aegean Sea to the west and the Hellespont to the north. The region also encompasses the Plain, the Simoeis River, and the citadels of Dardanos, Abydus, Arisbe, Percote, and Colonae.

DARDANOS. The Trojan citadel at the tip of the "fishhook" on the Hellespont. Trojan naval hulls harbor in the shadow of Dardanos' keep.

GARGARON. One of Mount Ida's many peaks, it overlooks the mountain passes into Mysia.

HATTUSAS. The administrative and military center of the Hittite empire in Asia Minor

HEIGHTS OF HERACLES. The southern extension of the Wall of Heracles, the mountain range located west of the Scamander River

HELLESPONT. The narrow body of water separating the Troad from Thynia

KILLA. A small Trojan encampment located due south of Abydus and northeast of Dardanos

LEMNOS. This island, located west of Troy, is a thriving trade center and slave market where the Trojans exchange their spoils for war matériel.

LESBOS. The huge island is located west of Mysia and south of the Troad. Its chief cities, Antissa and Mytilene, are trade centers.

LYCIA. Situated northeast of Rhodes and east of Caria, Lycia borders Cilicia. Xanthus is the nation's chief citadel.

LYDIA. Located south of Mysia and north of Caria, Lydia remains neutral during the Mysian Wars. During the Trojan War, Lydia joins Priam in his attempt to repel the Greeks.

MOUNT IDA. Home of the Trojan gods, Mount Ida separates the Troad from Mysia.

MOUNT ISMARUS. Located in western Thrace, Mount Ismarus faces the Aegean. The Cicones live along the mountain's southern slopes, which overlook their citadel at Zone.

MOUNT OLYMPUS. Home of the Greek gods

MYRINA. A port city and slave market located on Lemnos' western coast

MYSIA. The warrior nation located south of Mount Ida. Pitane is the seat of the Mysian court and a major military base for the Mysian fleet and army. Chrysa and Cyme form important frontier posts from which the Mysians attempt to launch military expeditions against their neighbors. Mysian ships are built along the beaches before Cyme.

PAEONIA. West of Thrace, Paeonia remains neutral during the Mysian Wars.

PERCOTE. A Trojan citadel located northeast of Abydus

PHOENICIA. An ancient region of city-states located at the eastern end of the Mediterranean Sea. Modern coastal Syria and Lebanon roughly mark the region's borders.

PHRYGIA. The vast hinterland extending from Troy's eastern borders into the heart of Asia Minor. The peoples of this region come under the influence of the Hatti.

PITANE. Chief city and citadel of Mysia. The city is a confused jumble of mud-brick buildings that sprawls in all directions.

PROPONTIS (SEA OF MARMARA). The broad inland sea that connects the Hellespont with the Bosporus and the Black Sea. For all practical purposes, Propontis is a Trojan lake, owing to the fact that all access to it is controlled by Priam.

RHODES. The large Greek island located south of Caria

SATASPES. A Trojan garrison town east of Dardanos

SCAMANDER. The largest river in the Troad. Running west from the Phrygian highlands, Scamander passes the great Trojan fortress at Thymbra, joins the south fork running down from the heights of Ida, and runs swiftly north across the Plain until it empties into the Hellespont.

SCYROS. The island of Scyros rises from the Aegean between Euboea and Lesbos. In advance of their invasion of the Troad, the Greeks fortify the island's citadel.

SESTUS. Chief city and citadel of the Thynian peninsula. Sestus is laid out like the hub and spokes of a chariot wheel, with the keep in the position of the hub and the streets running out from the center. Near the keep the streets are narrow; as they work out from the keep, they become broader, and this design makes the heart of the city easy to defend, because large bodies of invading warriors cannot approach the base of the keep in mass.

SIMOEIS. The second largest river in the Troad. The course of Simoeis roughly parallels the Hellespont until, like Scamander, it turns north and empties across the Plain into the sea.

TENEDOS. A small Trojan island west of Besika Bay, Tenedos is home to the Shark and the Whale.

THRACE. The mountainous region north of Propontis, which was first conquered by Kalitor

THYNIA. Today, this region is known as the Gallipoli Peninsula. Thynia is the focus of the northern wars fought by Kalitor; it is the home of a barbarian people who wear their hair in topknots. Brought under control according to a grand strategy planned by Pharos in the years before Dymas is born, Thynia is allied with Troy and lends military support to various Trojan enterprises.

THE TROAD. The home country of the Trojans, taking in the Plain, Ilium, Dardania, and all of the land between the Hellespont and Mount Ida

WALL OF HERACLES. The low coastal mountain range that separates the Plain of Ilium from the sea. The southern tip of the Wall slopes down to Besika Bay before rising again to become the Heights of Heracles.

XANTHUS. The primary port city and citadel of Lycia

XANTHUS' LAIR. A royal manor located several leagues south of Troy up the valley of Scamander

ZONE. Built below Mount Ismarus, Zone is the chief citadel of the Cicones.

A NOTE ON MILITARY ORGANIZATION
AND THE TROJAN ORDER OF BATTLE

Under the House of Dardanos, supreme political authority is vested in the king. Priam exercises this authority through a Grand Council of Trojan elders — statesmen, diplomatists, and retired generals. Supreme military authority is exercised by the Military Council, which consists of generals who are on the active list, commanding regiments and other bodies of warriors whose numbers exceed one thousand spears. Rather than involve himself directly in all military decisions, Priam appoints as chief of the Military Council a general of experience and skill, and this officer also sits on the Grand Council as Priam's military adviser. In times of war and crisis, firm distinctions between the Grand and Military Councils tend to blur, because nearly all Trojan elders have at one time or another held independent command in the army. As a result, during wartime, the Grand and Military Councils often meet in joint session, making strategic decisions through unified votes.

THE TROJAN REGIMENTS

The largest permanent unit in the Trojan army is the field regiment. Traditionally, Trojan regiments are named for animals (i.e., the Boar, the Kite, the Lion, the Eagle, the Shark), and regiments are subdivided into battalions, companies, platoons, and tens. Battalion, company, and platoon functions follow, according to custom, a certain logic associated with the body parts of the totem animal that is carried on the regimental standard. In a typical regiment — the Bear, for example — the Bear's Head consists of the Nose, the Eyes, and the Teeth. The Nose, which first scents the enemy, is a platoon-sized unit devoted to the task of staff intelligence. The Eyes are devoted to reconnaissance, usually going forward in company strength, and the Teeth are hard assault companies charged with the Head's defense. Clearly, the Bear's Brain — the general in command and his staff — controls the whole. The Paws, light infantry armed with javelins and rounded shields, comprise the shock battalions of the regiment, and the Bear's Body, consisting of two or more heavily armed battalions wearing body shields, makes up the regiment's main-line strength. The Bear's Rump or Quarters contain up to four companies of reserves, and these — in the event of a retreat — also form the rear guard through which the front line units retire. In the normal course of events, each general in command of a Trojan regiment holds a seat on the Military Council and receives his orders direct from that body.

In times of war, regiments and elements of regiments may be combined into temporary commands that attain the status of a field army. At such times, one regimental commander, on the basis of merit, is elevated above his contemporaries and given unified command of all regiments assigned to him for a specific task. During the raid on Scyros, for example, Polydamas is given temporary command of a field army consisting of the Shark, the Bear, the Lion, an allied regiment of Thynians from lower Thrace, and assorted companies of Mysian archers; elements of the Whale, also under his command, transport his army to and from Scyros. At sea, each Trojan war and merchant hull carries between fifty and seventy-five warriors.

THE TROJAN ORDER OF BATTLE

Home Base	Regiment	Approximate Strength*
Troy	The Imperial Blues	3000
	The Imperial Guard	3000
	The Household Guard	1500
Dardanos	The Boar	4000
	The Kite	4000
Thymbra	The Leopard	3000
	The Eagle	3000
	The Wolf	3000
Abydus	The Mustang	2000
Arisbe	The Bear	2000
Percote	The Lion	3000
Sestus	The Hawk (two battalions)	1000
Greater Thynia	The Hawk (roving battalions)	1000
Tenedos	The Shark	1000
	The Whale	3000

*Measured in senior spears; juniors are not counted in a regiment's main-line strength but may be fully integrated with the regiment in battle.